Murder under the Sun

ALSO BY FAITH MARTIN

DI HILLARY GREENE SERIES
Book 1: Murder on the Oxford Canal
Book 2: Murder at the University
Book 3: Murder of the Bride
Book 4: Murder in the Village
Book 5: Murder in the Family
Book 6: Murder at Home
Book 7: Murder in the Meadow
Book 8: Murder in the Mansion
Book 9: Murder in the Garden
Book 10: Murder by Fire
Book 11: Murder at Work
Book 12: Murder Never Retires
Book 13: Murder of a Lover
Book 14: Murder Never Misses
Book 15: Murder at Midnight
Book 16: Murder in Mind
Book 17: Hillary's Final Case
Book 18: Hillary's Back
Book 19: Murder Now and Then
Book 20: Murder in the Parish
Book 21: Murder on the Train
Book 22: Murder under the Sun

MONICA NOBLE MYSTERIES
Book 1: The Vicarage Murder
Book 2: The Flower Show Murder
Book 3: The Manor House Murder

TRAVELLING COOK MYSTERIES
Book 1: The Birthday Mystery
Book 2: The Winter Mystery
Book 3: The Riverboat Mystery
Book 4: The Castle Mystery
Book 5: The Oxford Mystery
Book 6: The Teatime Mystery
Book 7: The Country Inn Mystery

MURDER UNDER THE SUN

FAITH MARTIN

JOFFE BOOKS

Joffe Books, London
www.joffebooks.com

First published in Great Britain in 2025

This book is a work of fiction. Names, characters, businesses, organizations, places and events are either the product of the author's imagination or are used fictitiously. Any resemblance to actual persons, living or dead, events or locales is entirely coincidental. The spelling used is British English except where fidelity to the author's rendering of accent or dialect supersedes this.

Cover art by Nick Castle

ISBN: 978-1-80573-176-4

CHAPTER ONE

Hillary Greene rolled onto her side on her narrow bed, picked up her mobile phone, and listlessly turned it on. She scowled at the inoffensive screen informing her that the time was 7.45 a.m. and briefly contemplated whether she could be bothered to check out the status of the current temperature. It didn't take her long to decide that there was little point; she already knew that it would be hot.

Very hot.

For the last ten days in July, the UK had been sweltering in one of its increasingly frequent heatwaves, with all the weather forecasters apologetically warning that there was no sign of a respite on the horizon. In fact, temperatures already regularly reaching into the thirties were set to climb inexorably higher still during the upcoming week.

Hillary, like many of the nation's non-sun-loving population, had become fed up with television scenes of dogs lying in children's paddling pools, sun-burned Brits licking ice creams on various beaches, and end-of-news clips featuring opportunistic inventors coming up with large-brimmed hats sporting battery-operated fans and other such daft contraptions.

She sat up, feeling hot, sticky, sweaty and downright grumpy. If she'd managed to get four hours of sleep, she'd be surprised. Even people living in regular houses were griping about the night-time temperatures, but here on her narrowboat, the *Mollern*, she didn't even have the protection of bricks and roof-tiles to help shelter her from the unrelenting sun.

Even though, at the very first prediction of hot weather, she'd been canny enough to move from her usual mooring in the tiny hamlet of Thrupp a few hundred yards up the Oxford canal, to where a line of willow trees provided shade for at least three-quarters of the day, the boat inevitably resembled an oven before it was even noon.

If it continued for much longer, she might be forced to start sleeping on the flat roof of her boat, and just hope that she didn't roll over in her sleep and find herself taking an unexpected dip into the khaki waters below. Come to think of it, she might not even mind that, if she thought the water would be cool!

With a sigh, she trudged the few steps towards her bijou bathroom and turned on the shower, but even set at the bluest of blues on the temperature dial, the water still came out tepid. After having lived on the boat for more years than she now cared to contemplate, she had the art of the two-minute shower down pat and soon emerged temporarily sweat-free and a little — just a *little* — refreshed.

But she knew that by the time she'd had a glass of orange juice and a slice of toast, walked along the towpath to her car parked in the Boat pub's car park and driven the ten-to-fifteen-minute commute through the rush hour to Thames Valley Police Headquarters, she'd be feeling as hot and sticky as before.

She switched on the radio only to hear an announcer gleefully informing her that yet more 'record' temperatures were predicted for various spots inland. She promptly said something very uncomplimentary and turned it off again.

Her mood was not improved, half an hour later, when she was sitting in a queue waiting for the first set of Kidlington's traffic lights to turn green. Puff the Tragic Wagon, her ancient

Volkswagen Golf, gave a derisive snort when she turned on the air conditioner and she hastily turned it off again, not wanting the old boy to overheat before she even made it in to work.

Naturally, once she got there, she found that any spot in the Police HQ's car park that could offer any hope of shade had already been snaffled — probably by those tricky sods in the fraud squad. When she finally walked away from her car, she confidently predicted that by the time she came back to it, she'd be able to put a ready meal for one inside, shut the door, wait ten minutes, and it would be cooked.

'Good morning, Hill,' the desk sergeant called out cheerfully as she pushed her way inside and breathed a slight sigh of relief. Here, at least, the air was cooler.

'What's good about it?' she snarled back, making the sergeant grin.

'Some of us like the heat,' he called cheerfully after her departing back as she made her way down the stairs into the basement, where the Crime Review Team hung its collective hat.

Formerly a serving detective inspector, Hillary had taken a slightly early retirement, only to be lured back less than two years later into rejoining the service as a civilian consultant working cold cases.

The majority of the CRT unit consisted of computer and various forensic experts applying new and modern science to solve older cases, and the public only became aware of their hard work when 'historic' crimes were finally brought home to offenders who must have thought that, after five, ten, or even in some cases twenty years, they had got away with their maleficence.

But within this mostly office-bound and highly structured machine, there was a tiny section, consisting of Hillary and her team, who conducted actual murder investigations in the 'old-fashioned way'; cases that remained unsolved and always open. These were chosen by Chief Superintendent Roland 'Rollo' Sale, who regularly trawled the archives and passed on those cases he thought might profit by Hillary

Greene's expert eye. These cases called for a thorough review of the original investigation, including the reinterviewing of witnesses and suspects, as well as following up on those avenues that the senior investigating officer at the time wouldn't have had the time or the resources to do themselves.

As Hillary knew from her own days as a DI, murder cases always threw up long-shots that were never chased up, and loose ends that a fast-moving investigation simply didn't have the time or manpower to tie off. What's more, after some years had passed, witnesses who might not have spoken out at the time for various reasons could sometimes be persuaded that, with the passage of time, their reasons for holding back were no longer so imperative. Thus it was now her job to take on old murder cases and cast a fresh, new, and totally unbiased eye over them, and see if it was possible to find justice for the dead.

* * *

Down in the basement, for once, the lack of natural daylight was a help rather than a hindrance, but even here, where the sun couldn't penetrate, the build-up of ambient heat, day after day, was already making her white linen blouse stick to her back.

She trudged wearily to the former stationery cupboard (that human resources would insist on calling her office) and slumped into the single chair it could comfortably house. Her hair, a bell-shaped cut of chestnut-brown — now turning salt-and-pepper in a few places — was already inclined to cling to the back of her neck and her cheek, and as she checked her emails and dealt with the usual round of paperwork, she tried to ignore a small bead of sweat that wanted to run down the side of her nose.

A ping on her computer alerted her to a message from her boss asking her to come to his office, and a small sigh of satisfaction escaped her. Unless she missed her guess — and she rarely did — she was pretty sure that the chief super had a new assignment for her, and not even the oppressive heat could dampen the small but insistent flicker of excitement that always tingled through her bloodstream on such occasions.

* * *

'How was she killed?' Hillary asked a few minutes later, her eyes fixed on the file sitting on the desk in front of the room's only other occupant.

Rollo Sale, a white-haired veteran cruising towards his retirement, offered her a glass of chilled water which she accepted with a grateful nod, and then leaned back in his chair. He was already in his shirtsleeves and like most people nowadays, was looking flushed with the heat and generally tired.

'Battered over the head in the hallway of her home,' he said flatly. He ran a hand around the undone collar of his shirt and shook his head. 'You'll see why I want it looked at again when you've had the chance to study the files in more depth. It just rankles that someone could kill a woman in her prime — and what's more in her own home, where she should feel and *be* safe — and then get clean away with it. As far as I can see, the original investigation was thorough enough but . . .' He gave a brief shrug of his rather beefy shoulders and spread his hands in a telling gesture. 'Just do your best with it, yeah?'

If there was a better hint for her to get out of his office and leave him to slowly melt in miserable peace, she didn't know what it was, and with a sympathetic smile of acknowledgement she grabbed the file and without another word left the room, stepping out into a corridor that was thankfully quiet and momentarily deserted.

She didn't go far — in fact, only two doors down, to where her team of two hung out in their 'communal office', in which you could just about fit two desks and two chairs, with a single filing cabinet shoehorned into a slight alcove in the back wall, just for the fun of it. A plastic spider plant trailed over the desk belonging to Claire Wolley, whilst no such frippery was permitted on the spartan and almost freakishly neat desk belonging to Gareth Proctor.

Claire noticed her standing in the doorway first. In her mid-fifties, her short black hair was fast turning grey. Inclined to plumpness, she was feeling the heat as much as anyone, and already her face was flushed, despite the small battery-operated fan that she was wafting enthusiastically in front of her. Her brown eyes widened slightly as she saw the folder in Hillary's hand.

Like herself, Claire had once worked for the police, spending her career in the domestic violence and rape unit, before retiring when her pension fell due. Also like herself, she had been lured back to work as a civilian, but in Claire's case probably because she and her husband needed the second income, rather than out of restless boredom, as had been the motivating factor with Hillary.

'Is that our next case I spy?' she asked, nodding at the buff-coloured paper folder in Hillary's hand. Unlike the rest of the CRT, who seemed to work in the digital world only, Hillary's cases often came from the archives, where paper had ruled supreme. Which didn't worry her one bit.

Hillary nodded. 'Want to set up the board?'

As Claire reached into the gap between the two desks to pull out a cork noticeboard (no fancy *CSI* computer-generated simulations here!) Hillary noticed Gareth sit up just that little bit straighter in his chair, if it were possible.

Whereas Hillary and Claire were coppers through and through, Gareth Proctor had spent his working life in the army, before an explosion out in a foreign desert had put an end to all his long-term plans. Which is how, at the age of thirty-four, he'd found himself back on civvy street with a bad limp in his left leg, and only limited movement of his left arm, shoulder and elbow. Six feet and one inch tall, he still maintained his blond hair in a short, military-style cut nearly four years later. A thin white scar that intersected his left eyebrow did little to mar his good looks however, and pale blue eyes watched her intently as she came in and perched on the corner of Claire's desk.

When he'd first gained a place on Hillary's team just over three years ago, he'd still been very much the soldier, inclined to bark out 'yes, ma'am' and 'no, ma'am' as if accepting orders from a superior officer. Though he still couldn't bring himself to call her by her given name, at least he didn't bark out 'ma'am' quite so forcefully nowadays, but he still managed to look as if he was somehow sitting at attention behind his desk, as he was doing now.

Under her guidance and training he was fast becoming a first-rate criminal detective, and she was pleased and relieved to see him slowly building a new and satisfying life and career for himself, away from the military.

Claire, having unfolded and set up the murder board to await its first item, returned to her desk and her handheld fan. Hillary wondered, a little enviously, how many batteries she must have got through during the last three weeks. Although she had two larger electric fans on her boat, she was wary of running them too long in case she ran down the generator. Perhaps she should get her own wide-brimmed hat and attach a whole slew of the mini-gadgets to it? She could always attach a ribbon and tie it firmly under her chin if the hat threatened to helicopter away.

'All right, let's see what we have then,' Hillary muttered. Opening up the file she began speed-reading the bare details, which she then related to her team.

'Our murder victim is one Mrs Imelda Phelps, aged forty-one years at the time of her death,' she began briskly, and after turning the top page, was slightly surprised to uncover a rather professional-looking head-and-shoulders photograph of a very beautiful woman, which she promptly carried over to attach to the board. 'Ah, she was a professional model, apparently,' she continued reading the details on the form, and nodded at the photograph. 'Which probably explains this studio shot. I didn't think it was a family snap, somehow. The original SIO . . .' she quickly shuffled the papers until she found what she was looking for, 'was DI Diane Clovis.'

Hillary paused, eyes narrowing as she quickly wracked her memory and came up with nothing. She looked at Claire. 'Ring any bells?'

'Vaguely, guv,' Claire said. 'I think she was in Robbery most of the time. I seem to remember she worked serious crimes for a bit. She must have been retired for years now. What date are we talking about?'

Hillary looked at the top of the first form. 'Imelda Phelps was murdered on the twenty-third of June 2010. Head injuries, weapon never found.' She recited the bare facts then paused as all three of them turned to look at the face of the woman who was destined to become very familiar to them over the course of the next few weeks.

'She's certainly a stunner,' Claire said, stating the obvious, and Hillary nodded. According to cold hard statistics, Imelda had been five feet ten inches tall, with long auburn hair and hazel eyes, and weighed just over eight and a half stone at the time of her autopsy. But such bare facts did little to prepare you for the reality of the woman's physical attributes.

Although at the age of forty-one her modelling career must have been on the wane, she had been one of those women who aged well — *very well*. In fact, without having seen any photographs of her in her teenage years or early twenties, Hillary wouldn't have been surprised if she had been at the peak of her beauty only after she'd hit her thirties. Sharp cheekbones, narrow nose, shapely lips and arched brows all contributed their individual gifts to her beautiful face, but there was something else, something indefinable and elusive that made you want to keep on staring at her image.

'The camera loves her, that's for sure,' Hillary mused.

'And someone took a blunt instrument to that head?' Claire muttered darkly.

Hillary quickly rifled through the folder again until she found the summary of the autopsy report. 'Hmm . . . with something long and thin — possibly metal — although no helpful trace evidence was found.'

'A poker?' Gareth made his first contribution to the discussion. 'Did she live in a house with an open fire?'

Hillary again rifled through the folder. Her first order would be for Claire and Gareth to go through the laborious but needful task of making copies of the Murder Book for each of them — digitally where it could be managed, but by the use of a photocopier otherwise. The Murder Book was a constantly updated file that Hillary insisted all members of her team contributed to as and when they completed their assignments. It then became something they could all consult at any given point and was designed to stop them going over the same ground twice, and ensuring that they all had an up-to-date overview of the investigation.

'Here we are. She lived in Chippie,' she used the locals' shortened version for the pretty market town of Chipping Norton that lies to the north and west of the county, 'in a large family house on the outskirts of the town. From the looks of it,' she studied the photos of the house for a few seconds, 'I'd say it was built in the mid-nineteenth century, so originally there'd have been fireplaces. It still has chimneys, anyway, but chances are it was converted to central heating. Even so, lots of people still keep ornamental fire surrounds and brass fire sets and what not. As I recall, this address is in a smart area of the town.'

Which meant the family wasn't short of a bob or two.

She turned to the forms detailing her next of kin and briefly read the summaries. 'Her husband Thomas was, probably still is, a successful businessman. She had two children, a boy named Jonas, who was . . . twenty at the time, and away at university. The second child, a daughter called Jessica or Jessie for preference, who was only seventeen. She was the first to find her mother's body, on returning home from school.'

'Poor kid,' Claire muttered. 'I bet that still gives her nightmares to this day.'

Hillary closed the folder and absently began to use it to fan her face. 'We need to get set up,' she said, her mind racing ahead. 'Claire, see about getting everything relating to the case from Records up here, so you and Gareth can set about copying and collating.'

Claire rolled her eyes dramatically and groaned. 'Just what I need. Carting heaving boxes of paper about in this heat.'

'Charm some of the fitness freaks in the computer room,' Hillary advised her.

Claire raised an eyebrow. 'Do I look like I could successfully vamp a twenty-five-year-old?'

Hillary grinned. 'All right then, challenge their machismo. You know that always works. Tell them any wimp can use gym equipment, but only real men can lug bulky awkward boxes around in thirty-degree heat and not run home crying to their mummies.'

Even as Claire guffawed, Hillary saw Gareth glance down beside his desk, where his cane lay flat against the floor, out of everybody's way. She knew what he was thinking of course. Once, he'd have made short work of such a task himself.

'Gareth, I want you to hit that,' she said briskly, pointing at his laptop, 'and start printing off whatever you can find about the crime on the internet. Then get on with finding out the current whereabouts and details of everyone concerned. Make me a list of any witnesses who are now deceased and find out the current status and whereabouts of DI Clovis.'

'Yes, ma'am,' Gareth said promptly, already reaching out to start hitting the keyboard.

Hillary nodded. 'Right. I'll be in my office all day going through this and making my own notes,' she waved the file in the air and disappeared back to her stationery cupboard — which had risen in temperature about two degrees in the half an hour or so since she'd left it.

Grimly, she contemplated coming to work in future with a bikini on under her clothes, then locking the office door behind her and stripping off. And if, before that, she could get one of the scientific boffins to set her up with her own private sprinkler system that she could turn on and off at will to hose herself down at regular intervals, well, wouldn't she just have herself her own private little Shangri-La?

* * *

It was nearly four thirty by the time Hillary had finished going through the preliminary file on the Imelda Phelps murder and jotting down notes and ideas as they occurred to her.

She stretched, yawned and rose, feeling a little stiff after sitting for so long and made her way to the communal office. Her head had that fuzzy head-cold feeling that she sometimes got when she'd been concentrating on paperwork for too long, and when she stuck her head around the door, she could see a similar expression of weariness on Claire's face.

Gareth was still sitting straight in his chair, but even he had perspiration patches in the armpits of his white shirt and looked at her hopefully.

'All right, let's all knock off half an hour early,' she said, Claire brightening visibly at this. 'If we stay down here much longer, I'm worried we'll poach.'

'I've almost finished tracking down everyone's whereabouts, ma'am,' Gareth said, 'and one of them, the original SIO, is still living here in Kidlington.' He then named an address that Hillary thought was in one of the large housing estates somewhere at the back of the big Sainsbury's supermarket on the Kidlington roundabout.

Hillary glanced at her watch. 'OK. I'll just nip up there first then and see what she can remember of the case.' In her experience, murder detectives tended to remember the ones they couldn't close. 'With a bit of luck, she'll have some insights that aren't written down in black and white, which'll mean that we can hit the ground running tomorrow.'

'Guv, do you mind if I just hit the ground crawling?' Claire asked wearily. 'And maybe whimpering a bit? The temperature's not set to get down below twenty-six tonight, apparently.'

Hillary grinned. 'Crawling and whimpering's just fine. I might just join you.'

At this, even Gareth cracked a smile, and with a brief wave, Hillary bid her team goodbye, went back to gather her things together then headed back out up the steps and into the foyer, where a group of uniforms were just coming in after what sounded like a successful raid of a stolen goods cache.

Hillary unlocked Puff, opened the door and quickly stepped back to avoid the resulting wave of heated air. She waited a few minutes before getting in and winding down both the front windows, the heat from the seat penetrating uncomfortably through the pale blue linen trousers she was wearing. Tentatively, she touched the steering wheel, checking it out to see if she could handle it with her bare hands. She winced, but decided it was bearable. If it got any worse, though, she'd have to start bringing in driving gloves.

Or oven gloves.

With a brief prayer she turned on the ignition, and silently blessed her car as he started first time. Wasting no time in starting off — craving that blissful hit of a breeze that momentum brought with it — instead of turning right, she indicated left and headed away from her usual route home.

* * *

She found former DI Diane Clovis's house with the aid of the postcode and her rarely used satnav, and better yet, found just beyond it a parking space that was shaded by a large cherry tree. As she walked back to the house, she surveyed her baking surroundings, a feeling of slight depression settling over her.

The houses weren't that new but they had that skimpy throw-them-up-quick look of modern homes that would have made her parents weep. A handkerchief-sized lawn, rendered brown and crispy after a month of no rain, had a no-nonsense concrete path running directly through the middle of it, leading her towards Diane's front door. Old-fashioned lace curtains hung at the single downstairs window, but they looked more grey than white. The door, painted black, was badly in need of a fresh coat.

As Hillary rang the bell and glanced about, she couldn't see a single soul.

The door opened suddenly, pulled open with a yank, as if whoever was inside was getting ready to vent some spleen. The man regarding her looked to be somewhere in his seventies and not particularly friendly. Once tall and well built, he now looked slightly stooped and paunchy, with a beer belly that hung over a pair of khaki shorts and was barely contained by a sleeveless t-shirt in a shade of very-off white. His feet were bare.

'If you're selling something, we don't want it,' he informed her shortly.

'Mr Clovis?'

The man nodded, but Hillary was already pulling her ID out of her bag. 'I'm Hillary Greene. I'm working with the Thames Valley Police in the CRT unit. I was hoping I could have a quick word with your wife, Diane.'

The man blinked then gave a slight shrug and stepped back. 'Better come in then. Di's in the kitchen — it doesn't get the afternoon sun. She'll be asleep, but I'll wake her up. For what good it'll do you,' he muttered, not quite far enough under his breath so that she couldn't catch it.

Hillary frowned, not liking the sound of that last aside, but followed him into a hall barely big enough to accommodate them both, and he immediately swivelled and stepped past the first door on the right, opening the door beyond that. As he stepped aside for her to enter, she walked into a reasonably sized kitchen; done out in blue and white, it looked as if it hadn't been redecorated in twenty years and revealed a woman sleeping on a sunbed that had probably been dragged in from the less-than-generous patio in the back garden, where its twin still stood.

'Di, love, it's one of your oppos,' the man suddenly bellowed, making Hillary jump.

The woman opened her eyes and scowled. Hillary knew that Diane Clovis had been fifty-one years old at the time of Imelda Phelps's murder, which must now put her around sixty-six or -seven. She was stick-thin, with long hair that would have looked better (and would surely have felt cooler?) put up in a chignon or ponytail and had obvious liver spots on her bare hands, arms and upper sternum, which were all cruelly revealed by the thin, faded sleeveless cotton sundress that she was wearing.

'Who, Donnie?' she muttered thickly.

'Someone from work,' the man shouted back.

Hillary hoped Diane Clovis would find and put on her hearing aid, but her husband's next words made her heart sink even further.

'She's getting a bit . . . well, out of it, I suppose. Some days are better than others. Not sure how much sense you'll get out of her today, to be honest. This bloody heat don't help any, that's for sure. Even I'm starting to feel dozy. Tried to get hold of a couple of those big white electric fans from Argos to cool the air down a bit, but they were too bloody expensive. I'll get her a cold drink from the fridge, that might help.'

As he began to set about the task, Hillary drew up a wooden kitchen chair and sat beside the sun lounger, but it looked as if the older woman's eyes were already beginning to close again.

'Diane?' Hillary asked, not loudly but firmly. 'I'm from Thames Valley. Do you remember the Imelda Phelps case?'

'I remember her.' It was Donnie who answered, coming back with a glass of something in a shade of vivid orange. 'That good-looking model that got done in . . . what, getting on for twenty years ago now, am I right?'

Hillary watched as the man rested a meaty hand on his wife's bony shoulder and squeezed. 'Have a drink, love. Make you feel better.'

But Diane merely gave the glass a brief scowl and turned her head away. Her spouse sighed and took a gulp of the drink himself. 'Bloody social services. She should be in a home where they can look after her properly, but they say they don't have any vacancies. And if they did, I don't suppose they'd have the staff,' he added gloomily.

'Diane?' Hillary tried again, but she already knew it would be hopeless. 'We're taking another look at the case. Do you remember Imelda?'

'Wasting your time I'm afraid. 'S'no use, she'll be sleeping again in a minute,' her husband predicted fatalistically, then looked at Hillary again. 'I remember the one you mean, though. I remember all her murder cases,' he said proudly, giving a brief nod at the silent woman. 'Well, she only worked on four. The other three weren't much to write home about — a couple of gang things — knives and that, and that bloke what drowned his wife in the bath. But that murder of the model, yeah, that was a big thing. They made a big fuss of it in the papers and everything. A proper sensation it were, for a while. Neighbours were right chuffed to think that they knew the officer in charge of the case.' For a moment he smiled, reliving past, vicarious glories. But then the smile faded, and he sighed. 'Weren't her fault the case wasn't solved,' he added defensively, giving his wife a troubled look. 'She did her best, worked like a dog she did,' he added aggressively, as if Hillary was arguing with him. 'There just wasn't nothing she could get a hold of.'

Hillary, admitting defeat, got up and put the chair back where she had found it. 'Believe me, no one is saying your wife and her team didn't do a good job,' she said, and meant it. From her first run-through of the thing, she had found no fault so far with the original investigators or their efforts.

'So, it's being reopened then, is it?' he said, and nodded. 'Good thing, I suppose. I often wonder if the sod who did it ever did it again.'

'No unsolved case is ever closed, Mr Clovis,' Hillary corrected him gently. She handed him one of her cards. 'If Diane has a good day sometime soon, can you give me a call? I'd like to talk to her, if possible.'

Donnie Clovis grimaced. 'Me too,' he said bleakly. 'Been a while now since we talked about anything that wasn't gibberish. Her thinking it's thirty or forty years ago, and me wishing that it were.'

Hillary nodded, unable to think of anything to say in response to that which could possibly help. With a murmured thanks she turned away, the old man following her politely out and opening the front door for her.

Hillary returned to Puff and drove listlessly home, trying to shake off the gloom cast by the Clovises and the quietly relentless awfulness of their situation. They were clearly struggling to make ends meet on their joint pensions, and Diane's medical condition was enough to sap the joy out of anyone.

Trying to cheer herself up, she turned on the radio, which she kept permanently tuned to a station that played only sixties music, and sang (slightly offkey, it had to be said) about a 'Waterloo Sunset' along with the Kinks.

* * *

Donnie Clovis left his sleeping wife in the kitchen and stepped out in a back garden that was only just slightly bigger than the front. In his hand he had his ancient mobile phone, and after a bit of awkward fiddling, finally found the number he was searching for.

'Hello. Mitch? Yeah, it's me. Don . . . Donnie Clovis. Yeah, mate, I know, it must be years. Your son still working as a journo? Great. What, newspapers gone the way of dinosaurs? Yeah, I suppose it's all online nowadays,' his voice became slightly anxious. 'But they still want stories, yeah? Whaddya-call-ems, exclusives and the like? Yeah, as a matter of fact, I just might have. A nice juicy murder of some model. What? No, no, this was years ago now. But it was a big thing at the time and they're looking into it again. Should be worth a few quid to know about that right? Your boy could do all right by it, I reckon, rustle up some interest, stick his nose in, find out what's what . . .'

He cajoled, listened and bargained for a few minutes, and in the end reluctantly agreed to settle for twenty quid. He'd pick it up from Mitch, on his lad's behalf, first thing tomorrow morning.

It wasn't much, Donnie mused as he clicked off the phone, but it should be enough to buy a bottle of some cheap supermarket's own-brand booze, if nothing else.

CHAPTER TWO

After checking in at the office first thing the following morning and doing the usual admin chores, Hillary pleased Claire by opting to take Gareth with her to the first of the family interviews. Although it was barely ten o'clock the day was already uncomfortably warm, and Claire had brought in a precious portable electric fan from her home and was quite happy to stay in the office and continue collating the massive amount of data currently stored in the boxes that were now lining the office walls.

Back out in the car park, Hillary decided to give Puff an easy day, and opted instead for Gareth to use his car to drive them to Bicester, the market town where Thomas Phelps now lived. (It was a decision for which Gareth was very grateful, since his trust in Puff to get them anywhere without coughing his last was negligible.) His car, an anonymous-looking dark hatchback, had been converted to allow him to drive easily and safely with the restricted movements of his left leg and arm, and once they were on the main road between the two towns, he was able to get up enough speed to create a pleasant breeze through the open windows.

As they went, Hillary took the opportunity to read through the report on the dead woman's husband that her team had put together for her yesterday.

Thomas, who'd been forty-five at the time of Imelda's murder and so must now be somewhere around sixty, had sold his business less than two years ago, allowing him to retire early and live very comfortably indeed. She wasn't quite sure that she would personally have chosen to move to a new-build home in one of the modern housing estates that were being thrown up around the medieval market town if *she'd* been handed a couple of million pounds, but she supposed everyone had their own ideas about these things.

Perhaps his second marriage, to a woman more than a decade younger than himself with children of her own from a previous marriage, had had something to do with it. According to her information, Philippa Burgess had three children, two of whom had now grown up and left the nest, leaving her with only the thirteen-year-old Martine still at home. Maybe there was a good school nearby they'd wanted her to attend? Or maybe the second Mrs Phelps had relatives in the area?

It didn't take them long before they reached the housing estate — all cream stone and red roofs — and began, with some difficulty, navigating their way around the myriad number of roads and little cul-de-sacs with 'charming' names. The silver birches and weeping willow saplings that had been interspersed throughout the front gardens tried to take away some of the screaming newness of tarmac and concrete with only limited success.

The Phelps residence was one of the largest of housing styles on offer, boasting three storeys and the biggest area of plot the stingy planners had permitted. On a hot day, with blue skies and sunshine bouncing off newly planted and colourful bedding plants, she supposed there were worse places to be, but as she walked up the paving-stone path towards the neat new porch and pristinely painted front door, she found some of the depression that she'd managed to shake off after visiting the Clovises oddly creeping back.

'Nice,' Gareth said, looking around approvingly. 'And totally out of reach for most of us,' he added, without bitterness.

Hillary could understand that there was something here about the military-neat and clean uniform spaces that would appeal to him, but it left her cold. Give her a slightly smelly canal bordered by unruly wildflower- and weed-strewn hedgerows any day.

The door opened, revealing a tall, slender woman wearing a long summer dress in rainbow colours. Her fading corn-coloured hair was held back off her face in an old-fashioned head band in matching rainbow colours, and faded pink flip-flops adorned her suntanned feet. Pale blue-grey eyes regarded them a shade nervously.

'Hello, Mrs Phelps? I believe my colleague called you earlier on this morning?' Hillary began, showing her ID. Claire, who'd done the arranging, had made sure that Thomas would be at home today, and Hillary had, for the moment, no real objection to the second wife being present also. Sometimes the attitude of a second wife to the woman who'd once held the same position as herself could be very revealing.

'Oh yes, of course. Please, come on in. I have to say, Tom and I, we've been wondering what it's all about ever since we got the phone call.'

Hillary gave a non-committal smile and introduced Gareth. She saw Philippa notice his stick and scarred left hand and quickly step back to give him more room as they both moved into a reasonably spacious hall. On one side, a row of coat hooks was occupied, whilst beneath them, shoe racks were stuffed to capacity with various footwear. Open doors showed views of both a large kitchen-dining area and a lounge, with all the walls painted a very pure white. Laminate wood flooring flowed everywhere. In the lounge, black-leather sofas and chairs with chrome frames glinted in the harsh sunny light.

'We're in the kitchen — I hope that's all right?' the woman asked, turning to lead the way. Here, the black-and-white monotones continued, with shining white cupboards and black marble worktops overlooking a black marble island, which was in turn surrounded by tall stools done in black leather with a single chrome pedestal.

It made their hostess's rainbow-coloured outfit stand out vividly which, for all Hillary knew, had been the main purpose in wearing it. In one corner, a low black-leather sofa corner unit sat in front of a white-painted coffee table on which resided a single pot plant, not currently flowering.

The man seated on the sofa, with a cup of iced coffee in front of him, diffidently got up to greet them as they approached. 'Tom, this is, er, Mrs Greene and Mr Proctor.'

Hillary held out her hand and shook his firmly.

Thomas Phelps was around five feet seven or so, which would have made him several inches shorter than his tall, willowy model wife Imelda — and also his second one. Dressed in pale blue slacks and a plain white loose-fitting shirt, he was slender in stature, and still good-looking in a romantic-poet sort of way, with his once black hair now an attractive shade of grey, and brown eyes watching them warily from a face that had high cheekbones and a firm chin with a slight cleft in it. Given his comfortable wealth, she could understand why someone like Imelda had chosen him for a spouse.

Coupled with her own magnificent looks, Hillary was sure that they must have made a very handsome and no doubt sought-after couple back in the day — a veritable ornament for any dinner party or social gathering.

'Thank you for agreeing to see us, Mr Phelps. I'm a retired detective inspector, now working for the Crime Review Team at Thames Valley in Kidlington. We are currently looking again into Imelda's case,' Hillary explained simply.

'Oh, I see,' Thomas said, glancing at Philippa, then back to Hillary. He suddenly noticed Gareth's stick and quickly indicated the rest of the sofa, that bent at a right angle around the corner of the wall. 'Please, sit down.'

Hillary did so, leaving a cushion's worth of space between herself and Thomas Phelps, whilst Gareth sat in the middle of the space standing catercorner to them. He unobtrusively brought out a notebook and pen, as Hillary reached for her mobile. 'Do you mind if I record our conversation, sir? It's just a good idea to have a reliable record of everything that's said, but if it makes you uncomfortable at all . . . ?'

Thomas shrugged. 'No, it's fine. Go ahead.' He sat back down again, his pale blue slacks falling immediately back into their immaculate crease. 'Have you had some new information come to light about Imelda's . . . death? Is that why you're reopening her file?'

Philippa Phelps, after hesitating uncertainly for a moment, retreated to the island where she began to wash salad leaves and make herself conspicuously busy.

'No, sir, nothing like that. It's just that nearly fifteen years have passed now since Imelda's murder, and we like to take another look at such cases periodically. It's sometimes surprising what new things can come to light after some time has passed.'

Thomas nodded but looked unconvinced, moved his gaze to his wife, who had begun to chop and de-seed some tomatoes, then looked away again. 'I see. So, what can I do to help?'

Hillary settled back against the sofa, leaning slightly to the right, the better to see him and monitor his reactions. 'I understand you were at work at the time of the incident?'

'Incident?' Thomas repeated softly, his lips twisting slightly as he stared down into his lap.

'I'm sorry, sir,' Hillary said, and meant it. 'There's no right or wrong way to talk about things like this, I'm afraid. Some people like to keep the painful memories at bay with the careful language, as they find that it makes it easier for them to disassociate themselves from it all, whilst others . . . well, don't. I'm not here to upset you — I know talking about painful things, even things long past, can be difficult.'

Thomas shifted a little on his seat and sighed. 'No — I'm the one who should apologise. I realise you have a job to do and, well . . .' He trailed off and shook his head. 'Just ask what you need to ask, and I'll try not to be such a diva.' He gave a strained smile and lifted his head to meet her gaze squarely.

'Thank you, sir,' Hillary said softly. 'You were at work that day, yes?'

'Yes. In the office. I owned and ran a furniture wholesale business back then and worked out of the Oxfordshire warehouse. We had more than twenty of them, scattered throughout England and Wales.'

Hillary nodded. 'You arrived at work at the usual time, around nine in the morning?'

'Yes, and left at five thirty, again, as usual.'

According to the original investigation, his secretary Anne Raft had confirmed this. Diane Clovis's notes had made it clear that the woman hadn't seemed particularly devoted to her boss — and certainly showed no signs of being the adoring workmate so popular in golden-age crime fiction, who'd be willing to lie for him. But, against that, his office had been on the ground floor, with large, low-lying windows that opened easily onto a relatively small and secluded private parking area outside. And since he worked in it alone, it meant that it would certainly have been possible for him to slip out and return unseen. What's more, his home was less than a five-minute drive away.

So if he had planned to nip home and dispatch his wife, it was possible for him to have done so.

But it would have been risky. Very risky.

According to the notes, Anne Raft had denied that her boss had given her an unexpectedly elongated lunch hour or given instructions not to be disturbed at any point. Which meant that she could have wandered in at any time — and if she'd found the room empty, she would surely have wondered why Mr Phelps had taken to leaving via the window, rather than through the door that took him into the outer office.

So, this man had an alibi — of sorts — for the early afternoon of his wife's death which, according to the pathology report, was when Imelda was mostly likely to have been killed.

Although the original team had canvassed the neighbourhood extensively, nobody had been found who had seen either Thomas's car, or the man himself, at or near his residence at the time of his wife's death. But then, most of the neighbours were either at work themselves, or were out and about shopping or doing other errands.

'I understand your daughter found her mother's body when she came home from school?' she asked next. 'That must have been very traumatic for her,' she added gently.

'Yes,' Thomas said shortly. 'It was.' His lips formed into a firm line, the first indication she'd had so far that he was unhappy about the way her questions were going.

Hillary began to tread very carefully. 'I imagine the family liaison officer would have given you details about psychiatric services or counselling opportunities that might have benefited Jessica?'

'Jessie didn't want any of that,' Thomas said at once. 'She had us, her brother and myself. We looked after her.'

'And her grandmother too?' Hillary knew that Imelda's mother was living in Cheltenham at the time, which was less than an hour's drive away.

Thomas shrugged. 'Imelda and her mother weren't particularly close. Although she visited from time to time, Jessie and Jonas weren't close to her either.'

Hillary glanced across at Philippa, who was now washing strawberries under the cold water. 'I understand some rather distressing facts came to light in the subsequent investigation. Facts about Imelda's private life?' she began delicately.

'If you're talking about the lover she had that none of us knew about, then yes, they certainly did,' Thomas said. Although the words themselves were rather brutal, he didn't *sound* particularly angry, nor did he try to sound sophisticatedly amused about it; rather he sounded resigned, almost disinterested. Perhaps, after all this time, the knowledge of his dead wife's infidelity had lost any ability to hurt either his emotions or his pride? Or was he just trying to give that impression?

Or perhaps time had nothing to do with it? They had only his word for it that he *hadn't* known about Dermott Franklyn. There was nothing to say that their marriage hadn't been in trouble for some time, and that he'd grown indifferent to his beautiful wife long before someone had battered her over the head.

Although their friends and neighbours, when questioned, all said and apparently believed that the Phelpses were a strong and united couple, who could really tell what went on behind closed doors? And the fact that Imelda had had a younger lover — and for quite some time — was surely an indication that she, at least, had been dissatisfied with her lot. They had not long celebrated their twentieth wedding anniversary after all, so familiarity had had plenty of time to breed contempt.

Maybe Imelda had even been contemplating a divorce?

But if that had been the case, then Diane Clovis and her team had never picked up any hint of it, and Hillary doubted very much that Thomas Phelps would admit to it now.

She decided to leave this avenue until she had a better feeling for the case and changed direction.

'Your son, Jonas, was at university — where was that again?' she asked, although she knew the answer perfectly well.

'Bath. Studying architecture. Jonas has done very well for himself,' Thomas informed her, sounding perfunctorily proud.

The original team had confirmed that Jonas Phelps had indeed attended two lectures that morning, but his whereabouts on the afternoon of his mother's death had been less solid. He claimed to have worked in the library for a while, then studied in his room. At the time, Jonas had no car of his own, however, and the team had been unable to find any trace of him on Bath's CCTV at the railway or coach stations. And none of his friends had admitted to lending him a car. But some friends could be very loyal, she knew, especially at that young and impressionable age.

'You told DI Clovis that you had no idea who might have harmed your wife,' Hillary pressed on. 'Has that changed, in the years since?'

'No. Unless it was Franklyn, I can't think why anyone would want to hurt Imelda.'

'I've seen some of her stock studio photographs. She was very beautiful,' Hillary said, no inflection in her voice at all.

Apart from flicking a quick glance towards his current wife — who was now preparing a tall glass jug of iced cloudy lemonade — Thomas didn't react, other than to nod.

'She was formerly a model, I understand?'

'She still was,' Thomas corrected. 'Doing catalogues for big retail clothing stores, stuff like that. She could make a binbag look stylish.' This time there was no indication of pride — perfunctory or not. Merely a statement of fact.

Hillary let her glance travel around her. There were no personal touches that she could detect here in the kitchen — no family photos or well-thumbed books on the shelves, no magazines lying around or newspapers opened out at the crossword or sudoku sections; nothing at all, in fact, to indicate hobbies or personal preferences. And she had the feeling that the lounge that she'd glimpsed earlier would be the same.

Was it just that this couple had embraced the minimalist style? Or was there a deeper, more psychological explanation for it? Imelda's world would have been one of photography, colour, glamour and fashion. Had Thomas Phelps, when he'd buried his first wife, made the decision — consciously or not — to leave all that behind him, and attach himself to a very different personality altogether?

'I understand you're retired now, sir?'

'Yes. Why not? It makes sense to take it easy later in life, doesn't it? Phil, Martine and I all like to take long summer holidays abroad and enjoy ourselves. Time is a luxury, particularly nowadays, don't you think?'

Over at the kitchen island, Hillary thought she saw Philippa tense a little. Did she disapprove of having herself and her child dragged into the conversation? Or had she found something in the rather innocuous comment that had taken her unawares?

'I imagine Imelda liked trips abroad too?' Hillary asked, again keeping her tone bland and even.

'Of course, but we were both so busy back then. We got away when we could — at Christmas every year — skiing in Switzerland mostly. And at Easter we always went somewhere too — Amsterdam, Paris, city breaks and the like. Imelda adored Paris — I used to tease her that it was her American side coming out.'

'American side?'

'Her mother was one of those rich American socialites who toured Europe on the lookout for an equally rich husband, or at the very least an impoverished but titled one. You know the sort I mean — all diamonds and two-faced politeness.'

'It sounds as if there's no love lost between you and your mother-in-law,' Hillary said, this time allowing a small smile to cross her face.

Thomas shrugged. 'I wish it wasn't such a cliché, but it's true,' he acknowledged ruefully. 'I never particularly got on with Catherine. I always thought she was to blame for some of Imelda's less attractive traits.'

Hillary lifted one eyebrow, and Thomas waved a hand vaguely in the air. 'Yes, all right, I can see I need to enlarge on that. Catherine was brought up in the States by strict parents herself, so I suppose it's not all her fault. She was raised to be, how shall I put it, ladylike at all times; to never be seen to put a foot wrong, or worst of all, make a social faux pas. The worst of crimes, in her book, were either to sully your reputation or give any of your peers a reason or cause to laugh at you behind your back. The woman was obsessed about that kind of thing.'

He sighed. 'And it definitely rubbed off on Imelda. I suppose it didn't help that both sets of Catherine's grandparents came from what they called 'old money' — the Carpenters having made a fortune in hardware, and the Porterhouses in trucking. By the time Catherine was born, the whole clan of them fancied themselves New England royalty and raised Catherine to see herself in the same way.'

'She does sound like a bit of a gorgon,' Hillary mused. 'But then, some Americans can be very conservative, can't they — especially if they've grown up to live their lives in a restricted social circle. So, are you saying that her snootiness was instilled in Imelda?'

Funny that, Hillary thought. After reading most of Diane Clovis's reports, she hadn't picked up any indications that their murder victim had had a repulsive personality.

'Only in some ways,' Thomas said defensively. 'And never knowingly. She did her best not to be a carbon copy of her mother — in fact, she went out of her way to rebel against everything her mother stood for. As you can imagine, that made for a very tense mother-and-daughter relationship. But some things do get ingrained, don't they, no matter how you try not to let them?'

Hillary nodded. Interesting! Was it possible that Imelda had looked down her nose at the wrong person, perhaps? Someone who hadn't appreciated being condescended to by a rich, pampered, beautiful woman? That might well produce enough animus to make someone take a blunt instrument to their tormentor's head in a moment of rage or instability.

'I would imagine that having a mother like that would have made Imelda determined to have a better relationship with her own daughter, Jessie?' she said casually.

At this, Thomas hesitated visibly, his eyes dropping into his lap for a moment, before he shrugged. 'I'm sure she would have wanted that. I only wish it had worked out that way though.'

'Oh?'

'You have to remember that Jessie was only seventeen when she lost her mother. And those teenage years can be very trying. And it didn't help that Jessie didn't take after her mother in either looks or temperament.'

'They argued?'

'No. Yes. No — it wasn't that so much, as they just found it hard to make a connection with each other. I'm sure it would have smoothed itself out had they been given the chance or the time . . . I'm sure, if she'd lived, Immy and Jessie would have become much better friends, the older and less judgemental Jessie became. A lot of mothers and daughters *do* grow closer with time, don't they?' he insisted, on the defensive now. 'Only they were never able to. It's just another thing that man took away from us.'

'That man?' Hillary echoed sharply.

Thomas's head snapped up. 'What? Oh, sorry. That's just how I've always referred to whoever did it. As *"that man"*.'

'You don't think it could have been a woman then?' Hillary pressed. She knew that the medical report had been clear that the wounds inflicted on Imelda could have been caused by either sex, providing they were reasonably fit and able-bodied.

Thomas shrugged. 'I don't know. I've just always tended to think that it was a man, that's all.'

Hillary nodded. She could see that underneath his tan he'd now become somewhat pale, and that lines of strain and stress were appearing around his eyes and mouth. And over at the island, Philippa too was becoming restless. Time, she thought, to call a halt.

She leaned forward and ended the recording on her phone. 'Well, I think that's all for now, Mr Phelps. Thank you for your time. I'll probably have to come back again in the future, just because further questions are sure to arise which will need your input. But for now, I think that's all.'

Thomas Phelps couldn't quite hide the look of relief that crossed his face as he rose to his feet. Once again, they politely and formally shook hands. Thomas pretended not to notice the slight difficulty Gareth had in rising from the sofa, merely waiting silently before walking them back to the door.

Once outside and back in Gareth's car, Hillary waited until they were heading back to Kidlington to speak.

'So, what did you make of that?'

Gareth smoothly overtook two cyclists who were taking up one half of the road, and said slowly, 'I think he wants us to think that the lover did it.'

'Hmm — no brownie points for that,' she said with a smile. 'But did you get the impression that he believed it himself?'

'Can't say as I did, ma'am,' Gareth said after a moment's thought.

'No. Me neither,' she said flatly.

* * *

When they got back to HQ, Claire looked up eagerly, and Hillary obliged her with a rundown on how the interview had gone.

Hillary had already transferred the recording to Gareth's phone, and without needing to be asked, he began transcribing the notes for the Murder Book.

'By the way, guv, I thought you might like to see this,' Claire said, punching something up on her tablet, and then turning it around so that Hillary could see it. 'It hit the internet not half an hour ago.'

Hillary saw that it was the website of one of the Oxford newspapers, and informed anybody who was interested that 'the tragic murder of the beautiful local model Imelda Phelps' was once again being investigated by the Thames Valley Police, and that 'the beloved mother of two' had yet to receive justice nearly fifteen years after being 'brutally bludgeoned to death in her own home.'

Hillary swore fluently. 'How the hell did they get on to this so quickly?'

'The husband's the only one you've informed so far, guv,' Claire pointed out.

'I don't think so. For one thing, we've only just come from his place. Besides, I can't see him or his second wife wanting it all raked up again in the public domain. He must have had a bellyful of publicity the first time around.'

'Well, I don't suppose it will raise that much of a fuss,' Claire tried to look on the bright side. 'Will people really be that interested in something that happened fifteen years ago?'

Hillary shrugged and nudged the device back her way. 'Let's hope not.'

She checked her watch. 'OK, it's lunch time now. We can . . .' she broke off, then said, 'By the way, is the mother still alive?'

'What, Imelda's mother you mean? Hold on, I was just doing her . . .' Claire quickly unearthed a notepad from under a pile of files and flicked through the pages. 'Yeah, here we are. Catherine Burton. Aged sixty-two at the time of her daughter's murder. Living in Cheltenham . . . Yes, she is still with us — at least I couldn't find a death certificate for her. And was still living at the same address this time last year, according to the electoral register. She'd be what . . . seventy-six or seven now, right?'

Hillary nodded. 'Have you got a telephone number for her?'

'Not yet, guv, but I could find one easily enough. Want me to ring her?'

'Yes. See if she's in and would speak to us this afternoon if possible. Fancy a run across to Cheltenham?'

Claire looked at Hillary carefully. 'Only if we can take my car, guv. The air conditioner works a treat.'

Hillary felt slightly offended on Puff's behalf, but not enough to fight his corner. 'Fine,' she agreed with a grin.

'Why the rush anyway?' Claire asked curiously.

Hillary shrugged. 'Thomas Phelps's description of her roused my curiosity, that's all. I just wanted to see if she really is the gorgon he described. Besides, Diane Clovis's interview with her barely rated a few lines, and if we're going to build up a full and accurate picture of our murder victim, I think her mother is as good a place to start as anywhere.'

'I'm sold,' Claire said. 'Especially if we can stop off at a pub somewhere on the way for an iced drink?' she wheedled cheekily.

Hillary laughed. 'Now *I'm* sold!'

CHAPTER THREE

They reached the spa town of Cheltenham a little before three o'clock, just as the afternoon sun reached its zenith, and the lovely spa town felt as if it was literally baking under a cloudless azure sky. The creamy Cotswold stone buildings shimmered, as did the asphalt that had been rendered tacky by the high temperatures. Claire checked her satnav attentively as they approached the area where Imelda's mother had lived for most of her life in the UK.

'According to the estate agent's website I googled, it's a really swanky area, guv,' Claire muttered, and quoted from memory: '"*A discreet and delightful cul-de-sac of impressive and generously proportioned Georgian architecture*" no less. And not a house that would go for under two mil,' she added enviously. 'And even *that* was the smallest, most modest des-res of the lot.'

Hillary glanced around at the growing signs of affluence and nodded. 'Makes sense. She's the daughter and granddaughter of canny American businessmen, and she married an MP whose family owned a fair portion of Northamptonshire. Not quite the heir to a title, but perhaps she found being the wife of a prominent member of parliament an acceptable alternative.'

'He died nearly twenty years ago now,' Claire informed her. 'Kept his seat — Conservative, of course . . .'

'Of course.'

'. . . for nearly thirty years. Mind you, around here, if you cut 'em they'd bleed blue blood,' Claire continued cheerfully. 'So I reckon this place of Mrs Burton's will have had plenty of nice, shady trees planted around it, don't you? Hold on — this is it, I think.'

The satnav had just told her to turn right and that she had reached her destination, and as they did so, the two women found themselves facing a genteel crescent with beech, plane and various ornamental cherry trees planted strategically in front of each of the ten or so houses. And there, in the middle of the circle, there was even a private garden, laden with lilacs and laburnums; ringed by highly decorated Victorian wrought iron and made complete by a notice on the only gate that firmly informed you that the garden was 'Strictly Private' and 'For the use of residents only,' who had, presumably, been given a key to the padlock on the purchase of their homes.

Shade abounded.

The houses reminded Hillary of some of those that could be found in Bath; the four at the far end were, strictly speaking, terraced, in that they all shared adjoining walls, but the three-storey edifices, with large sash windows and squarely placed front doors, all looked far too grand to care. The other houses spreading around and off from these were all detached, but the gap between them was negligible. All had wide stone steps reaching up from the pavement, as well as that uniform look of well-kept smugness. Here, no window was in need of cleaning, no geranium dared droop in their black-painted window boxes, and no chimney or wall was anything less than well-pointed and pristine.

'Crikey. You could film an episode of *Downton Abbey* here, guv,' Claire said with a grin.

Although several cars — Daimlers, Jaguars and the odd classic sports car — lined the narrow road, outside the home of Catherine Burton, the road was clear. What's more, a large plane tree provided plenty of shade, and Claire parked with a sigh of satisfaction in its densest part.

As they climbed out, the swish of muted traffic was the only sound to be heard. It was as if every bird in the town was too stunned by heat exhaustion to offer so much as a chirrup.

Wasting no time, they walked up the three stone steps and rang the doorbell. They hadn't rung ahead, for Hillary was quietly confident that no woman in her mid-seventies would be out and about during the worst of the afternoon heat, and her confidence was rewarded when the door was opened by a middle-aged woman who, when asked, confirmed that Mrs Burton was indeed 'at home'.

The guardian of the gate admitted them into a blessedly cool, traditionally black-and-white tiled hall with a genuine 18th-century grandfather clock ticking away ponderously in a shadowy corner, and Hillary wondered if she was the traditional housekeeper of old, with a comfortable set of rooms in the attic and a properly deferential manner, or whether she was the modern product of a domestic cleaning agency and went home every evening to a home and family of her own.

She rather thought the latter — but sometimes, you never knew.

Hillary produced her identification and for the first time saw evidence that the woman had been disconcerted. She was somewhere in her mid-fifties, with salt-and-pepper hair cut neat and short, but with a pleasant wave in it that mitigated her somewhat plain face.

'It's nothing alarming, I assure you. Purely routine,' Hillary said.

The woman did her best to look convinced, murmured a request for them to wait, turned and left them.

Claire glanced at Hillary nervously. 'Do you think we'll be expected to curtsy?' she whispered.

Hillary grinned, but quickly wiped it off her face as the woman returned. At least, Hillary mused, they weren't going to be kept waiting the requisite five minutes or so, just so that they could become properly aware of their place.

'Please come this way. Mrs Burton has ordered tea and refreshments.'

Hillary said a polite thank you, her eyes narrowing in concentration as the woman opened a set of double doors that led into a quietly splendid front room. Like most Georgian houses, the ceilings were high, the room square and the windows massive, which would normally have allowed in floods of natural light. Today, however, the shutters had been semi-closed in an attempt to keep out most of the ferocious sun, lending the room a dim and curtailed light. The Aubusson carpet and Chippendale furniture looked like the real deal to Hillary, as did the paintings by Fragonard that hung on two of the walls.

The woman who rose to greet them matched the room to perfection, in that she clearly came from another era. She stood upright and tall, with nothing of a slouch in her spine. Her hair was pure white and sat on top of her head in an imperious-looking chignon. She was wearing a white summer dress that reached mid-calf and was almost certainly acquired from a private salon in Paris somewhere. On her feet were neat court shoes with a modest heel, also in white. A row of pearls lined her neck, looking incongruously lovely against her crepe-paper-like skin, slightly marred by liver spots.

But the thing that most struck Hillary was the old lady's bone structure, which age couldn't destroy, and it was clear at once from whom Imelda had inherited her good looks. The same hazel eyes that had gazed back at her from the murdered woman's photograph now stared at her, assessing and questioning.

'Police?' she asked, as if doubting it could be true.

'Civilian consultant to the police, Mrs Burton. My name is Hillary Greene. I'm a former detective inspector, and I now work with the Crime Review Team. We are currently reviewing your daughter Imelda's case.'

A flicker of something crossed Catherine's face and was gone before Hillary could quite catch it, and then she was sinking gracefully back onto the sofa. 'I see. Please, be seated. My housekeeper will be bringing tea and cakes shortly.'

Hillary hadn't noticed that the other woman had already left them, and introduced Claire. The old woman barely registered this introduction however, keeping her eyes firmly fixed on Hillary as she accepted the offer to sit.

The second sofa in the room faced Catherine Burton over a small occasional table with an exquisite marble top, and Hillary made no attempt to bring out her phone and set it to record, trusting that Claire would have already done so — out of sight — on her own device. Instead, she reached into her bag and got out her seldom-used leatherbound notebook and a silver Parker pen that had been a long-neglected Christmas gift from her mother.

As she'd thought, Catherine Burton seemed to expect nothing less and Hillary suddenly felt as if she'd wandered into one of those lavish Agatha Christie television productions, where she was playing the part of the hapless flatfoot, whilst Poirot observed the proceedings with his gleaming green eyes and used his little grey cells to assess all the clues.

Alas, today, her own little grey cells would just have to do.

'I just wanted to get a bit of background on your daughter, Mrs Burton, and hoped that you could help me. I understand Imelda was an only child?'

'Yes. I'm afraid her birth was very difficult. I nearly died, and the doctors advised me to have no more children.'

The words were said crisply and with a matter-of-factness that defied any need for sympathy or comment, so Hillary gave none. Merely nodding, she carried on. 'She married young, I understand?'

'She was twenty. The same age as I was when I married,' Catherine corrected her primly.

'Her husband — Thomas. Did you and your husband approve of him?'

'He was sound enough, I suppose. He seemed to suit Imelda anyway. Their marriage was very successful. My husband was very fond of Jonas, his grandson.'

Hillary's lips twitched. What a glowing testimonial! 'Were you also close to your grandson back then? Or were you closer to Jessie?'

'Jessica was a rather difficult child, I'm afraid. I felt rather sorry for her.'

'Oh? Why?' This flicker of genuine emotion on the part of her witness was the first hint she'd had that the old lady might unbend a bit, and she hoped the trend would continue.

Catherine shrugged one elegantly bony shoulder. 'She just seems to be one of life's misfits, Inspector Greene. Have you spoken to her yet?'

'Not yet.'

'Well, when you do, you'll see for yourself.' And she gave a dismissive shrug.

Hillary hid a small sigh. So much for her unbending then! But she wasn't about to give up yet, and deliberately softened her voice. Although she doubted that she could get Catherine Burton to become positively chatty, if she could just get her to provide more than a bare sentence or two in response to her questions, she might let down her guard enough to say something revealing.

'What happened to your daughter must have come as a great shock to you, Mrs Burton, and I'm sure it's still raw after all this time.'

The older woman inclined her head regally. 'Thank you.'

'I've often found that mothers know the most about their children, even more than their partners in fact, which is why I was anxious to speak to you first.' She didn't think it was diplomatic to tell her that, actually, she'd been second on the list. 'You're obviously a woman of intelligence and experience — did you, or do you now have any ideas who might have committed the crime?' She hoped that the hint of flattery and appeal for her input might just be enough to encourage Catherine to rise to the challenge, so she wasn't all that surprised when the old lady slowly nodded her head.

'I have an opinion, yes. But it's purely personal. I have no evidence whatsoever for my beliefs.' Her thin lips firmed into a tighter line, making Hillary worry that she'd be too stiff-necked to say anything more.

She gave a brief smile. 'I'd still be obliged if you'd tell me, nonetheless,' she said. 'The opinions of those closest to the nucleus of the crime, such as yourself, should never be ignored. And I'm sure, as a responsible and upright citizen, you're aware of your duty to help the police with their inquiries,' she added. She considered that reminding a woman like this of her civil duty was at least worth a shot.

She thought she might have gone a little overboard on the law-and-justice bit though, because for a moment Catherine's sharp hazel stare narrowed on her a little ominously, as if suspecting that she was being manipulated or managed, but after a tense moment, the danger passed.

'Very well,' Catherine conceded coolly. 'My first thought was that my poor daughter was attacked by some stranger who had become obsessed with her, and I said as much to the investigating officer at the time, but apparently she could find no evidence for this. After that was ruled out, I decided that the most likely suspect was that Brightman woman; I always suspected she was rather more unstable than most people believed. I told Imelda that it was a mistake to go into business with someone like that, but as usual, my daughter thought she knew better.'

Hillary, who had been expecting the name of Dermott Franklyn to feature prominently, had to quickly readjust her thinking. 'This is Connie Brightman we're talking about, yes? If I remember correctly, she and your daughter were in a business partnership for a time. Designing, making and selling jewellery, correct? I can't quite recall the name of it . . .'

For the first time Claire spoke. 'Cotswolds Gems, ma'am.'

'Ah yes, thank you, Claire,' Hillary murmured. She understood why her friend had used the very formal 'ma'am' instead of her name or her more usual 'guv', of course. In this rather overwhelming setting, informality had become verboten.

Catherine sighed. 'It sounds much grander than it really was — and I wouldn't, personally, have called it a partnership as such either. Certainly not an *equal* partnership. Imelda put up all the funding, naturally, and she was also responsible for all the selling too — almost exclusively to her circle of friends, I might add. All the Brightman woman did was design and make the pieces — ghastly modern stuff it was too. I saw some examples of it, and it seemed to consist of soldering bits of metal to each other in irregular shapes, and sometimes setting stones into them — and mostly semi-precious stones at that. Even polished pebbles, I believe.' The old lady shook her head. 'It was hardly Fabergé or Asprey. Fortunately, the enterprise was fairly short-lived.'

Hillary knew from her preliminary perusal of the original files a little about Connie Brightman and the small business she and Imelda had set up — in Imelda's case, probably just to augment her income from her sporadic modelling assignments, and to give her something to do to stave off boredom. But Hillary seemed to recall from DI Clovis's reports that for Connie Brightman it had been her sole source of income, and she'd been very unhappy indeed when Imelda had decided she'd had enough and shut the operation down after just a few years.

'I understand Miss Brightman was very upset when the partnership ended, given that she'd been reliant on the business for her livelihood,' Hillary said, careful to keep any hint of censure from her voice.

'Yes, that is so. Of course, it was very wrong of Imelda to encourage her in the first place,' Catherine said stiffly. 'I told her so at the time. You have to understand, my daughter had passing fancies and never stuck at anything for very long. I imagine, once she'd charmed all her friends — and the acquaintances of those friends — into buying their wretched geegaws, she just couldn't be bothered to do a proper marketing strategy, and simply turned her attentions to the next thing that caught her eye.'

'Leaving Miss Brightman high and dry?'

'As you say,' Catherine conceded with a cool tilt of her head. 'I was there once, at Imelda's home, when she received a phone call from the woman not long after dissolving the enterprise, and I could hear her shouting and carrying on even from where I was sitting. She must have been shouting down the telephone line — and the language she used! Imelda just hung up on her. In my opinion, the woman was unstable, possibly even unhinged.'

Hillary nodded. She'd have to check the notes again, but from memory, she thought that Imelda had died some two months or so after the demise of the business. So, if Connie Brightman *had* been enraged enough to strike back so violently, she'd taken her time about it. On the other hand, perhaps the passing months had only allowed her resentment and anger to grow until she had reached a boiling point?

Of course, Catherine might merely have latched onto the 'outsider' as the killer of her daughter simply because she couldn't conceive of anyone more intimately connected to Imelda killing her. Such as her husband, her lover, or either of her two children, for instance.

'Did you visit with Imelda often?' she asked casually, wondering if her assessment would match that of her son-in-law.

Catherine sighed. 'Not very often, no. I always found it something of a trek to her place, and I've never been fond of driving. I've given up my car now and use taxis.'

'Were you aware of your daughter's affair with Dermott Franklyn, Mrs Burton?'

The old woman stiffened. 'There was no affair,' she stated coldly.

In her peripheral vision, Hillary saw Claire's head shoot up in surprise.

'I believe the original investigating officer found plenty of proof that there was, in fact, a rather long-lived liaison between Mr Franklyn and Imelda,' Hillary contradicted her quietly, choosing her language carefully.

'Rubbish,' Catherine said, waving a ring-bedecked hand imperiously in the air. 'I raised my daughter better than that. Oh, I know that sort of thing goes on nowadays as it did back then, and nobody seems to bat an eye over it, but Imelda would never have allowed her standards to slip that far. A lady's reputation and her good name, once gone, is gone forever, as I constantly drummed into her. If that man said they had been . . . together . . . he is simply lying. Or he's a fantasist.'

Hillary didn't argue. She knew it would be pointless. Let the old lady keep her head buried in the sand if it helped her to cope.

'You said your first thought was that Imelda might have been attacked by an obsessive stranger. Did your daughter ever mention to you if someone was stalking her?'

'No, she never said as much,' Catherine admitted, relaxing a little now that the conversation had taken a more acceptable turn. 'But it wouldn't have surprised me.'

'Oh?' Hillary asked sharply.

'What else could she expect? Her so-called modelling career — fah! Making herself so conspicuous. It was just asking for trouble, and I told her so.'

Hillary nodded, as if in agreement. 'I understand Imelda signed up with an agency when she was just eighteen?'

Catherine gave a slight sniff. 'She had a portfolio of herself done when she was sixteen — without informing me I might add, and then tried to persuade me to give consent to her signing a modelling contract shortly afterwards. Naturally, I refused.'

'Naturally,' Hillary murmured. 'You were trying to protect her. I can't imagine that she saw it that way though. Teenagers, especially thwarted teenagers, can be very volatile and dramatic.'

In response, Catherine merely shrugged, her lips once more thinning into a tight, forbidding line.

'I take it your husband agreed with your refusal to go along with Imelda's chosen profession?'

'Of course he did. He was a member of parliament, and the Sunday scandal sheets in this country are notorious for muck raking. We felt as if we were walking on eggshells for years, especially during a general election, just waiting for some nasty little journalist to write up a feature on her, in a bid to smear poor Arthur. But she had no consideration for us at all — all she did was laugh and say that nobody cared about that sort of thing anymore.'

'It must have been a difficult time for you — all of you,' Hillary said diplomatically. She could tell the old lady was beginning to get restless. Doubtless all this raking over of their dirty laundry was going very much against the grain, and since she now felt that she'd got all the insight she needed into the relationship between murder victim and mother, she decided that there was nothing to be gained in alienating Catherine further.

Far better to leave her to settle for a bit, and then come back when she'd recovered her equilibrium.

'Well, thank you very much, Mrs Burton, you've been most helpful. I'm afraid I may need to come and see you again at some point, as we're only in the early stages of our investigation.' And added, just to sugar-coat the pill a bit, 'I take it that you want to be kept fully informed of any progress?'

'Naturally,' Catherine agreed, and rose from her sofa as Hillary and Claire did likewise. Just then the door opened and the housekeeper came in with a tray. On it was a solid silver tea set, with bone-china cups and saucers, a plate of wafer-thin cucumber sandwiches and another of tiny cakes that could only have come from a French patisserie somewhere in town.

'I'm sorry, but we're just leaving,' Hillary said to her.

Without a word, the housekeeper deposited the tray on the table, turned and led them out. Passing through the cool marble hall, Hillary stopped momentarily in front of a small gallery of framed photographs mounted on the wall. Most were of the MP husband, debating in the Commons or pictured with minor royalty or the odd film star of yesteryear. There were no photographs of Imelda at all, and only one of Catherine.

In it, she was pictured being presented with some sort of silver salver, surrounded by a small group of women who were all wearing their conservative best, and ranged in age from their early thirties to their mid-sixties. A small gold plaque attached to the bottom of the framed picture drew her eye.

Mrs Catherine Burton
Voted Woman of the Year 2011
By the Women's Charity League

Once outside, the heat hit them like a blast furnace, making Hillary realise just how well air-conditioned the interior of the house had been.

'Blimey! No wonder Imelda married early and left home the first chance she got,' Claire said as they made their way to her car. 'What a dragon.'

Hillary climbed into the passenger seat and buckled up her seat belt thoughtfully. She was beginning to get a better picture of their murder victim now and wasn't so sure that things were quite as black and white as Claire was making out. 'She's certainly of the old school,' she agreed. 'And I'm beginning to think that Imelda choosing to pursue a modelling career wasn't dictated so much by her obvious physical attributes as by a desire to hit back at her mother.'

Claire grunted. 'Good on her, I say. Mind you, guv, if that was the case, wouldn't she have gone in for nude shots or something? She never did though. Clovis never found anything remotely like it in her background. The raciest thing in her portfolio were some run-of-the-mill underwear shots — and those were only for a catalogue for good ol' M&S.'

Hillary looked up at Imelda's childhood home and frowned. 'I don't think we're dealing with something as simple as teenage rebellion. If she'd been a real wild child, she would have run away at sixteen and really kicked off the traces. Instead, she chose the more conventional route of marrying and having children. Which tells me that Imelda couldn't throw off her mother's influence as thoroughly as she would have liked.'

'Don't look now, guv, but we're being watched,' Claire said, nodding her head slightly to her right.

Hillary, instantly distracted, picked up on her line of sight and saw a woman watching them from the shady depths of the private garden. Around Catherine Burton's age, but much smaller in stature, she gave Hillary the impression of a small curious bird, watching them with unabashed interest.

Hillary gave her a brief smile and a little friendly wave as Claire pulled away.

* * *

Back at HQ, since it was nearly clocking-off time, she told Claire to leave typing up her notes until tomorrow morning, and left her in the office, filling in Gareth on the interview.

She went to her own office, which felt distressingly airless, and after just five minutes or so, was glad to lock up and leave.

She had planned to interview Imelda's children as her next priority but after the trip to Cheltenham was inclined to change her mind. Tomorrow, she wanted to visit Chipping Norton and assess Connie Brightman herself. It wouldn't hurt to take a look at the Phelpses' one-time home either, just to get a general impression of the lie of the land.

Back on the *Mollern*, she began the now-familiar process of opening up all the windows on the shady side of the boat, then took a brief shower before slipping into a lightweight, roomy kaftan. Leaving her feet deliciously bare, she padded through to the galley and poured herself a cold lemonade and listlessly checked her fridge, where she found a few frugal ingredients that might just about make up a salad.

Outside, the usual feathered pirates — mostly comprised of bolshy mallards — began to demand their own dinner.

Hillary tossed a handful of brown bread chunks out of the open window and told them to think themselves lucky.

CHAPTER FOUR

That night it was almost impossible to sleep, with the heat barely dissipating with the setting of the sun, and then turning unbearably humid just for good measure. Hillary supposed she must have catnapped on and off, but she was awake long before dawn, and after lying on top of her bed, gently steaming (physically and mentally) for an hour or so, got up and went for a sluggish early morning walk.

By the time she arrived at HQ on the dot of 9 a.m., she felt as if she'd already put in a full day's work. Popping her head into the communal office on her way to her stationery cupboard, she saw Claire slumped in her chair, face practically thrust into the slowly revolving electric fan, looking as bleary-eyed as herself.

Gareth, looking as crisp and fresh as a daisy, was reading something on his laptop, and looked up at her far more eagerly. Although it's a well-known fact that misery loves company, she decided to give Claire a break, and nodded over at the former soldier. 'Give me half an hour to update the boss and check my emails, and then we'll head out to Chippie, OK?'

'Yes, ma'am,' Gareth nodded, and visibly hesitated to say something.

'We'll take your car,' Hillary helped him out dryly. 'Oh, and give Ms Brightman a call, make sure she's going to be in. And if not, find out where she's working and ask her if she can arrange to spare us ten minutes or so.'

Gareth, trying not to look relieved, nodded and returned his attention to his computer screen.

* * *

The north-west Oxfordshire town of Chipping Norton had been settled on high ground, and was usually the first to know about it whenever cold and snowy weather put in an appearance during the winter months. Pleasant, bustling, full of vernacular architecture, it boasted a huge, eye-catching former mill with a tall chimney that nestled in a little valley which had long since been turned into flats for the seriously rich.

It turned out that Imelda Phelps's former marital home missed out on a view of this local landmark by a cat's whisker, but nevertheless was located firmly in a plot that bore all the hallmarks of a 'desirable area.' Wide, tree-lined roads gave access to large gardens and detached houses ranging from Georgian to Victorian with some mandatory 'modern eyesores' thrown in, which seemed to mostly consist of glass cubes and steel.

The former Phelpses' home was early Victorian, probably updated inside to within an inch of its life: comprised of traditional red brick with white-painted gingerbread trim, it had a lovely old wisteria growing up three of its four walls, and boasted a wide, neatly raked pale gravel driveway.

'Wonder who lives there now?' Hillary mused as she and Gareth inspected it from the idling car.

'I can find out quickly enough,' Gareth offered, reaching for his smartphone, but Hillary waved a hand to stop him.

'No, don't bother. Even if someone was in and let us look around, too much time has passed for us to get anything meaningful out of it. Besides, the people who bought it from Thomas Phelps might have moved on, and the present owners might have no idea that a woman was murdered in their hallway. And if that's the case, you know what they say. Ignorance is bliss.'

Gareth nodded, then looked in the rear-view mirror and frowned. 'Looks like the neighbourhood-watch scheme is working on all four cylinders,' he said, making Hillary glance at him curiously. 'Look behind you,' he advised.

Hillary did so and saw a Jam Sandwich pulling up behind them, and the sight of the marked police car made her eyebrows rise. 'Whoever phoned in and reported us as suspicious characters must have timed it just right. Dispatch must have caught them just as they were passing — we haven't been here five minutes.'

She pushed the button that electronically rolled down the window as the constable in the driver's seat stepped out and casually approached. Right now, she assumed his partner was running Gareth's licence plates. 'It has to be your fault,' Hillary told her companion wryly. 'You must look like a burglar.'

Gareth's lips twitched. 'What does that make you then, ma'am?'

'The safecracker, I suppose,' Hillary muttered, already reaching into her handbag for her ID, as the constable began to bend down to look at her through the open window.

'Morning, Constable,' Hillary said, flapping open the little leather wallet that showed her photograph and designation.

The constable, who looked barely eighteen to her but was probably as much as three or four years older, clearly recognised her name, because she saw his pale grey eyes widen a little. Although she wasn't, strictly speaking, still 'in the job,' her many years as a DI (plus her enviable solve rate) had earned her a solid reputation that even new recruits were aware of. 'Nothing to worry your guv'nor about, Constable,' she told him genially. 'This residence was the scene of a homicide back in 2010, and the CRT are currently taking a second look at it. Don't worry, we're just getting the lie of the land and will be moving on in a minute. Actually, you can do me a favour. Do you know the best way to get to . . .' She quickly checked the address for Connie Brightman and relayed it.

The constable nodded. 'Yes, ma'am. Go straight on . . .' She listened as he continued to give directions, and when he'd finished, thanked him politely. She watched him retreat back to the Jam Sandwich where he began to talk animatedly to his partner.

'Better get going then,' Hillary advised Gareth languidly. 'Apart from upsetting the locals, if we stay in one place too long we're likely to melt. What's the temperature already?' Although Gareth's air-con unit was pumping out a cooling draught, she could still feel the ambient heat seeping through the windscreen.

'Twenty-eight, ma'am,' Gareth said, checking the dashboard display with a quick flick of his eyes.

'And it's not even eleven yet,' she muttered, and fought back a huge yawn.

Gareth, wisely, said nothing, and concentrated on the road.

They may only have driven for a few minutes, but in those minutes, they might as well have travelled to another world. Gone was the picture-postcard version of the Cotswold town, and in its place was a maze of semi-detached, council-built houses that looked identical, with dismembered cars and discarded children's toys proliferating in tiny front gardens far more than flowers or neat lawns. Here potholes abounded, and the render on walls had a dirty, grimy look to it.

As they parked and stepped out onto the pavement, Hillary could see at once that the local dog-walkers paid scant attention to the warning notices of stringent fines for owners who didn't clean up after their pooches, and she made sure to step carefully as she made her way to the front gate of number 28 Acacia Drive. Needless to say, there wasn't an acacia in sight.

As she pushed open the gate and approached the house, she could see that this half of the semi-detached had been turned into two cramped flats — with Connie Brightman occupying the ground floor. She pressed the bell under the Brightman name and waited.

After a minute that seemed to lag into two, the door was eventually opened, revealing a dumpy woman of five feet six or so, peering at them through small brown eyes. She had short dyed blonde hair and was wearing a jogging suit in a particularly lurid shade of turquoise. Hillary knew from the case notes that Connie Brightman had been thirty-one at the time of the murder, so must now be forty-six or thereabouts, but she looked much older. Her skin was sallow, her nails short and bitten, and she was sweating profusely.

Yellow-stained fingers showed she was a smoker, which probably hadn't helped her state of health much, and for a moment she stood stubbornly blocking the hallway. Then her rounded shoulders slumped a little. 'You the fellah that called this morning?' she asked, looking at Gareth. Her eyes missed nothing of the scar on his face, the walking cane he leaned on, or the slightly withered appearance of his left hand.

'Yes, ma'am,' Gareth said politely.

Hillary showed her ID and introduced herself.

'This is still about Imelda then, is it?' Connie guessed, her voice flat and definitely lacking in enthusiasm.

'Yes,' Hillary agreed simply.

A small, bitter smile flickered around the other woman's lips. 'Of course it is,' she muttered. 'What else should I have expected? It always was about dear Imelda when she was alive, so why should it be any different now that she's been dead and gone for years? You'd better come in, I suppose — you're letting the heat in.'

The hall of the house was obviously a communal area used by the upstairs tenant also, for a children's buggy stood in one corner, and Hillary knew from the notes that Connie Brightman had no children.

'This way then.' She opened the door to her flat and led them into what had once been a living room, but which now had to serve as both living room and tiny kitchen-diner.

'Sit down,' she indicated the two kitchen chairs that were tucked under a table currently awash with sketches and designs. She turned to drag around the single armchair the room boasted and sank back into it with a sigh.

The curtains on the front wall were drawn against the sun, but they were thin and worn, and still let in a significant amount of light. Hillary couldn't help but pick up one of the drawings to take a closer look. A pair of earrings, in beaten copper and with intricate scroll-work depicting a dragon's head on each, looked back at her.

'These are good,' Hillary said, and meant it. 'You clearly have a wonderful eye. I didn't know you still made jewellery.'

'I don't,' Connie said flatly. 'I just sell designs and stuff for this woman from Stow-on-the-Wold. She's another Imelda that one! Her rich hubby has bought her a little shop to play with, and she makes her own range of baubles and sells it to gullible rich tourists. Only thing is, she can't design to save her life. So she comes to me and buys my ideas and then cons people into believing they are her own. Does very nicely out of 'em too, but will she make me a proper partner? Will she hell. The cow.'

Connie reached into the pocket of her trousers and drew out a packet of cigarettes, then lit one from a small zippo-type lighter. Hillary resigned herself to not only enduring the heat, but to doing so without an adequate supply of breathable air. Gareth surreptitiously pushed his chair a little further back in a vain effort to avoid the worst of the smoke.

'Whatcha wanna know then?' Connie demanded. 'After all this time, you really think you're gonna get the bloke that did for Imelda?' She gave an inelegant snort. 'Fat chance. Your lot couldn't suss it out then, so I don't fancy your chances after all this time.'

'You think it was a man then?' Hillary asked, ignoring the insult to her colleagues and trying to keep her face turned from the bulk of the smoke without being obvious about it. She had the feeling that if she made her discomfiture plain, Connie would, as likely as not, deliberately aim more smoke her way.

'Stands to reason, don't it?' Connie said harshly. 'Women like her are usually done in by men, aren't they?'

'Women like her?' Hillary pounced on the phrase.

Connie drew on her cigarette with gusto, but thankfully tilted her head up and blew the resulting stream of smoke upwards at the ceiling. It had the automatic, unthinking quality of habit about it that made Hillary think this woman was used to smoking this way. Perhaps she had a partner who didn't appreciate a face-full of smoke either?

A quick glance around revealed no obvious signs of a male cohabitant though.

'You know — beautiful rich cows who think they just have to crook a little finger and everything falls right into their lap. And it does. Those sort of women, they go too far, don't they? Push their luck just that bit too much. And — bam!' She shrugged.

Hillary leaned back a little in her chair. 'She liked to push her luck, did she? Imelda?'

'Course she did! For a start, she led that poor wimp of a husband of hers a merry dance. And then there was that other fellah she had on the go for over a year or more. Head-over-heels about her he was, daft sod. He wanted her to run off with him — couldn't have given a toss about her kids or anything else.'

'You mean Dermott Franklyn?'

'Him, yeah. But there were others before him. Not so serious mind.'

Hillary blinked. There had been no mention of 'others' in Clovis's original investigation.

'She two-timed her husband with more than one man?' Hillary mused out loud, too worn out from last night's bout of sleeplessness to sound particularly excited about it. And she could tell her lack of shock didn't sit well with her witness, who had no doubt expected more of a reaction.

'Course she did! Oh, I'm not saying that she had more than one fella on the go at any one time,' Connie admitted reluctantly, narrowing her eyes and staring at her cigarette thoughtfully. 'No, I'm not saying she did *that.* But I know for a fact she had at least one fella before that Dermott came along — probably a whole string of 'em. Stands to reason, don't it? But I only caught her out and about with one other bloke before Dishy Dermott became such a long-term feature.'

Hillary took a moment to sort out this rather convoluted statement. 'You think she made a habit of having flings, but then settled down for a long-term affair with Dishy Dermott?'

'Uh-huh.'

'Do you think her husband knew?'

Connie snorted with laughter. 'What? Him? Nah. Lived with his head in the clouds that one. Too chuffed to have nabbed himself such a looker to see what was going on under his nose, I reckon.' Then she frowned and stared at her cigarette again. 'Or maybe he knew, but just didn't give a toss? Either way, he never made a fuss about things, not as far as I know. And I'd have known, believe me.'

'Were you close with the Phelpses, then?' Hillary asked sceptically, again making the other woman snort with mirth.

'Don't make me laugh. Too hoity-toity to treat me as anything other than the staff, them! Nah, I could just read that woman like a book, that's all.'

If that had been true, Hillary thought cynically, why was it that Connie hadn't been prepared when Imelda became bored enough with Cotswold Gems to bring their little business to a close? Because, from what DI Clovis's team had established, it *had* come as a nasty shock to her. But she was wise enough not to antagonise her witness and kept her thoughts to herself. Right now, she needed Connie Brightman to remain talkative and spiteful. 'You were living with your aunt at the time of the murder, I understand?' she asked instead.

'Yeah — Aunty Mae. She had a council house a bit like this one — but a whole one, I mean. Her and her husband had it ever since my uncle came home from the war. He'd been gone some years, though, when I moved in. She was finding it harder and harder to live on her pension, and was probably feeling a bit lonely, like. And I was glad enough to move out of Mum and Dad's place and get out from under their beady little eyes, wasn't I? So it made sense for both of us — I became her lodger, paid a bit of rent and enjoyed some freedom for a change.' She shrugged, stubbed out her cigarette in an over-full ashtray, and immediately lit up another one.

'I take it she's gone now?'

'Yeah — a few years after Imelda carked it. The council were charging too much for me to carry on living there, and 'sides, they wanted to move a family in and said I didn't need a house to myself, so they turfed me out, the buggers, and found me this rathole instead. And I've been here ever since.'

'You must have thought Cotswold Gems was your chance at a better life?' Hillary asked, not without sympathy.

'Too right,' Connie said bitterly. 'Only ever worked in garage forecourts or stacking shelves in supermarkets before then. But I could always draw, even at school,' she added proudly.

Once again, Hillary selected a sheet of paper from the tabletop — this one of a bracelet linked with a clever paper-clip-inspired design of enamel in red and green. Again, to Hillary's admittedly unprofessional eye, it looked as though it would be very striking when turned into reality.

'You never thought of studying design at university? Or doing a Guilds or something?'

Connie grunted. 'Me? Couldn't afford it for one thing — had to leave school and start earning, or Mum and Dad would have boxed me ears,' she explained without any obvious malice. ''Sides, I was no good at book-learning and exams and stuff. But give me a soldering iron . . .' She sighed. 'Beautiful stuff, I made — proper quality,' she added angrily, as if Hillary had expressed some doubt about it. 'I did a better job than that cow in Stow does, I can tell you! Hands down! No, we never had no trouble selling my stuff — never. Just her ladyship couldn't be arsed to go out and drum up new customers. Too much like hard work for our Imelda.' Her eyes glazed a little as she recalled her glory days, then abruptly dulled. 'I had to sell off all the equipment when she shut us down, didn't I? Only bloody thing she left me, when the solicitors had got through with things. Oh, I tried to carry on making stuff on my own like, for a bit, and even sold some to some shops, but it was no good. I couldn't make it pay, so had to sell the gear. And then it was back to stacking shelves at Tesco. And now, it's the bloody factory.'

'According to what you told DI Clovis, on the day that Imelda died you worked that morning, came home at lunchtime, then watched television all afternoon?'

'That's right,' Connie said flatly. 'Bloody daytime telly is shit, but what else is there to do that don't cost money? All garden make-overs and DIY and antiques and stuff. Dead boring, but it passes the time I suppose.'

She sucked mightily on her cigarette, her eyes brooding.

Hillary nodded. 'But you had nobody who could confirm you were in? Your aunt, I understand, was out visiting a friend that day?'

'Down at the bingo more like with her cronies,' Connie said with a sneer.

'But you had no alibi for the time of the murder,' Hillary persisted quietly.

'Nope,' Connie said challengingly, once more sucking hard on her cigarette, and looking vaguely amused now. 'And I'll tell you this for nothing. That woman inspector might not have found anyone who could say I was here, but nor could she find anyone to say I was at Imelda's place neither. So there then! 'Sides, why would I do in the selfish cow? She wasn't worth risking jail-time for, let me tell you! Silly old bint, always swanning around and saying she was on the verge of signing some big new modelling deal. Living in la-la land if you ask me. She was over the hill, but never would admit it.'

'I saw a photograph of her not long before her death. She still looked fabulous,' Hillary pointed out mildly.

Connie merely grunted.

'Did you get the impression things were all right at home?' Hillary changed tack.

'What, with the gormless hubby? Far as I know.'

'What was her relationship like with her kids?'

Connie grinned. 'The daughter couldn't stand her, and I don't reckon that boy of hers gave her the time of day much either.'

Hillary nodded but didn't take the bait. She'd prefer to assess Jessie and Jonas Phelps herself, when she interviewed them.

'Did Imelda seem the same as usual? The last time you saw her?'

'Didn't see her much after she closed down the business,' Connie stated flatly. 'But before that, she seemed all right. Mind you, there was that time she seemed to go into hibernation for a bit. Can't think what that was about — she couldn't have been that fascinated with her home life.'

Hillary cocked her head to one side. 'What do you mean?'

Connie shrugged. 'Nothing much. It was just her ladyship was always out and about, but for some reason, for a while, she didn't seem to leave the house. Well, I never saw her anyway. I used to go there nearly every day, to discuss the jewellery and pick up whatever gold or stones had come in. She ordered everything and it came to her house, see? But for about a week, no more like two maybe, she kept putting me off. Had the metal and stones messengered over to me. I called her on her landline and she always answered, so I knew she wasn't out galivanting, but . . . it was just odd, that's all.'

'But you saw her eventually?'

'Oh yeah. Things went back to normal.'

'So she was probably just ill — had the flu or something?' Hillary proffered.

Connie shrugged indifferently. 'She didn't say as much.'

'Did she ever mention falling out with someone? Or being afraid of anyone?'

'Not to me. But I wouldn't be surprised if she hadn't rubbed someone up the wrong way. She was all me, me, me, that woman. People don't like it, do they? They get fed up with it.'

'Anyone specific spring to mind?' Hillary pressed.

But Connie just shook her head, her eyes slewing off to one side, idly following a column of smoke as it rose in the air. A little smile tugged at her lips.

Hillary sighed, then coughed as the smoky air caught at the back of her dry throat. She was sure as she could be that Connie had thought of something just then and was intent on holding it back, but she was now so desperate to get out of the smoky atmosphere and into some fresh air that she decided it could wait. It would give her an excuse to come back, and from past experience of this type of witness she knew that if she pushed it, Connie would only dig her heels in even further. Then she'd never get it out of her.

No, it was better to wait and let it stew for a while.

'Well, thank you for your help, Ms Brightman. I may call on you again sometime soon — just to see if anything else has come to mind in the meantime. You'd be surprised what memories come to the surface once your subconscious has been teased.'

She produced her card and handed it over. Connie took it with the air of one who is mentally wondering which rubbish bin she can toss it into first.

Gareth discreetly turned off the recording app on his phone, and manoeuvred himself to his feet, thanked Connie politely, and followed Hillary back out into the hall.

Once outside, Hillary took in several breaths of hot but blissfully smoke-free air, and leaned against the wall of the house for a few moments. This time, she couldn't fight off an enormous yawn, and put a hand over her mouth. 'Another five minutes in there and you might have had to carry me out,' she informed him.

Gareth's lips twitched. 'Back to Kidlington, ma'am?'

'Back to Kidlington,' Hillary agreed wearily. 'And on the way back, we're stopping at a pub somewhere and drinking a few quarts of something ice-cold.'

'Sounds like a plan to me, ma'am.'

* * *

Gavin Otterley stared at the archive footage his newspaper had published at the time of Imelda Phelps's murder, and wished he'd been old enough to cover the story himself, instead of still being in school and sitting his A levels.

He was pretty sure he'd have made a better job of it than the original reporter who *had* covered it.

Leaning back in his chair, he stared from his small bedroom window out over the streets of Osney Mead. In the distance, the famous creamy stones of the 'dreaming spires' of Oxford reflected golden light like some fabled city out of one of JRR Tolkien's novels. Like a lot of his fellow journalists, especially in this city of literary fame, he often dreamed of writing a novel himself one day. But, also like a lot of people in his profession, his reality was working from home in an industry that was practically all conducted online and left little room for the romance of dreams.

It irked him that he'd never smelt the ink or touched the paper still warm off the presses, let alone phoned in a 'scoop' to an impatient editor who had the ear of every crooked politician in town. He'd be lucky if his dozy editor even knew the whereabouts of a crooked corkscrew.

So instead of living the dream of being the street-savvy hard-bitten hero reporter so beloved of the films he watched and the paperback thrillers he devoured in his every free moment, he'd had to endure five years of small-city stories, low pay, and a sense of ever-growing disillusionment.

He'd started work on the Oxford paper fresh out of college, with London firmly in his sights, confident that youthful drive, intelligence and ambition would soon see him scrabbling up the journalistic ladder. Instead, here he was, *still* in Oxford, *still* struggling to afford the astronomical rent of his tiny flat, and *still* fighting for every by-line and taste of honey that he could get.

But, he had to acknowledge that he'd been given a break with the 'Model Mother' murder, as he was intent on dubbing it in a bid to drum up a modicum of interest from his employers and the jaded reading public alike. The tip-off from the friend of his father had allowed him to be the first to break the news of the new police interest in the old murder case, and the online piece he'd submitted had created the best splash he'd had for at least a year, so he was anxious to keep the momentum going. And since good stories were rare indeed, that meant that he had to build on the one he'd been gifted.

The only trouble with that was, left as it lay, the story would just sink back into nothingness. The public's fickle attention would wander, and with it would go his beloved by-lines.

So what could he do as a follow-up?

He'd already tried to contact the dead woman's husband, but Thomas Phelps had now blocked his calls, and wasn't answering any of his emails. He'd tried the son and daughter too, naturally, but had met with the same, stone-walling response.

Time to think bigger maybe?

He swung to and fro on his somewhat tatty swivel chair, tapping his lips with a pencil. He'd never actually used it to write anything with, it was just a habit he'd carried with him from primary school. And he liked to think it made him look thoughtful and intelligent.

At five feet six, slender, with rather long fair hair and a cheeky-chappie sort of face, he knew that he rather resembled a grown-up child. But this deceiving air of innocence had served him well, disarming people and encouraging them to open up, so that by the time they'd realised that they'd laid their souls bare to him it was too late, leaving them to regret their naivete and 'read all about it' in the papers the next day.

Yes, perhaps it was time to turn on his famous charm in person? Not with the husband though — Gavin was sure the likes of Thomas would see through him in an instant. The son too. No, the daughter was his best bet. Photographically too, if she looked anything like her late mother. He could just see it now — a photograph of the still-grieving daughter, wondering who had killed her beloved mother, and hoping

Gavin Otterley and his 'crusading' paper might be the vehicle to jog people's memories and provide that one vital clue that brought a killer to justice.

His editor would lap it up!

Or maybe the murdered woman's mother, if she was still in the land of the living, was the way to go? An interview with a grief-stricken mother always went down well with readers. With maybe a shot across the bows of the police added in for good measure.

In his small bedroom-cum-office Gavin grinned widely. A bit of police-bashing never lost its popularity with good ol' Joe Public, and since Thames Valley Police had never solved the case, it wasn't as if they could object if he pointed out their failings. Which meant that he'd have to tackle the new plod on the case and see if he could get a rise out of them. He reached quickly for his phone and rang Donnie Clovis's number, but it turned out the silly old sod couldn't remember the copper's name. He described her, but a fat lot of good that did him!

Gavin thanked him cursorily and hung up. Still, there was more than one way to skin a rabbit, and he knew some people who knew some people in Police HQ, so a few further phone calls later, he was furnished with the name of Hillary Greene.

He quickly began to tap out key words in his search engine and was soon whistling through his teeth. Apparently, the new investigator was a bit of a living legend. During her career as a DI she'd been awarded a medal for bravery and taken down some very nasty characters indeed. What's more, her solve rate was so impressive that the police PR team never failed to mention it at every opportunity.

Might there be an angle there? A little niggle or needle that he could use? After all, the original DI had been a woman as well, right? And she'd fumbled it. He could stir up every misogynist in their readership easy as pie by pointing out that another woman had been given a second bite of the cherry and get a bit of controversy going that way.

Hmm . . . On the other hand, the editor might not be so keen, since half their readers were women. He'd have to give it all some more thought.

Tapping the pencil thoughtfully against his lips, Gavin stared out of the window. At least it was evening time, and the worst of the heat was letting up a bit now. Not that he minded the heat himself — he was just waiting for the oldies to start falling off their perches so he could do a piece on 'killer weather.'

* * *

As Gavin Otterley gazed out over the city skyline and lazily pondered his options, several miles away, Hillary Greene gazed out over the Oxford canal. She was sitting at one of the garden tables set up outside the Boat pub, and was idly perusing the menu. Unable to face cooking anything, she'd wandered down to save herself the trouble, and was now contemplating the merits of the Caesar salad versus the poached salmon special.

On the table in front of her stood a pint glass of lemon and lime, awash with ice. She drank it thirstily and idly watched a busy thrush as it rooted about in a grassy tussock overhanging the canal.

She was feeling slightly guilty.

After her trip to Chippie, she simply hadn't been able to face another hot journey out and about, and so had contented herself with making a significant dent in the never-ending paperwork, only to find her eyes kept closing treacherously over her computer. For two pins, she could have put her head down on her folded arms and gone to sleep.

Was she in danger of becoming dead weight? She didn't like to think so. And she knew, realistically, that she couldn't be the only one suffering from the prolonged heatwave. But still . . . Was it a sign that she was just getting too long in the tooth? Perhaps it was time to think of retiring properly?

The crime novel that she'd written and had published was selling steadily. True, it wasn't troubling the bestseller charts yet, but her editor was hinting that if there was a second novel in the making, it would be viewed favourably. Perhaps she should just grow old gracefully and become a staid, stay-at-home woman of letters? Maybe that was all she was becoming good for?

Then she gave a mental head shake. And give up on the possibility of getting justice for the forgotten — such as Imelda Phelps? In a pig's eye!

Tomorrow, she promised herself stoutly, she'd hit the road with renewed vigour.

Then she yawned widely.

Well.

Maybe with something that might be mistaken for vigour.

CHAPTER FIVE

Hillary awoke the next morning feeling like an inert mass. Although she'd technically slept for more hours than the night before — probably out of sheer tiredness and necessity — the night had been unbearably humid, and her dozing had been interrupted and unsatisfying.

A sluggish shower, followed by a breakfast of cornflakes and lukewarm coffee didn't make her feel that much better, and by the time she'd listlessly parked Puff in a sliver of shade that would disappear before mid-morning, she had reduced her resolution about tackling things all gung-ho to a more modest determination to drag herself where she needed to be, come what may.

Heading down into the basement, she briefly detoured on her way to her stationery cupboard to give Rollo Sale an overview of the case so far and request expenses for two train tickets to London so that they could interview Jonas Phelps.

Rollo was apparently in a good mood (or already too hot and bothered to put up a fight) and merely waved away the expenses with a brief nod.

In the communal office, she dropped her bag next to Claire's desk and perched on her usual corner of it. Claire took this as an invite to fill her in on their progress — or lack thereof — so far.

'Guv, I finished going over the forensic reports yesterday,' she began. 'As you know, the SOCO's lifted plenty of fingerprints, consisting mainly of all the family members, a few friends and regular visitors, plus the cleaners from the domestic agency. I've run them all through the databases and they don't turn up at any other crime scene since 2010. Also, no similar MOs in either our region or nationwide.'

'Which means we're probably dealing with a one-off then,' Hillary mused. She'd always believed that was likely to be the case, but until it was confirmed, it couldn't be ruled out that Imelda had been the victim of a hitherto unsuspected serial killer.

'So, it was personal,' she continued, glancing across at the corkboard and the accumulated data it now held. The large studio portrait of the murdered woman was still the dominating feature. 'Not surprising — she was very beautiful. And women with looks like that often bring out the insecurities, fantasies and violent tendencies in other people. Either deliberately or totally unintentionally. And from what we're learning about her nature, neither can be ruled out. She seemed to have a knack of upsetting people in a variety of ways. As far as I can tell, she wasn't discreet, and didn't seem to have much empathy with the feelings of others. She could have underestimated her effect on people, and not realised that she was pushing someone too far.'

'You like the husband for it, guv?' Claire asked, interest creeping into her voice.

Hillary shrugged. 'You know the crime statistics on that as well as I do.'

The two women regarded each other thoughtfully for a moment, as, over in his seat, Gareth watched them closely. He knew that these two former officers had, between them, a vast amount of experience, and he was enjoying the process of learning just by observing them. But now he felt like he needed to do his bit.

'Or a lover, ma'am?' he proffered. 'Connie Brightman was convinced that the victim had been seeing other men as well as Dermott Franklyn. What if *he* found out she was seeing someone else?'

Hillary nodded. 'Yes, it's possible. I've come across cases where the lover doesn't regard the husband as being a real rival at all — or even relevant. They develop either a disdain for them, or perversely, a sort of vague fondness for them. Either way, they know the object of their affection has become bored with him, or indifferent, and so cease to regard them as a real rival. But the advent of another lover . . . younger than themselves maybe, or better looking, or with a bigger car or better job . . . yes, that's a possibility.'

She nodded at Gareth. 'How are you doing on tracing the whereabouts of all the witnesses?'

'About two-thirds of the way through, ma'am. I started with the more important ones, and only have those on the periphery of the inquiry to get nailed down.'

'OK. Leave those for now and compile a list of any potential new men who might have been in Imelda's life. That'll test your initiative and computer skills.'

Gareth grinned. 'Yes, ma'am.'

'There were no unknown prints found,' Claire pointed out. 'Which doesn't bode well for a secondary lover theory.'

'Unless the lover was a husband or boyfriend of one of her friends,' Hillary mused. 'We know the Phelpses' had quite a wide circle of friends — male and female — who visited the house from time to time.'

Claire sighed. 'Pilfering your bestie's man could earn you a whack on the back of the head all right,' she said. Then, regarding the photograph of the dead woman, she said, 'Do you think she'd go that far, though? I mean, Dermott Franklyn wasn't known to any of her circle. She met him at the gym, didn't she?'

'That's right. And the killer could've been wearing gloves, so whether it's someone known or unknown to her, on that front we're no better off. Which begs the question,' Hillary continued, 'Did the killer bring gloves as well as the weapon with him — or her?'

'Are we totally sure that the killer *did* bring the weapon to the house though?' Claire willingly played devil's advocate. 'We know the family say they didn't miss anything from the home, but how reliable is that as evidence?' She gave an amused snort. 'I know for a fact that my lot wouldn't be able to tell you where every object at our place is, and wouldn't have a clue if, say, the mop went missing.'

Hillary grinned, but Claire had a point. 'Well, we know the Phelpses' had cleaners in three times a week to do the housework. Presumably they brought the bulk of their equipment in with them, but it was certainly possible some items were stored at the house. And it's unlikely any of the Phelps family — including Imelda — would have clocked stuff like that going missing. Remind me of the pathologist's report on the wound again?'

Claire called up the report on her computer. 'Hold on . . . duh-duh-duh, cranial fissures . . . duh-duh . . . yes, here it is. "It's my opinion the wound was caused by a relatively lightweight object that was wielded with some force and probably rounded at one end. No particulates were found in the wound, so it was made of a material not likely to shed particulates or components." Well that's very helpful,' she finished glumly.

'What normal everyday household objects cover that description?' Hillary challenged her team, but after ten minutes of coming up with everything from glass paperweights to rolling pins, they were no further forward.

'We could speculate for hours and just run ourselves ragged,' Claire complained. 'And in the end, we're still left with two possibilities. Either the killer brought the weapon with them, in which case it was premeditated, or the killer improvised, and the family isn't aware of what was used.'

'Or the family were well aware what was used and opted to keep quiet about it,' Hillary corrected her.

Claire looked at Hillary then at the photograph of the dead woman. A long moment passed. 'The husband would cover for his kids,' she finally said.

'And vice-versa,' Hillary agreed. 'I know it's early days yet, but from what we're hearing, the Phelpses' weren't exactly ideal candidates to play Happy Families.'

'Is there anything about the placing and position of the body that helps us?' Gareth wondered aloud.

Claire obligingly called up the relevant photographs on her computer and turned the screen first to Hillary, then towards Gareth.

'Crumpled up, lying on her left side in the hall, half-under the console table, facing the door,' Hillary summed it up. 'We know from the path report that she was struck from behind, and we can see that she was found with her head facing the door. Clovis's team worked on the theory that either her killer was someone she might have been entertaining and that she was struck down whilst showing them out, or that she answered the door, the killer pushed their way in and they tussled there and then, and she just happened to end up that way.'

'Do we have a preference?' Claire asked, raising one eyebrow at Hillary.

Hillary gave it some thought then sighed. 'People answer their doors,' she said flatly. 'We don't expect to be attacked when we do. We can see from the photos that the door had no windows in it, so she wouldn't have known whether a stranger, friend or enemy, was on the other side of it.'

'SOCO found no signs that she'd entertained anyone,' Claire pointed out.

'All that means is that Imelda didn't make them a cup of tea or whatever,' Hillary took her turn playing devil's advocate. 'It doesn't mean she didn't invite whoever it was into the lounge. Say it was someone she knew. Someone she would have entertained in normal circumstances, and had done, many times before. There's nothing to say that an argument couldn't have started before she had the chance to play hostess. Or, for that matter, that the killer didn't clean up after themselves.'

Hillary swung one leg thoughtfully, then slipped off the desk and glanced at her watch. 'Right, I just need to check on my emails, then we're off to London to talk to the son. Gareth, can you phone him and set it up? If he insists, we can see him at his work, but I'd far prefer to see him in his home environment.'

'With a bit of luck he'll be working from home anyway, ma'am,' Gareth said.

'Yeah, since Covid a lot of professionals only go into the office every now and then, especially in the city,' Claire chipped in. 'Lucky sods.'

'The boss has given the nod to expenses, so we're going in by train,' Hillary said. 'I just can't face the motorway in this heat. All it would take is one accident, and we'd be sitting in a traffic jam for hours, baking in a tin can.'

'The same might happen if the points on the line melt or something,' Claire, ever the optimist, pointed out with a grin.

'Well one of you will have to take the chance with me,' Hillary said drolly, then made up her mind. 'Gareth, you come with me today. It might be useful to have a male take on another male. Claire, you and I can tackle the daughter tomorrow — with the same logic presiding. Whilst we're gone, you can take over the task of tracking down the current whereabouts of witnesses and doing a follow-up on the phone. Not that I'm expecting much to come of it,' she added.

In Hillary's experience, non-nosy neighbours who saw no evil, heard no evil and spoke no evil were unlikely to have undergone a personality transplant after nearly fifteen years.

* * *

They took the Park and Ride bus to Oxford station, cannily saving on the notoriously high parking fees at train stations throughout the land, and caught the next train out to the capital with minutes to spare.

Since the rush hour was long over, the carriages weren't that crowded, and they both managed to find a seat, facing each other, on the shady side of the carriage. Unable to study work documents where members of the public might see them, Hillary contented herself with watching the passing scenery as Gareth did whatever it was men did for hours on end on their smartphones.

Jonas Phelps had been twenty at the time of his mother's murder, which would make him thirty-five or so now. She knew from the background checks that Gareth and Claire had been doing that he'd graduated from his university with a good degree in architecture, and had since fared well, managing to forge a decent career in the arena of his choice, unlike so many of his fellow graduates, who were often forced to settle for whatever job they could get. It had meant him moving to the capital, but presumably that had been no hardship for him.

From what she could recall from the notes, his company specialised in doing expensive 'trendy' conversions in the city — turning unlikely, once industrial buildings into family homes and apartment living.

He'd married a woman called Jennifer Keele just over ten years ago, and the couple now had four children, aged from two up to nine. They lived in a new-build estate (ironically not one designed by his firm, which presumably he would not have been able to afford) in one of the more pleasant, leafy northern suburbs, and had a totally clean sheet. Not even a parking ticket.

It would be interesting to see how the murdered woman's only son had fared in the years after her death, and Hillary was looking forward to getting his measure.

Gareth had confirmed that, luckily, Jonas was indeed working mostly from home these days. He had been warned by his father that he could expect a visit and had expressed no objections to giving them an interview.

As she sat back and found her heavy eyes insisting on closing, she hoped she wouldn't nod off and suffer the ignominy of having Gareth shake her awake when they reached the city.

* * *

An hour later, as Hillary (who'd stayed awake — but only just) and Gareth left the station, her colleague was already looking up buses and timetables on his mobile. Hillary instinctively headed for a shady bench at a nearby bus stop to await the news, but he was already nodding his head.

'It's the 22A we need, ma'am. There should be a stop about . . .' he consulted the ever-obliging Google Maps, 'a five-minute walk from his address.' He glanced at his watch. 'One's expected along here in about ten minutes.'

Hillary nodded, glancing around the busy suburb. She did not like London. She did not like travelling to London, she did not like negotiating her way around London, she did not like the way it looked, or sounded or smelled. She'd always found it hostile and ugly, and as an added bonus, today the city was doing its best to be about two degrees hotter than the surrounding areas. Her animus wasn't only reserved for London, however — any large city made her skin itch.

Gareth settled himself comfortably on the bench beside her, resting his walking cane neatly between his knees. Glancing around thoughtfully, his eyes caught and followed a pair of attractive women who were sunbathing on a spot of grass about twenty feet away.

Hillary pretended not to notice. Although she knew all about Claire's husband and family members because her friend often talked about them (usually with an eye-roll or a snort of affection or frustration), Gareth didn't volunteer private or personal information, and she never liked to ask.

She assumed he had a regular partner, but maybe she was wrong. She made a mental note to try and draw him out more in the future. She'd had the feeling of late that Gareth had things on his mind. So far it wasn't affecting his work, but if he needed someone to speak to, it wouldn't hurt to offer her ear.

The bus, unlike any other of its species, which as far as she could tell, never arrived or left on time anywhere in the country, elected to arrive five minutes early, and she got on first, paying for two return fares to the stop Gareth had mentioned. It was a double-decker bus, but she knew her colleague would find the narrow twisty stairs impossible to navigate, so she retreated along the lower floor towards the back. She sat down on the empty seat just in front of the bench seat at the back, Gareth taking the seat on the opposite side of the aisle.

As the bus jerked away from the stop, she automatically put out a hand on the metal rail of the seat in front of her to stop herself pitching forward, and bit back a yelp of pain as the metal proved to be as hot as blazes. Obviously, it had been absorbing the full heat of the sun through the window for some time, and she swore at it below her breath as she put her now tingling palm and fingers in her lap and tenderly nursed them.

Once more, London hadn't disappointed her.

At least the journey wasn't too long, but having to stop and start every two minutes got on her nerves. Unfortunately, once they'd left the bus, they then had a short walk ahead of them which, ordinarily, wouldn't have bothered her one bit. But she could already feel her clothes were wilting in the heat and beginning to stick to her prickling, damp skin, and she only hoped her deodorant was as foolproof as the blurb on it had promised!

Imelda's son had made his home in the sort of homogeneous house that was large without being attractive, sported only the tiniest of gardens that consisted of a closely cropped lawn with a single flowering shrub of some kind in the middle of it, and a paved driveway big enough for three cars.

Hillary wasted no time walking to the door and ringing the bell. She could feel the sun on her bare head threatening to give her a headache and was anxious to nip it in the bud. She wanted to be on her top game with Jonas Phelps. Whilst the murdered woman's husband had been outwardly helpful and had answered all her questions, she knew he'd also been keeping a tight rein on what he said.

She could only hope the murdered woman's children would be more forthcoming, and she needed to be alert to all the telltale pauses in the conversation, every eye-flick or other interesting body language on display.

The door was opened by a woman who stood about five feet five in wedged sandals. Her hair was cropped uncompromisingly short and was of an indeterminate brown colour, and she had eyes that were a shade darker and that were set just a little too close together. Her dominant feature, however, was definitely her nose, which was large and could, if you wanted to be kind, be described as 'Roman'. She was dressed in dark blue slacks made of some kind of synthetic stretch material, and a large, plain white t-shirt that was several sizes too large, and which Hillary suspected she'd bought deliberately in order to fit over her a bit like a tent.

But the smile that lit up her face was genuinely sweet, and her voice was warm and welcoming. 'You must be the police consultants? Please, come in. Jonas is in his study, but I'll oik him out of it for you.'

'Thank you, Ms . . . ?'

'Oh, I'm Jennifer, his wife. Please, don't mind the mess. The three oldest are at school, and the littlest is at daycare, but I never seem to get the chance to clean up their things.'

And indeed, the living room she showed them into was cluttered with various toys, the odd item of discarded clothing, and a large shaggy dog that lay panting in one corner, and merely thumped a plumy tail in greeting before resting his shaggy head back on his shaggy forepaws and going back to sleep.

Hillary half-wished she could lie down beside him and do the same.

'Don't mind Sausage Roll, he's friendly,' Jennifer Phelps advised them, before disappearing for a few moments and then reappearing with one of the handsomest men Hillary had ever seen. In every way, he seemed to be the polar opposite of his wife. Whereas her hair was nondescript brown, his was a pure black, so deep it almost seemed to have blue overtones to it. Probably inherited from his father's side of the family, Hillary guessed. Whereas Jennifer's nose was large, his was perfectly proportioned, and from either side of it, perfectly spaced hazel-coloured eyes (a replica of his mother's) looked back at her. Where Jennifer was short and dumpy, he was lean and easily over six feet tall. He was also dressed in a crisp white shirt that fitted him perfectly and showed that he was no stranger to a gym and a regular workout routine. His white slacks were loose-fitting but elegant.

If his job as an architect ever came under peril, surely he could follow his mother's chosen profession with little effort. His was the sort of face and body that could sell anything from million-pound sports cars to toilet rolls.

'Mrs Greene is it?' Jonas said, his gaze going from her to Gareth.

'Yes, sir, thanks for seeing us. This is my colleague Gareth Proctor.'

'Well, sit down, sit down.'

'Oh yes, sorry, I should have said!' Jennifer apologised, looking a little flustered. 'Don't know where my manners are — I think it's this awful heat. I don't like it. Speaking of which, I'm sure you'd like something cold to drink? Or would you prefer tea or coffee?'

Hillary gratefully accepted the cold drink, with Gareth doing the same, and she hurried off.

Hillary looked around and spied the usual three-piece suite in dark maroon leather. The living room was one of those all-white-walls jobs, with laminate flooring for easy cleaning, ideal when you had messy kids to deal with.

She took one chair, Gareth the other, leaving the sofa for the Phelpses. But after Jennifer had delivered a jug of iced lemonade and glasses to the coffee table set equidistant between the furniture, she turned and left, saying she had the lunch to see to.

Hillary wondered if she was being diplomatic, but as she caught Jonas's eye, he gave a small smile.

'Jenny is an amazing cook, which means I'm constantly spoiled. I think it's quiche today, with a salad recipe that top chefs would probably kill to have, if only they knew about it. She also bakes the most delicious breakfast rolls you've ever tasted.'

Hillary smiled and asked if he minded if they recorded their conversation. Like his father before him, he made no objection.

'Thank you, sir,' she said, as he reached forward and poured out the drinks and handed her hers.

'Oh, call me Jonas.'

'Thank you. I imagine your father has been in touch?' Hillary began lightly. 'And told you we're taking a second look at your mother's case?'

'Yes. He was very pleased about it, as you can imagine,' he said, then gave a quick scowl and shook his head. 'That is, I didn't mean to imply that he had any grievance with the original investigation, or with your colleague's efforts to find out who killed Mum,' he added. 'We're all sure that they did the best they could but . . .'

He shrugged.

'I understand,' Hillary said quietly. 'It was never solved. And that must have been hard to live with. You were away at university at the time it happened, isn't that right?'

'Yes. I came home as soon as Dad called me. Jess was in a right state, as you can imagine. She was the first one to find Mum.'

'Yes, I'm so sorry. I haven't talked to her yet — I thought I'd leave it until I'd got a better picture of your mother and her life back then. The last thing I want to do is cause more distress to your family. Is Jess, er, reconciled to what happened now?' she probed delicately.

Jonas gave a twisted smile. 'As much as she can be, I guess,' he muttered, and shrugged his impressive shoulders.

He obviously didn't want to talk about his sister, so she quickly moved on.

'I imagine some of the revelations that emerged afterwards about your mother's private life came as a bit of a shock?'

'You mean the lovers?' he asked flatly, meeting her eyes with a gaze that matched his tone.

'Lovers?' Hillary echoed. 'From DI Clovis's files, she was only aware of Dermott Franklyn. And he'd been seeing your mother for quite some time — nearly three years in fact.'

Jonas nodded, then again gave a brief shrug. 'Lover, then.'

But Hillary was curious. Apparently, Connie Brightman wasn't the only one who thought Dermott Franklyn had simply been the last in line.

'Did you ever suspect your mother was unfaithful? I mean, you were, what, twenty at the time. Sometimes teenagers see, hear, and suspect far more than their parents might suppose.'

Jonas's lips gave that odd little twist again — not quite amusement, not quite pain. 'I just never gave it much thought. You don't, do you? Kids, I mean. The thought of parents having any kind of sex life . . . brr . . .' He gave a mock shudder. 'When we found out about it, I was sort of surprised, and I sort of wasn't. I mean, we had no hint that she was having an affair — none at all — but once I *did* learn about it, I wasn't surprised.'

'You were close to your mother?'

Jonas stared down into his glass, absently swirling it, setting the ice-cubes tinkling. 'Not really.'

'Ah. Closer to your father then?'

Again, there came that shrug and lip-twist. 'Not really. It's Jess who adores Dad. And vice-versa.'

'Ah yes. Fathers are closest to their daughters, and mothers to their sons. Isn't that how Freud insisted it was supposed to work?' she said lightly.

'Couldn't tell that by me,' Jonas said flatly. 'To be perfectly honest, I came to the conclusion long before I reached twenty that my mother couldn't really have wanted kids. And I blame my grandmother for that.'

'Catherine Burton? Yes, I've spoken to her.'

Jonas gave a proper laugh this time. 'I don't suppose she's changed much. Still playing Lady Muck in Cheltenham?'

Hillary gave a smile. 'No comment.'

Jonas merely nodded. 'It figures.'

But Hillary wasn't going to let him off the hook so easily — not now that he'd offered her something so meaty to chew on. 'What made you think your mother didn't want you or Jess?'

Jonas's hazel eyes — so disconcertingly identical to those of the woman under discussion — moved from Hillary and wandered over his own children's toys scattered around and so much in evidence. After a moment or two of thought, he somewhat wearily shook his head.

'I could just feel it, that's all. Oh, she went through all the motions, don't get me wrong; the Christmas presents we pestered her for, the perfectly catered birthday parties until we were twelve or so, turning up at school concerts or sports days. She made sure that all the "what-a-good-mother-does" points were ticked off. But it was never for *our* benefit. She didn't care if we won the egg-and-spoon race, or who got an essay prize. She was only concerned that the other mothers noticed her presence. That the teachers approved that she showed up for the PTA meetings. Again, I blame Grandmother's influence for that. Never let it be said that she let her image slip. One thing you could always rely on — Imelda Phelps would be seen to be doing the right thing.'

For the first time he sounded more bitter than resigned.

'That sounds rather a heavy burden for her to have to carry around,' she mused quietly.

Jonas gave her a quick look, a flicker of surprise crossing his face. 'You know, I've never really thought about it like that. I mean, seeing it from her point of view.' His shoulders slumped a little. 'I shouldn't have been so self-centred, I guess.'

'You were young,' Hillary said simply. 'You hadn't had time enough to grow and gain experience or perspective. But now that you have, looking back on it — what kind of woman was your mother?'

There was silence for a while, then he shrugged. 'I just don't know. I'm sorry, but I don't. My lasting memories of Mum are all tied up in how she *looked,* not how she *was*. She was always at the hairdresser, always shopping for clothes, or shoes, or make-up. Oh, I know that was to do with her job, but . . . I think she was probably angry that she didn't ever make it to the super-leagues. Perhaps she felt life had done the dirty on her? Perhaps we were never going to be enough — not Dad, me or poor Jess. Perhaps that's where the likes of Dermott Franklyn came in.'

'A boost to her ego?'

'I suppose. Perhaps it made her feel vindicated, somehow. Or maybe it was just a reaction to all that "always act like a perfect lady" crap that Grandmother fed her?' He glanced at Hillary then back down into his glass, as if lemonade and ice could provide him with the answer. 'All I can tell you is that she never managed to shake off all that conditioning. Wherever we went, whoever was watching, she was always playing the role of Imelda the perfect lady.'

'I wouldn't have thought having an affair with a younger man fitted in with that,' Hillary pointed out.

'True. I suppose she just had to rebel somehow — and perhaps that's how she did it.'

'What else do you remember most about her?'

'The need to be the centre of attention all the time,' he responded promptly. 'She loved being adored. All that "look at beautiful, perfect me" nonsense. Well, she was beautiful,' he added, his tone softer now, 'but perfect? Who of us is?'

Hillary nodded. 'It sounds as if you had a bit of a rough ride of it. With Jess being your father's favourite and your mother being too self-absorbed to pay you any attention, you must have felt as if you'd been left out in the cold?'

'Poor little me, you mean?' Jonas said, this time with a genuine grin. 'Not really. I had a friend — Patrick Deemster, lived a few streets away from me. He was an only child, and his parents were great. I practically lived there. Every day I'd go home from school with Pat to his house, more often than not eating with them too. First thing in the morning, I'd call in there on our way to school. Rachel and Terry — Pat's parents — were very nearly mine too, in all but name. And that carried on when we left primary school and both went to the same local grammar.'

'Didn't your own parents object?'

'Why would they? Dad didn't mind, and I don't think Mum noticed most of the time. And whenever it was pointed out to her, she'd insist that it was because I felt sorry for Patrick, being a lonely only child and all that crap. That way she earned brownie points for raising such a thoughtful and considerate son. See how her mind worked now?'

'You sound as if you didn't like her much,' Hillary mused. She was careful not to sound judgemental, but only curious or intrigued.

Again, Jonas Phelps's eyes wandered sadly across the room at all the evidence of his own children's occupation of the house, and for a moment, he was silent.

'You know, I probably didn't,' he admitted sadly. 'Don't get me wrong, she was my mother, and as such I loved her. But I'm trying to be honest here. It was always a perfunctory sort of love — an obligation because I was her son, and that's what you're supposed to do.' He gave a frustrated shake of his head, as if displeased with the explanation, and tried again. 'Let me put it this way — if I'd met her as an adult, and a stranger, I wouldn't have wanted to cultivate her company. Do you understand what I'm trying to say?'

'Yes, I think so. Do you have any idea who might have killed her?'

'No, not really. I know they looked into her toyboy quite a bit, and that woman who helped Mum run her jewellery business for a while. But nothing seemed to come of it.'

'Do you think your father knew about her affair . . . or affairs?' she asked quietly.

Jonas shot her a quick look. 'Dad was at work when it happened. That was proved,' he said, his voice hard and his tone flat.

'I'm sorry, I don't mean to be offensive. I'm just trying to get an idea of how things were. Your father wouldn't have been the first man to know about his wife's infidelity but turn a blind eye to it. After all, they were both grown-ups, and all-in-all it seems to me, looking at it objectively, that their marriage seemed to work pretty well. Or did it? Did they argue much?'

'No. Dad is too placid and laid-back, and Mum thought it was unladylike to rant and shout. And you're right, I shouldn't be so sensitive. I know the husband or wife is always the first suspect in a murder case, but if you're seriously looking at Dad, I can tell you now, you're wasting your time.'

'I take it that goes for your sister too?'

Jonas went back to that curious lip-twisting, shoulder-shrugging demeanour again. 'Jess found her own solution to the lack of motherly love,' he said cryptically.

'Care to elaborate?'

But this time, he wasn't to be drawn. 'I have no doubt you'll figure it out for yourself when it's her turn.'

* * *

Half an hour later they were walking back to the bus stop. Although Hillary had taken her witness back through the last time he'd seen his mother, and his movements on the day of her death, nothing had popped out at her.

Now, as they walked, they talked.

'That was interesting, ma'am,' Gareth began.

Hillary felt like giving a lip-twist and shoulder-shrug of her own. 'Wasn't it just. Tell me, what struck you the most about that interview?' It was part of her job to help train him up and get him thinking like a cop, but apart from that, it was always useful to have a sounding board on which to check out her own impressions and thoughts.

'Only the obvious, ma'am. He didn't really have a good word to say about her, did he?'

'Hmm.' That wasn't what had interested her the most about the interview, but she could see why it was a top priority with the ex-soldier. She rather suspected he adored his own mum!

'His alibi seemed pretty solid,' Gareth went on. 'He's really the only one in her immediate family who has one that strong. Even his sister's isn't that good, since she could have killed her mum on returning from school, and waited before reporting it.'

Hillary regarded him thoughtfully. 'You don't want it to be him?'

Gareth gave her a hurt look. 'I have no opinion on it, ma'am,' he said, a little stiffly.

Hillary shook her head. 'Don't get huffy. I know I've successfully drummed it into you to keep an open mind. What did you make of his choice of wife?'

'Ma'am?' He was more cautious now.

Hillary didn't take it personally. 'It struck me that she was so obviously the opposite of his mother. Plain, not beautiful. No interest in fashion. A good cook, a loving mother — and four kids.'

'You mean he went out of his way to make sure that his own life didn't resemble that of his childhood in any way?' Gareth said, slowly nodding. 'Yes, I see what you're getting at.'

At the bus stop now, Hillary leaned against the pole, felt it instantly begin to burn through the thin material of her blouse against her shoulder, and quickly straightened up. They had the place to themselves, but she kept her voice low.

'Well, if nothing else, our murder victim is beginning to come into focus now. So far, she's left behind her a cuckold of a husband, a disapproving mother, an irate business partner, and a disaffected son. And from what Jonas said of his sister, I don't have high hopes that Jessie will have anything good to say about her either. She's not making it easy for us to catch her killer, that's for sure.'

She paused, looked around her, and then surprised Gareth by saying, seemingly at random, 'I bloody hate London.'

CHAPTER SIX

Around the same time that Hillary and Gareth were waiting for the bus to take them back to the train station, Gavin Otterley was parking up in a swanky little cul-de-sac in Cheltenham.

As he climbed out of his regretfully unimpressive car, he saw the curtains twitch in the house opposite the one that he was visiting, and bit back a happy smile. The area might be upmarket and upper class, but he was reassured to see that prurient nosiness was no respecter of such trifles.

He bounded up the short set of steps in front of the impressive Cotswold stone townhouse, and pressed the doorbell, running through his opening gambits. He had several, depending on who it was he was hoping to pump for information, and he was rather hoping it would be the old lady herself who answered his summons — on the whole, he had a good track record getting *them* to talk. But a quick glance around at his wealthy surroundings told him that the odds on that happening were fifty/fifty at best. Which meant that he was not too surprised when the woman who appeared behind the opening door was not Catherine Burton herself but an obvious minion of some kind. Private secretary perhaps?

Middle-aged, snooty and unimpressed; these were his immediate thoughts as she ran her eyes over him, and he bit back the usual surge of resentment that he felt when things didn't go his way and put on his best smile. Not the cheeky-chappie smile, which experience had told him would definitely not work on a customer such as this. He was glad he had donned his best trousers and shirt but now regretted leaving the matching jacket in the car. He'd thought that the furnace-like heat of the day would be regarded as a good excuse for leaving it off, but this woman was clearly not most people.

'Yes, sir? How may I help you?' she asked coolly.

'I was hoping to speak to Mrs Catherine Burton? Is she at home?' Gavin asked, using his best Oxford accent in an attempt to counterpoint the demerits he'd earned for his lack of sartorial elegance.

But she was having none of it. 'Do you have an appointment?' she demanded, a slightly raised eyebrow suggesting that she harboured serious doubts about such an eventuality.

'I'm so sorry, I didn't realise one was needed,' Gavin said, sensing that he was fighting a losing battle.

'May I ask the purpose of your visit?'

Gavin felt his heart sink even further. In the good old days, when asked awkward questions like this, his heroes had been allowed to use all sorts of lies, evasions and downright dirty tricks to gain access to places and snatch a quote; but alas, in this day of litigation and nervous editors, he knew better than to misrepresent himself. Instead, he tried diplomacy.

Which, he well knew, was not his strong point.

'I wondered if Mrs Burton had any thoughts about the Thames Valley Police taking a second look at her daughter's case? We at the *Oxford—*'

'Mrs Burton doesn't speak to reporters, sir,' the woman said flatly, interrupting him before he could even name his newspaper — which was perfectly respectable and read by a (usually) discerning clientele. Worse luck. Gavin had always dreamed of working for a Fleet Street rag that sold to millions, and told cheap and cheerful lies, and paid their reporters massive bonuses for really juicy and salacious scoops.

'But surely she would be glad of the opportunity to give her side of the stor—'

'Good day, sir.'

She didn't exactly slam the door in his face, but it shut with a decided and emphatic 'snick'.

Gavin swore. He swore standing in front of the door, he swore walking down the steps, he swore walking to his car, and he swore as he looked slowly and enviously around at the affluent houses, with their smug sash windows and shared private garden.

He stopped swearing when he saw the curtain in the window opposite quiver yet again.

Then he began to smile.

As he crossed the road and made for the curtain-twitcher, in her drawing room, Catherine Burton watched his progress, her lips set in a thin, grim line. Her housekeeper, having just reported his impudence, had now retired to make her a fresh batch of Pimm's.

As she watched the short, fair-haired young man climb her neighbour's front steps, she could feel anger and resentment roiling in her midriff. It was disgraceful that this sort of thing was allowed to go on in a civilized society. If her granddaddy had had his way, muck raking newspapers would have been eradicated — their premises and presses burnt down, and their proprietors along with them!

She watched in sheer frustration as the door was opened to the reporter by that silly little milksop of a woman, Eloise Featherstone. The daughter of a lord she might be, but she didn't have the sense of a hen. No wonder she'd never married. Who would have her, even with her blue-blooded connections?

Who knew what tale he would spin her, and she, the silly chump, would swallow it all like a gullible guppy. And Catherine shuddered to think what *she'd* tell *him* in return. The fact that they hardly exchanged more than a polite 'good morning' whenever they happened to cross paths wouldn't prevent the chatterbox from making up all sorts of silly things to please and flatter her unexpected visitor. She could almost hear her now! 'Oh, poor Catherine, yes it was such a tragedy what happened to her daughter. But of course, she never talks about it . . .'

She made a 'tcha' sound of sheer disgust and moved to sit down on the sofa. Her housekeeper would be back soon with the now much-needed Pimm's, and it wouldn't do to be seen snooping out of the window.

She forced a look of unconcern onto her face, but her mind was busy mentally running through her list of acquaintances with clout. Alas, since the death of her husband, she had to admit that list had shrunk considerably, not least because most of the people who could have helped her were of her own generation and a fair number of them had inconsiderately shuffled off this mortal coil.

But there had to be *someone* who could curb the excesses of the press? She simply wouldn't tolerate having to endure all that nightmarish publicity again. Now, who did she know in Oxford who owed her a favour . . . ?

* * *

The next morning, Hillary awoke, as usual, feeling damp, hot and seriously fed up. So far, the weather pundits were predicting a possible break in the heatwave at the beginning of next week, but even that respite would be brief, with another area of high pressure moving in again after the usual thunderstorms had passed.

It didn't improve her mood when Puff resolutely refused to start, and she was forced to ring her usual mechanic to come over and check him out, and then Claire to ask if she could come and pick her up.

Claire duly arrived a little after nine, careful to keep her own opinions on her boss's car to herself, and with her air-con on full blast.

'We won't bother calling in at the office,' Hillary told her as she did up her seatbelt. 'Let's head straight over to Jessica Phelps's place. You have her address, right?'

'Yes, guv — she's in Bicester.'

'Like her father,' Hillary mused. 'I wonder if it's just a coincidence she ended up living so close to him, or if she moved there deliberately so that she could be near him after he remarried?'

Claire gave a snort. 'If I were Thomas Phelps's second wife, I would be hoping it was the former. Grown-up daughters with serious daddy issues can be a pain in the backside, in my opinion.'

She sounded so adamant that Hillary suspected her friend had personal experience of this phenomenon and gave her a sideways look.

'That sounded heartfelt,' Hillary said, careful to keep her voice light.

Claire sighed. 'Sorry – didn't mean to bring my problems to work. My son's having some issues with his wife. I'm hoping they'll get themselves sorted out sooner rather than later. But you know how it is.'

Hillary didn't, never having had children, but she sensed Claire wasn't comfortable talking about her problems on the job, so she decided to drop it for now, and got back to the matter in hand. 'You arranged with Jessica for her to be in?'

'Yes, guv, I called her yesterday afternoon. She didn't sound all that keen to me. Oh, nothing obvious — just a feeling I got.'

Hillary was fully prepared to back Claire's feelings. As an officer who'd dealt with domestic violence for most of her career, Claire knew how to read people even over the telephone.

'Noted. She's a vet, right? Works at a clinic in town?'

'Yes, guv. Never married, no kids. Has a mortgage, no record.'

Hillary nodded. And wondered — just how much was Puff going to cost her for repairs this time?

* * *

Imelda's daughter lived in a 1960s-build house in a small maze of similar houses near St Edburg's Church, with a compact front garden that was packed with neatly tended plants, and not a paving stone in sight.

Large horse-chestnut trees that had been dotted strategically around by the far-sighted planners offered some respite from the morning glare, and as Claire led the way up the small semi's grassy path, Hillary regarded the square Norman tower of the old church. Its clock, she noticed, was telling the right time, which was not always the case with old churches.

Her thoughts on matters ecclesiastical quickly fled as the door was answered by a woman with Imelda's auburn colouring, but none of her beauty. Now thirty-one or thirty-two years old, Hillary thought she could still see the remnants of the seventeen-year-old girl that Jessica had once been, when she'd discovered her mother's body.

Her face still had some of the rounded smoothness of someone much younger, and the same plumpness seemed to have spread to her body in an adult version of puppy fat. She was wearing plain stretch slacks in navy blue, matched with a white short-sleeved blouse that was already showing signs of dampness under the armpits.

'You must be the police?' she said.

In response, Hillary and Claire both showed her their ID cards, which she regarded briefly, before stepping back to let them in.

The house was as compact inside as out, and Hillary suspected that it consisted of little more than a living room and kitchen downstairs, and probably only one bedroom and a bathroom upstairs. The front door opened straight into the main room of the house, which had room for a small sofa and one armchair. The single window was large, but even so, the house seemed dim. On a hot day like today, that was probably an advantage, but Hillary suspected that in the winter she had to keep a light on permanently.

'Please, sit down.'

There was no accompanying offer of tea or coffee, but that didn't bother either of the women. Claire chose one end of the sofa, and Hillary quickly chose the armchair, which meant she'd have a good view of Jessie Phelps's face throughout the interview.

Their witness perched nervously on the edge of the sofa, her knees tightly clamped together, and cleared her throat. 'So, you want to know about Mum?'

'Yes. I'm sorry, I know this must be dredging up bad memories for you,' Hillary apologised. 'You were the first member of your family on the scene?'

'Yes. I came home from school, and there she was. Well, to be more accurate, I came home from my friend's place. Maggie's.'

So here was another of Imelda's children who wasn't in any hurry to return to the family home at the end of the day. 'What time would that have been, do you think?' Hillary already knew the answer to this from DI Clovis's notes, of course, but she was interested to see if Jessie's recollections had changed much over the years.

'About five . . . maybe a quarter past. I just opened the front door, took one step inside and there she was. On the floor. With red stuff on the hall tiles. I remember how shocked I was . . . I mean, not just that I was surprised at finding her there, but about finding her looking so . . . untidy.'

Hillary blinked. *Untidy?*

As if belatedly sensing that her choice of words seemed odd, Jessie's face was immediately suffused with a dull shade of red. 'I'm sorry, that didn't sound right, did it? I mean, that's not what . . . I just . . .' She gave up the effort of trying to explain herself and sighed heavily. 'You have to understand that Mum always looked perfect, you know? Always dressed in the right outfit, her make-up immaculate, with not a hair out of place. Seeing her like that was so . . . bizarre. I mean, I'd literally never seen her like that. I'm sorry, I expect this sounds awful to you. I'm just trying to explain . . .'

But her words dried up again, and instead she held out her hands in a telling 'what can I do?' gesture.

'It's all right, Miss Phelps, just say whatever feels right,' Hillary reassured her. 'I'm sure you were in shock, and you were just a teenager, after all. You can't expect to process what you saw or felt very easily.'

'Oh, I've always been the same, really. Socially awkward and all that. Can never say the right things to people. I much prefer animals. I know where I am with animals. If they bite or scratch me, I don't mind. I know it's not personal.' She tried to give an upbeat smile that didn't quite come off.

Her hands began to twist themselves into shapes on her upraised knees. Hillary was pretty sure Jessie Phelps had no idea she was displaying her nervousness and distress so obviously. And whilst dealing with a witness in such a heightened state of emotion could often be useful, as people tended to blurt out truths they might otherwise be able to hold back, too much angst could also be self-defeating.

She would just have to keep an eye on her witness very carefully and try and keep the interview on as even a keel as possible.

'Can you tell me what happened, after you'd opened the door and found what you found?' she asked, careful to keep her words as bland as she could.

Jessie jerked her chin up and down in an awkward-looking nod. 'I backed out. I remember that. Then I went next door, to Mrs Forrester's place, and rang the doorbell. Then my knees seemed to give out and I sat down on her front doorstep. When she opened the door, I told her what had happened. She went round to see for herself and . . . well, came back and telephoned for the police and an ambulance and all that. She helped me up and sat me down in her kitchen and made me drink sweet tea. Then, at some point, Dad was there. Mrs Forrester must have called him too. Later there were policemen and women. I gave a short statement, then Dad took us to Grandmother's house, and I fell asleep.'

After every short sentence, Jessie took a shallow, agitated breath. But beyond that, Hillary also detected a feeling of rote about it, as if she was remembering having said these words before, over and over again fifteen years ago, and had now fallen back into that same, near-mindless repetitious mode.

Which made sense, since this was almost exactly what she'd told DI Clovis in her original statements. And in itself, that wasn't suspicious — but it wasn't what Hillary needed. She wanted this obviously intelligent but highly strung woman thinking new thoughts and remembering things anew.

So she tried a question that Jessie wouldn't have been asked more than once. 'Did you notice any changes in your mother's behaviour in the days or weeks before she died?'

She had thought this was a fairly innocuous query and had chosen it for that reason, so she was surprised to see a look of panic flash across Jessie's face. Somehow, she had done the opposite of calming her down, and instead had managed to hit a nerve.

'No!' she said quickly and much too loudly, then she swallowed hard and tried to pull off a nonchalant shrug. 'I mean, why would I?' she said, lowering her voice a few octaves and decibels. 'I barely saw her really. She was always out and about, and even if that wasn't the case, she was far too busy with . . . er . . . the usual stuff.'

Jessie dragged her eyes from Hillary and moved them across the room towards the slightly open door which led, presumably, to the kitchen. The effect of what she saw there was instant. Some of the tension drained out of her shoulders, and the smile that came to her face was the first genuine one that Hillary had seen from her.

Hillary glanced behind to see the door move slightly, and instantly tensed in alarm. Why hadn't she heard footsteps? Why hadn't she sensed someone else's presence? All her copper's suspicion and needful paranoia flooded through her. She half-turned on the chair, instinctively prepared to jump to her feet, ready to deal with some protective male stomping in and demanding that she leave.

Or worse.

Then the most enormous rabbit that Hillary had ever seen in her life entered the room. It was easily the size and weight of a King Charles spaniel — possibly even bigger. It was ginger and grey in colour, with a mandolin shape over the top of the body. It had surprisingly long legs, a pointed muzzle and an unusually narrow-looking head. Its nose, however, as was habitual with its species, was constantly twitching, and it had a bunny's signature huge, velvety-looking ears.

It ignored Claire and Hillary completely, hop-walking across the carpet to put its front paws on Jessie's knees. Although she knew she shouldn't anthropomorphise animals, Hillary had the distinct impression that it had somehow picked up on its owner's distress and had come to offer moral support.

'Hello, Jester, you can't be hungry again?' Jessie cooed at it, reaching down to lift it up effortlessly into her lap. Which couldn't have been any mean feat — Hillary gauged the animal must have weighed twenty pounds at least, if not more. It was so big that it spilled over Jessie's lap and its backside ended up half on Claire's legs.

Claire gave its fur a tentative pat but Jessie ran her hands luxuriantly from the tip of its never-still nose, down over its ears — flattening them against its arched back — and then all the way down to its flanks in one long, smooth movement. The fur was so dense that Hillary could see it rippling.

Hillary had no doubt that this procedure was a very common occurrence for both woman and rabbit.

'This is Jester,' Jessie said with a smile, her hands continuing the long stroking movements automatically. 'He's a Flemish Giant. I called him Jester because he was a bit of a clown when he was a baby.'

'He's magnificent,' Hillary said, and meant it.

Jessie beamed. 'He's my best friend, aren't you, Jester?' She buried her hands in the warm spot between the rabbit's ears and tickled. Its eyes closed in bliss. 'I've always loved animals, so I suppose I was destined to be a vet. Mind you, at school I loved botany too, and it was a bit of a toss-up which one I chose for my degree. But in the end, the animals won out over the plants. Well, they can love you back, can't they, whereas a daisy can't.'

'Did you have a pet as a child?' Hillay asked gently.

'A cat, yes. Smudge — because he had a white smudge on his black nose. Mum wouldn't have a dog — she said they were too messy and needy. But cats can look after themselves. Speaking of looking after someone . . .' She nodded down at the enormous rabbit. 'I really must take him to his pen outside. He needs some fresh grass.'

So saying, she rose to her feet, again manoeuvring the animal without effort so that its front paws were now resting against her shoulder and she was cupping its copious bottom in the crook of her bent arms.

'Mind if I come with you?' Hillary said, giving her little option to say 'no' as she too rose to her feet. Claire, caught off guard, quickly put away her notebook and pencil and joined her. 'I so admired your front garden, and I take it the back one is a little larger? They usually are, aren't they?' Hillary offered by way of explanation.

As she'd expected, this more friendly topic went down well, and Jessie nodded with something at least approaching enthusiasm. 'Sure — mind you, I'd like a bigger plot, but . . .' She shrugged and led them down a narrow corridor, where there was a back door. Off to one side, they passed a kitchen that housed little more than a sink, a cooker, a fridge and about a foot of Formica-topped workspace.

Opening the back door for her, Hillary saw at once the square tower of the church looming to one side and a colourful, oblong-shaped garden surrounded on all three sides by a mixture of native trees and shrubs. In one corner, chicken netting surrounded the wooden hutch that denoted Jester's lodgings, but Jessie headed instead to another spot along one hedge, deep in the shade, where a long wooden frame, again covered in chicken netting, was set out over a patch of grass. Closely cropped areas of grass scattered all around the lawn showed that Jester's munching grounds were rotated on a regular basis.

Jessie lifted the frame with the bottom of one foot, keeping perfect balance as she did so and thus demonstrating that this was a procedure she could probably do in her sleep. Hefting her companion down and scooting his bum under the wooden bottom board, she let it fall back carefully over him.

'I worry about red kites,' she said, then laughed again. 'Silly really — they're more into carrion than live prey, and not nearly strong enough to be able to pluck Jester into the air. I should really be more worried about the plants . . .' She broke off, as if appalled by something, and her voice began to wobble. And for the second time, a look of near panic crossed her face.

Again, Hillary didn't understand why, but this time she was determined to try and track it back to its source.

'The plants?' she prompted, looking around the flower borders, a thoughtful frown on her face. The gardens out here were as lovely and well-tended as those out front. 'I'm not an expert — I don't even have a garden of my own, but this all looks lovely.' She thought she recognised a variety of country-garden favourites — geraniums, pinks, foxglove, snapdragons, various fuchsias and hollyhocks.

Jessie looked at her miserably. 'Oh, don't mind me. I've always been a worrywart. Dad says . . . It's just I always have to warn my patients . . . I mean, their owners, about the dangers in their gardens. Take lilies for instance — every part of it is toxic to cats — the stem, leaves, flowers, pollen and even the water in the vase if you've had some in the house. That's why you won't see any in my garden.'

'Ah, I see,' Hillary said. But she wasn't at all convinced that she was. Even granted that Jessie Phelps was one of those individuals who preferred animals to people and found conversation and social intercourse with her own kind awkward, she was sure that there was far more behind her behaviour than the usual case of nerves and unease in the company of strangers.

In fact, she would have bet a year's salary that the girl was desperate to keep something from her, and was terrified that she would inadvertently let that something slip.

'Do you know, I really do need to be getting back to work soon. You can't imagine how busy vets are,' Jessie said. 'Do you think we could wind this up quickly?'

She walked so fast back towards the house that even Hillary had trouble keeping pace with her.

Once inside, Hillary had to make a snap decision. Should she dig in her heels, or should she acquiesce? If she'd still been a serving DI and Jessie had been a person of interest in a current case, there would be no debate. But that was not so here. Jessie was, until proved otherwise (if she ever was), a victim of a crime, and a crime that was nearly fifteen years in the past. And Hillary was here on sufferance, and really couldn't afford to push her luck. If this woman dug in her heels and refused to speak to her at all, there'd be nothing she could do about it.

'Of course, we wouldn't want you to miss any appointments,' Hillary agreed, keeping her voice light and mild. 'But as I said to your father, we will probably have to come back at some point in the future and speak to you again.'

'Sure, sure, that'll be fine,' Jessie said eagerly, giving Hillary the impression that she was so relieved to be rid of them that she would have agreed to anything. Already, she was opening the door to let them out.

The door then closed behind them so fast that it almost caught Claire's heel as she stepped off the small outside step and onto the grass path.

'Well, I've had the bum's rush before but that was a doozy,' her colleague said drily.

CHAPTER SEVEN

'Talk about being all over the place,' Claire muttered as they walked back towards her car. 'She was practically jumping out of her skin. She really wasn't comfortable talking to us, was she? Just the nervous type, you think? Or something more to it?'

'Both,' Hillary said unhelpfully, her mind busily working. 'You noticed she had no trouble hauling that enormous animal about? She's physically very strong. I wonder if she was as strong as a teenager?'

'Strong enough to bash her mother over the head with something? I don't see why not,' Claire said. Given her professional career in rape and domestic violence units, she had no trouble in accepting a seventeen-year-old girl as the murderer of her own mother. 'She was about as close to her mother as I am to my mother-in-law. And in case you're wondering . . .' she trailed off deliberately, a grin on her face.

'That's not close,' Hillary obliged her. 'Seriously though — DI Clovis only had her version of events to go on. The original investigation couldn't find any neighbours or witnesses who saw Jessie arrive home from her friend's house. And the friend who vouched for what time she left her house might have lied for her. Teenage girls can be very loyal. What if Jessie arrived sometime before she said she did, got into an argument with her mum, and things got out of hand?'

'Possible,' Claire agreed. 'The trouble is, what did she do then? We know from forensics that they found no traces of blood on the kid's clothes, so she'd have had to have gone upstairs and changed. Washed. And again, forensics came up with nothing. Then what did she do with the clothes? They weren't stashed anywhere in the house — the search the original team did was as thorough as you could hope for.'

Hillary sighed. 'And again, no witnesses saw her out and about between school and arriving home — so it's unlikely she stashed her clothes in a skip or someone else's rubbish bin. Again, she might have gone back to the friend's house, who was a latch-key kid, so the parents would have been absent until they returned from their own places of work. But lying for Jessie about the time she left is one thing; actually helping her pal hide bloodstained clothing is something else again. I just can't see it somehow.'

'Agreed,' Claire said. 'Besides, most teenagers can't keep a secret — not one that huge or that brutal. Not for long anyway.'

Hillary sighed. 'That's the trouble with negative evidence — it only proves what didn't happen. Not what did. But just because we can't find any evidence that Jessie killed her mother, doesn't mean to say that she didn't. The girl went on to become a vet and could also have been a botanist — it's not as if she was lacking in brains.'

'But maybe her backbone wasn't up to it, guv?' Claire murmured. 'If she was a bundle of nerves just talking to us about it fifteen years later, she must have been a basket case when it actually happened — and if she'd just killed her mum . . . Can you really see DI Clovis not clocking it?'

Hillary grinned. 'Not really. But Jessie's definitely hiding *something*.'

'Oh yeah,' Claire agreed happily. 'Which gives us somewhere to start. How long are you going to give her before trying again?'

Hillary shrugged. 'Depends where the rest of the interviews take us.'

For a moment, the two women walked in silence back to Claire's car. Then her friend shook her head. 'Guv, did the way she doted on that rabbit give you the heebie-jeebies just a little bit? Because it did me. I felt a bit as if I'd stumbled into one of those psychological horror movies — you know the kind, where the lead character is obviously a bit "off" and something really creepy is going on in the background.'

Since they'd now reached the car, Hillary paused before opening the passenger door, giving the question some thought. 'I wouldn't go that far. In fact, it made *me* feel rather sad. I got the feeling she needed so desperately to love something that wouldn't hurt her back for doing so. I wonder if that's the reason she doesn't have children? She's scared stiff even her children won't love her?'

Claire paled a little. 'Because she doesn't believe her mother ever loved her?'

Hillary grimaced. 'Maybe. And perhaps she was right to think that. But we mustn't fall into the trap of demonising Imelda. Remember, there's two sides to every story and we can never get our murder victim's side — only that of the people who existed around her. Let's never forget that she would have her own demons to cope with. Chances are, she did the best she could, and she wouldn't have been the first by a long chalk if that best hadn't been good enough.'

* * *

Back in the house, Jessie waited until the two policewomen had left the garden, then immediately reached for her mobile phone and hit a speed-dial number.

It was answered instantly.

'Daddy? Yes, they've just gone. No, it was awful. I was so scared in case I said the wrong thing. I was so careful not to say anything about . . . you know . . . that I'm sure they were suspicious and suspect me.' She listened for a while, and then smiled. 'That would be wonderful! Can you come right away?' She hesitated, moving nervously from one foot to the other. 'Dad . . . what if they find out? You know, about what I did?'

She listened for another few moments, then took a long, shaky breath. 'Thanks, Dad, I'd really like to talk about it. I'll put the kettle on, shall I? I baked a coffee and walnut cake, your favourite . . .'

* * *

As Jessie Phelps talked on the telephone to her father, and Hillary and Claire made their way back to Thames Valley HQ, in Chipping Norton, Connie Brightman walked back towards her flat, laden down with shopping bags.

She didn't recognise the large black car that was parked outside on the road in front of her place, but she knew that it was an expensive model, and as such, looked out of place in this area. She glanced at it curiously as she went by, but it had darkened glass, so she could only just make out that it contained two people, one in the driving seat and one in the rear.

She trudged to her front door, let one bag drop onto the step and shuffled around in the side pocket of the other one for her key. As she did so, she heard the car door open behind her, and looked around to see where the occupants of the car were going.

She half-suspected that young lad over the street was a dealer of some kind, and wouldn't be at all surprised if his supplier and his bodyguard had come calling with whatever it was he was peddling.

But she saw instantly that she was wrong. Only one person had got out of the car, and they were now opening the gate to her house. What's more, Connie instantly knew who it was.

Her heart lifted. Today might well turn out to be her lucky day.

The moment she'd seen the story about Imelda appear in the papers she'd seen the opportunity it represented, and she had, that very morning, sent an email to the reporter who'd written the item, hoping it might be worth a few quid. So far, he hadn't responded, but she was confident that he would get around to her sooner or later.

But here, walking towards her, was a far better source of potential income. 'Well, well, well,' Connie Brightman drawled. 'Look what the cat's dragged in. Changed your mind, have you? I thought you might,' she said smugly. 'I suppose you'd better come in.'

* * *

Back at Kidlington, Hillary left Claire in the communal office to fill in Gareth on the interview with Jessie Phelps before typing up the notes for the Murder Book, whilst Hillary went to her office and belatedly logged on to her computer to check her emails.

After sending off a memo to Rollo on her latest thoughts and findings, she phoned her mechanic, who had good news. He'd swung by Thrupp to take a look at Puff (she'd left the car keys for him with the landlord of the Boat) and the diagnosis was nothing serious, nor — for once — ruinously expensive. He also promised to have her beloved Volkswagen back in the land of the living by the end of the day.

Feeling far more chipper, she collected Gareth from the office and set off for Moreton-in-Marsh in the neighbouring county of Gloucestershire. A beautiful old market town in the Cotswolds, it was typical of that breed — full of tourists, old mellow-stone buildings, narrow streets with nowhere near enough parking, and shops that were doing their best to fight off the insidious proliferation of their online competition. The pubs all had a profusion of hanging baskets frothing with colour, and there was no litter in sight — which was usually a sign that the local council was trying to win some kind of 'Beautiful Britain' award for the town and were forking out for street cleaners.

As Gareth drove, Hillary read through the updates that her team had managed to pull together on her next witness.

Dermott Franklyn had been thirty years old at the time of the murder, a full eleven years younger than his lover, but she doubted that the age gap would have worried either of them much. Why should it? That would make him forty-five or so now, and she wondered, idly, if he'd aged well.

The photograph of him in the original file showed a blond, blue-eyed athletic man of six foot, with a squarish face and prominent jaw. He'd been a rower at Oxford (never quite good enough to make the Oxford–Cambridge boat-race team, but worthy enough to become a reserve) and was the product of a wealthy family, from whom he had been set to inherit a minor fortune. Originally from Norwich, he'd obviously fallen in love with Oxford and its environs, for according to his list of residences, he'd never moved back to East Anglia.

Nor had he married, although that didn't mean he couldn't have had half a dozen or more partners since he'd lost Imelda.

'I think we're nearly there, ma'am,' Gareth said, checking the satnav. They'd now gone nearly all the way through the town and were on the verge of coming out the other side. Hillary noticed some brown 'heritage' signs that told her that there was an arboretum and a bird-of-prey centre close by, and then, just before they emerged back into the countryside proper, Gareth was turning off to the right, and climbing a slight but persistent incline.

Below them, the view began to open out into a wide, beautiful valley of rolling hills and farmland. And as Hillary watched, a huge bird of prey circled lazily in the air some distance away. She knew it was far too large to be a native species and presumed that the falconers at the bird-of-prey centre had some eagle or other out and about, showing off its paces to their visitors.

'I bet that puts the wind up the local sparrows,' Hillary murmured.

Gareth gave a long, low whistle — not in response to her comment — but because of the house that now appeared around a bend in the one-track lane.

Low, with a vast expanse of grey slate roof, it was a mixture of old and new; Cotswold stone, almost smothered with ancient wisteria gave way here and there to large sheets of gleaming, slightly darkened glass. A traditional cottage garden met modern design with a generous patio and steel-rimmed flowerbeds in a pleasing mix that screamed professional garden designer. As Gareth parked under a three-car timbered lean-to, that was itself attached on one side to an outbuilding that was probably a granny annexe, Hillary wondered how much it would all sell for. Two million? No, probably more, given the very desirable area and outstanding view.

It was now just gone noon, and as she stepped out of the car, she felt the sun instantly attack the top of her head, making her scalp start to itch. She was dressed in her usual 'summer survival outfit' of loose-fitting white linen slacks teamed with white open-toed sandals, and a pale green cotton blouse that suited her bell-shaped head of auburn-turning-grey hair and sherry-coloured eyes to perfection.

She wished she'd thought to bring a white straw hat with her, but knew it wouldn't have looked professional, so she hurried instead to the front porch, where the lilac-coloured wisteria cascaded around her. In May, the perfume coming off it must have been heady.

'He's expecting us, ma'am,' Gareth assured her, reaching her side at a more sedate pace.

Hillary had set up a vague schedule for their interviewees that they were following as best they could, and so far, nobody had refused their request for a chat, although Dermott had vetoed an earlier day that they'd pencilled in for him, claiming work commitments.

Hillary pulled the genuinely old, wrought-iron bellpull that hung beside the oak-panelled door, and somewhere inside, she could hear it clanging. No out-of-place electronic door buzzer for 'The Eyrie', it seemed. She wondered if the name of the house referred to the view from the top of the hill, or if Dermott had chosen it because eagles did indeed soar across the vistas that he could see from his home.

The door was opened by the man himself a moment later, and Hillary's musings as to whether he'd aged well were instantly answered. He had. And then some.

For a start, he looked a good seven years or so younger than she knew him to be, and his body had clearly never heard of 'middle-aged spread'. His blond hair hadn't begun to thin either, and the only sign of his advancing years showed in his face, which had become a little thinner and even more square than before. Which had, somehow, only enhanced his good looks.

'Yes?'

Hillary held out her ID, which he checked thoroughly, as he did Gareth's. He also noted her companion's ramrod straight posture along with the cane he had to use, and she thought she saw a look of sympathy cross his face.

Gareth's expression didn't change.

'You're the police reinvestigating Imelda's murder, yes?'

'I was a former DI for Thames Valley, sir, now working as a civilian consultant for the Crime Review Team. No unsolved murder case is ever closed, so technically it's still an ongoing investigation. But yes, we are taking a second in-depth look at Mrs Phelps's murder.'

'A nice distinction, I'm sure,' Dermott said dryly, standing aside and giving a nod at them to come in. 'Well, you can't make more of a hash of it than the original lot, I suppose,' he conceded.

The hallway floor was composed of traditional and probably original flagstones, so dark and worn with age that they were almost black. And, in this heat, they felt deliciously cool under the thin soles of Hillary's sandals. The hall almost instantly made way for a room that had once probably consisted of three or more rooms — a sitting room, drawing room, scullery? — but had now all been knocked into one large open-plan living area, so beloved of aficionados of 'modern' living.

The rear wall was almost all glass, and led out onto a decked veranda that drew the eye like a magnet to the vast and beautiful view of the valley it overlooked.

'Come on out — there's a good shady overhang, and I've just made some iced lime water,' Dermott said, catching the direction of her gaze. 'There's usually a breeze out here as well, even on the stillest of days.'

Hillary didn't need asking twice, and as Dermott drifted off into the kitchen area towards a huge American-style refrigerator, she stepped through the open sliding glass doors and out onto the deck. Here several wooden tables had been set out and she chose one with four chairs around it.

Gareth, without being asked, drew one chair a little further away from the table and towards the glass wall of the house, and sat down, taking out his phone and setting it to record. Dermott arrived a few moments later with a slightly green-tinged jug of water, tinkling with ice, and three tall glasses.

He poured out three, leaving Gareth's at the foot of his chair with a slightly amused smile, before turning back to pull out a chair opposite Hillary. When asked, he had no objection to the interview being recorded.

'This is gorgeous,' Hillary said, with a nod to the panorama set out behind him. 'Do you ever get used to it?'

Dermott shrugged. 'I suppose so. Sometimes. Familiarity breeds contempt, so they say, don't they?'

Hillary took a sip of her lime-flavoured water. 'Imelda was very beautiful too,' she said quietly.

Dermott raised an eyebrow. 'And did I eventually tire of looking at her as well?' he mocked gently. 'The answer to that is no, I didn't. I would have been quite content looking at her for the rest of my life, if some bastard hadn't taken her away from me.'

Hillary, getting the measure of her man instantly, mentally removed any kid gloves she might have considered using.

'But she didn't feel the same way about you, did she, sir? According to what the original SIO could discover, Imelda had no intention of leaving her husband and children.'

Dermott smiled grimly. 'Not then, maybe, no,' he admitted. 'But she would have changed her mind eventually.

When her daughter had left the nest completely, like her son had, and it was just her and Tommy-the-Terrible. She'd have seen sense then.'

He sounded so confident, even now, that it made Hillary wonder if he wasn't right. 'What makes you so sure?' she asked, genuinely interested in his reply. If it was only down to bravado or a false sense of his desirability it would tell her one thing. And if there was something more solid behind his self-belief, it would tell her something else.

'You think I'm full of myself, don't you?' Dermott said, as if he'd been reading her mind. 'That I'm just some wealthy jerk who also got lucky in the genetic lottery that governs the good-looks department, so I'm doubly used to getting my own way?' He gave a shrug of his still-impressive shoulders, reminding her, oddly enough, of Jonas Phelps, Imelda's son. He too was a good-looking, fit man with more than his share of handsome features.

'Those are your words, not mine, Mr Franklyn,' Hillary chided him calmly. 'Is that how you see yourself? Is that how you think Imelda saw you?'

He turned his glass around on the table, watching the ice move. 'You're a sharp one then, aren't you?' he said, nodding as if to himself. 'Fair enough. Let's see — did Imelda think me a spoiled brat? Possibly she did. At first. But not later, not when she really got to know me. We met at the gym — she needed to keep her slim figure, and I needed to keep in shape for the rowing. The moment I saw her, I felt . . .'

He suddenly stopped, and then threw his head back and laughed outright. 'Oh hell, what can I say that doesn't sound corny? I felt the earth shift beneath my feet? Well, it did! I felt my heart start to pound? Well, it did. I felt my throat go dry? Yep, it did that too. All of that and more. I just looked at her and knew. So go right ahead and laugh it up. But that's exactly what happened. And you know what? I was right.'

He lifted his head from the contemplation of his condensation-soaked glass and met Hillary's eyes with a fierce gaze, the last three words of his diatribe coming out without any self-deprecating humour at all. 'I've never found anyone else since that comes even close to her.'

He lifted his glass then, gave Hillary a mocking salute with it, and drank deeply. Hillary watched his Adam's apple move up and down, and got the sense of a powerful, healthy animal. A not unintelligent one either. She could easily see why Imelda would have been flattered by his interest. He was, in many ways, a perfect mate for her.

'I'm sorry to hear that, Mr Franklyn,' Hillary said — and meant it. Underneath the man-of-steel act, she could sense an old pain, held well in check. 'I take it the attraction was mutual?'

'Oh yeah,' Dermott said. 'Not that she didn't make me work for her, mind,' he added, and again that knowing but slightly abashed grin spread across his face. 'But I didn't care about that. She knew her own worth, and wasn't about to fall into my hand like a ripe plum, just for the asking — and why should she?' He looked up at Hillary. 'And now you're thinking that she was just one more upmarket, bored-housewife-cum-tart, am I right? Far too shallow to be taken seriously, and—'

'Wrong,' Hillary interrupted him, in no mood to hear a lecture. 'Please stop putting words into my mouth, Mr Franklyn. I don't like it, and it's very annoying.' If he preferred women who knew their own minds, then she had no problem providing him with one more to deal with.

He blinked a little at that, then his shoulders relaxed slightly, and his blue eyes definitely warmed. 'Fair enough,' he said, some of the latent aggression in his body relaxing somewhat. 'And I'm sorry. I'm just so used to defending her . . .' He shrugged the rest of his apology.

'Did she need defending?' Hillary asked curiously.

'Oh yeah. From anybody and everybody. The press, the bastards, went to town on her after she died, as if somehow her being a model, and an unfaithful wife, made her fair game. As if she'd been asking for it. I wanted to throttle the whole bloody lot of them,' he snarled.

'I can imagine,' Hillary agreed. 'And I have no great love for the press either. They tend to get in the way and make my job ten times harder. Occasionally though, they can be useful.'

'If you say so,' he said, clearly unconvinced. 'Mind you, her so-called friends were just as bad. I can just imagine them — mourning her at her funeral, then backbiting her over the booze and nibbles afterwards. Lying, miserable, mediocre cats, all of them. And their men would have been no better. All nudge-nudge, wink-wink, I daresay, pretending that if they just snapped their fingers that they all could have had her, if they'd wanted to. The absurdity of it! As if she'd have given any one of them so much as a second look.'

Hillary regarded him thoughtfully. Still so bitter after all these years. One thing was for certain — here, at last, was someone who genuinely mourned Imelda Phelps. She wasn't sure that her husband did, and she was pretty sure her children didn't. Not even her mother had shown any remnants of grief for her only child.

But here, in this lovely place and with this angry man, Imelda's memory still shone as brightly as ever.

'You really loved her,' Hillary paid tribute to him simply.

'Yes.'

'The outside world saw you as her toyboy though?'

'Oh yeah.' He grinned lazily. 'As if I gave a damn! They wanted to believe I was her fling, her way of cocking a snook at the world. A distraction that wouldn't last. But we were together nearly three years — and we'd be together right now if things had been different. She'd be here with me, sitting on one of these chairs, sipping champagne in the sun, right now.'

He looked around at the other empty tables and chairs and a muscle clenched at his jaw. 'I wouldn't have stopped until she'd admitted her marriage was over, you see. Wouldn't have stopped until she'd applied for and obtained a divorce. Wouldn't have stopped until she'd agreed to put *my* wedding ring on her finger. And she would have — because she loved me too. Oh, not as much as I loved her,' he added hastily. 'I don't want you running away with the idea that I'm some idiot who can't see what's right in front of his face. I know I was more in love with her than she with me. But they say that in every relationship there's the one who is loved, and the one who does the loving, right? Well, she was happy to be loved, and I was happy to love her. We worked. We fitted.'

Hillary shifted a little in her chair. Was he right? Or merely deluded? It was impossible to say without having ever seen them together and seeing how it had been for herself. But one thing she was sure of — this man had not been an unimportant part of Imelda's life. He'd been young, handsome, fit, healthy and wealthy. And determined to win her. That was a potent combination for anyone, let alone a woman who was in her forties and could see her youth and the beauty that she'd always taken for granted on the point of declining.

'You were pressing her to leave her husband around the time of her death?'

He nodded.

'But she was still saying no?'

He nodded.

'That must have made you angry? Frustrated?'

He gave a wry smile. 'Oh sure. But if you're thinking I got tired of the rejection, lost my temper and bashed her over the head, you're out of your mind. And you're not listening to me. I knew that soon she was going to be mine — fully mine — that it was just a matter of time and patience. And I was willing to wait for her.'

His blue eyes suddenly darkened. 'When I heard she was dead . . .' He got up abruptly and stood leaning against the wooden railing of the veranda, staring out in front of him blindly. The change of position had taken him out into the bright glare of the sun, which turned his blond hair almost white. He slowly shook his head.

'The worst day of my life. By far.'

Hillary watched him quietly for a while, took another long sip of her drink and sighed. 'Please come and sit back down, Mr Franklyn. I want you to tell me about Imelda.'

Dermott looked over his shoulder at her, then nodded, and returned to the table. 'You know which buttons to press, don't you, former DI Hillary Greene? Talking about Imelda is one of my favourite things to do. And now you're wondering if I'm just some sad sack, stuck in the past and unable to move on?'

'Are you?'

Again he threw his head back and laughed. 'Probably. So, go ahead — ask me about Imelda.'

'Did you notice anything odd in her behaviour in the months prior to her death?'

'Generally — no. There was a week or ten days or so when I couldn't get to see her though.'

'She wouldn't see you?'

'She wouldn't see *anyone*, as far as I could make out. She didn't accept any invitations out to see friends, or go to the gym, or attend her book club. She just seemed to drop out of sight altogether. I couldn't tease her out of her house for love nor money. But it didn't last. Like I said, it was about a week — ten days tops. Then she was back to her usual social whirl.'

Hillary nodded. This was the second time she was hearing about this bout of odd behaviour on the part of the murder victim.

'Did you form any idea about what was behind it? The most obvious explanation is that she was ill. A cold or stomach bug maybe?'

'Possibly,' Dermott agreed. 'But Imelda was remarkably healthy. I can't say as I ever knew her to be sick. I did, in my darkest moments, wonder if she might have met someone else, but I made sure it wasn't that. Like I said — she just didn't go out, period. Didn't seem to leave the house.'

Hillary looked at him quickly. 'And how do you know that?'

Dermott grinned mockingly back at her. 'Did I sit outside her house like some gumshoe from a bad private-eye movie and stake it out? Well, yes, I did, as it happens, off and on. When she turned down a particular offer of a meal out or a trip to the theatre, I'd drive over there to watch what happened. And no, she didn't leave the house and meet someone else. I also checked out all her usual haunts every day and night, and never saw a trace of her there either.'

'That sounds rather like obsessive behaviour to me,' Hillary said.

Dermott shrugged indifferently. 'Perhaps it was. It put my mind at rest though. And afterwards, when we saw each other again, I could tell that I'd had nothing to worry about. Whatever had turned her into a temporary hermit, it had nothing to do with a rival. A man can always tell.'

Hillary wasn't so sure about that, but she let it pass.

'Not long before she was murdered, Imelda shut down her jewellery business, and left her business partner rather sore with her, is that right?'

'Connie something-or-other? Yeah, she did. Imelda would get fads that would come and go, and then she'd move on to something else. The jewellery thing was just another one in a long line.'

'It left Connie Brightman high and dry though. It might have been nothing but a hobby to Imelda, but to her business partner it was her sole living and her way out of a humdrum job. It wasn't very nice of her to leave Connie flat like that.'

Dermott frowned. 'I know — I can't say as I liked it much. But Imelda didn't take criticism well and . . . let's be honest, I didn't really care what she did. When you love someone, you take them as they are — faults and all.'

'And what if *you'd* turned out to be just a passing fad too? Oh, I don't disagree that you lasted longer than most, but . . . ?'

Dermott nodded. 'I see where you're going with this, but you're wrong. I know that other detective, that Clovis woman, looked at me long and hard and sideways for it, but I had an alibi. I was on the river rowing at the time. Others saw me there.'

Hillary knew that. But he'd been on his own, in a single kayak, and not in a longer boat with a team. Clovis had speculated that he could have chosen a discreet bend in the river to tie up and slink off unseen. He could have left a car somewhere within walking distance, driven to his lover's house, killed her, and driven back and got back on the river in time to return the boat to the boathouse later on, and no one the wiser.

On the downside, there'd been no witnesses to suggest his arrival at the Phelpses' house, and no witnesses to him leaving the river.

'Yes, I know it wasn't airtight,' he jeered, as if reading her mind again. 'But I had no reason to kill her. Like I keep saying — all I had to do was wait.'

'Patient soul, are you?'

'Not as a rule, no,' he said coolly. Hard blue eyes met hard sherry eyes, with neither blinking.

'You must have wondered who killed her?' Hillary challenged him.

Dermott snorted then, a half-laugh, half-growl. '*You think?* I almost drove myself nuts thinking about nothing else.'

'And your conclusion?'

Dermott looked at her bleakly now. 'Take your pick. Sometimes I wanted it to be Thomas-the-Terrible, but I never really could make myself believe it. He wasn't so terrible, really, it's just how I liked to think of him. He was all wrong for Imelda — too dull, too ordinary, too . . . oh hell, just not right for her. But a killer?' He shrugged. 'Didn't have it in him.'

He paused, sighed and leaned back in his chair, staring up at the overhanging roof above him. 'Her son was too up-his-own-arse and barely gave her the time of day. Her daughter could be a bit neurotic, but she was only a kid — Imelda could have handled her if one of her tantrums turned really physical. Besides, what reason would either of them have to hurt their own mother? Nah. I thought about that Connie woman . . . but again, in any fight between the two of them, Imelda would have come out on top. She was fit and quick and nobody's fool. It's no use — I just can't picture any of them getting the better of her somehow. Does that make sense?'

Hillary nodded. To this man, Imelda was all but perfect — far too bright and strong to be caught out by an inferior; but again, she didn't agree with his assessment; her vast experience of human nature and the cut-throat realities of her work had seen to that. People could always surprise you. And it was only the work of a moment to hit an unsuspecting victim on the back of the head. And anyone at all could be caught out by an attack that came out of the blue — especially if you knew and trusted — or even loved — your attacker.

'So we're left with — what? A passing stranger?' Hillary mused out loud. 'Was Imelda the type who'd let a stranger into the house? Bear in mind, they might have a good cover story.'

'Possibly,' Dermott said, but without enthusiasm. 'I think it more likely than a member of her family. Possibly it *was* a stranger, but not necessarily someone that she didn't know.'

'Come again?' Hillary said, confused.

Dermott smiled. 'Sorry. Have you thought that it might have been work-related? Not the jewellery stuff, that was just pocket money. But her real work — modelling. And more specifically, that someone from that whole "Face of Experience" thing might have been mixed up in it?'

Hillary shot bolt upright in her chair. 'And just what,' she said sharply, 'is "The Face of Experience"?'

CHAPTER EIGHT

'You know — the modelling contract that she was so excited about,' Dermott said, his gaze sharpening at her obvious surprise. 'Her one last shot at the big time. Her family must have mentioned it to DI Clovis.'

But Hillary knew that they hadn't. Nowhere, in any of the old case files, was there any mention of an imminent modelling contract, let alone by name. But she was not about to reveal that to her witness.

'Or maybe she never told them?' Dermott swept on, too lost in his own thoughts to realise just how much he'd thrown her. 'Mind you, I know she'd been asked to keep it all hush-hush until the PR people were ready to announce the product launch, but she knew *I* could keep my mouth shut. Or it could be that she was just too nervous to tell anyone else in case she didn't get it — although she'd been one of the few shortlisted. Yeah, that makes sense. She would have felt humiliated if it had got out that she was in line for a big comeback only for some other model to get the top job.'

'Why don't you just tell me what you know about "The Face of Experience", Mr Franklyn,' Hillary said, forcing herself to relax back in her chair. 'Starting from the beginning, please.'

Dermott nodded. 'OK, but this is fifteen years ago, remember. I won't be all that hot on details. So, I know it was a fashion company — or was it for cosmetics? Don't ask me the name of it, I couldn't tell you. But they were going to launch a line of stuff for their . . .' and here he made quote marks with his fingers, his lips twisting into a grimace of distaste, '. . . "older woman" clientele. The forty-plus brigade. Imelda was torn between indignation at being approached for the "silver" market, and over the moon because it was going to be a really big thing. TV ads, magazines, billboards, products in all the top stores, the works.'

'How did all this come about?' Hillary asked. 'Who approached her?'

'Oh, just the usual way I suppose — through the modelling agency that she was signed up with. They arranged all the initial interviews, photoshoots, whatever,' Dermott explained. 'I remember Immy being really excited about one shoot — furs and diamonds were mentioned. Fake furs, I suppose,' he added, but with a frown of uncertainty.

'OK, and you say she was shortlisted?'

'Yes — I think it was down to her and two others. You know — to be their "Face of Experience". The way it was sold to her was that she was going to be the poster girl for the middle-aged. You know — you too can look like this if you use whatever the hell it was they were selling.'

Hillary smiled. 'You sound like you weren't all that impressed?'

Dermott shrugged. 'If it made her happy,' he muttered.

Hillary gave him a long, level look. 'But you weren't really that keen on her landing the assignment, were you?' she put it to him straight. 'Because if she got the job and became famous, you must have been worried that you might lose her. It was one thing to win over an ageing and bored housewife — but a well-known model? Her face on everyone's television screen? She was still stunning, after all. You'd soon have had some serious competition then.'

Dermott eyed her askance, then reluctantly smiled. 'Don't pull your punches, do you?' he grumbled. 'But yeah, you're right of course. I supported her, naturally I did, because she was so excited about it. But yes, secretly, I'll admit that I was always hoping that one of her rivals pipped her at the post. So you can imagine what a right bastard that made me feel when she died before they announced . . . Morgan Fisher!' He snapped his fingers in triumph. '*That* was the chap's name. I remember it now — I remember Immy talking about him. He was one of the head honchos of the firm — or was he the one in charge of the advertising campaign? I'm not sure, but that was his name.'

Hillary glanced at Gareth to make sure he'd got the name, and he nodded back at her.

'Anyway, the model they finally gave the contract to in the end wasn't a patch on Imelda, I can tell you that.'

Naturally not, Hillary thought silently. She tried to recall if she had ever purchased a 'Face of Experience' product and couldn't. But then, she'd never really bought into the whole shopping-as-therapy ethos.

'And this was all happening what — in the weeks or months before her death?' Hillary prompted.

'Yeah, that's right. So if someone she knew from that lot had called on her — maybe a photographer who said he wanted some more shots, or a so-called assistant who wanted further details . . . well, she'd let *them* in, wouldn't she?'

'It's an idea, certainly,' Hillary agreed. Given her looks, Imelda could have picked up a predator from either the company itself or the advertising people they were using — some chancer who tried the whole 'sleep with me, luv, I've got the ear of the big boss and can make sure you're a shoo-in' spiel. She could see how a situation like that could quickly deteriorate from farce to fatality.

And then there were the other two models also in the running for the big prize to consider. If one of them had access to someone friendly on The Face of Experience team, they might have been able to find out the names and addresses of their rivals. But it was a bit of a stretch to imagine them going so far as to kill off their competition . . . Or was it? Presumably a national campaign meant big money and — even more alluring — fame and approbation. Still beautiful at forty — still desired by men and envied by women. To be held up as the gold standard for a whole generation would be heady stuff indeed. It only needed for one of the other candidates to be desperate, or a little off kilter . . .

'Why didn't you mention any of this to DI Clovis yourself?' Hillary wanted to know.

Dermott looked surprised at this question for a moment, then slowly shook his head. 'I dunno really. Any number of reasons I suppose — mainly, I just assumed someone else would have mentioned it. I can't believe Immy could have kept it a secret from her husband, for instance. Also, you have to remember I was a total mess at the time and not thinking straight. In the end, I couldn't even go to her funeral — for her kids' sake, and because I knew how much she would have hated it. She wouldn't have been able to stand people sniggering at my presence. She was so old-fashioned about stuff like that. And not being there really did my head in.'

Dermott scowled, then clicked his fingers. 'Oh yeah, and sure as hell, that DI Clovis was getting under my skin, implying it was me who'd killed her, and trying to get me to confess. It was laughable, really, but after a while it began to seriously piss me off and by then I wouldn't have told her that rain was wet and the sun was hot. I suppose it made me generally uncooperative. And yeah, I daresay that makes me sound like a bit of a bastard, but like I said — I didn't really begin to get my head around things until months — years, really — after she died. I'm not sure my head's still right about it all, even now,' he concluded glumly.

Hillary glanced out over the magnificent view, both to give him a moment to compose himself, and also to prevent him from seeing her sense of growing excitement. But keeping it under control was difficult when she'd just uncovered a significant thread that the original team had missed.

She began making mental notes. Find the current whereabouts of this Morgan Fisher character and get his take on things. Get the name of The Face of Experience winning model and the other, losing candidate, and all the major players in the campaign. True, after all this time, it would be hard going trying to track down where they all were on 23 June 2010, but it was going to have to be attempted.

She could only imagine Claire and Gareth's reactions when they realised the enormity of the task ahead of them. But at least it gave them new ground to cover, which was a bonus. Because she'd been getting the worrying feeling that this case might be a really tough nut to crack.

But now — who knew what new leads they might find?

* * *

Hillary didn't let the grass grow under her feet, and as soon as they got in the car and started the journey back to HQ, she got out her mobile and rang Claire.

'Claire? We've caught a break. Get on the computer and find out all you can about a range of fashion and/or cosmetics called The Face of Experience that should have been set up and running sometime in 2010 or maybe 2011. I want to know the name of the company behind it, the name of the model they used for the launch campaign, and the current whereabouts of someone called Morgan Fisher, who had some sort of finger in the pie.'

She gave her colleague a quick précis of the interview, then hung up and glanced at her watch. It was now just coming up to three o'clock. 'What did you make of Imelda's lover then?' she asked Gareth.

'Seemed a bit over the top to me, ma'am,' Gareth said, after some judicious thought. 'It's been nearly fifteen years, so you'd have thought he'd have moved on more than he seems to have done.'

'Unless he was faking it,' Hillary added. 'Or overdoing it. Some people like to self-aggrandise. He looked the type.

Still, I think the emotion was genuine enough. I got the feeling that she was definitely someone special to him.'

Gareth slowly nodded. 'Ye-es, I thought so too. But I'm not at all sure that things would have worked out as he so blithely assumed they would, if she'd lived.'

Hillary thought that this was a rather insightful thing for a man of Gareth's relatively young age to realise, and she regarded him thoughtfully for a moment. He certainly was maturing fast, and she couldn't help but wonder if he was gaining this worldly-wise wisdom the hard way.

His face, as usual, gave nothing away, and she made a mental note to pay much more attention to him going forward.

He looked at her, as if wondering at her silence, and she quickly nodded in agreement with his assessment. 'No — me neither. But let's leave the man with his dreams, shall we?'

They were just five miles from the office when Claire rang her back.

'Guv? We've struck lucky for once!' she said, her excited voice prompting Hillary to put her on speaker phone, so that Gareth could hear her too.

'The company behind Face of Experience was called Dundas and had a fair range of shops and lines throughout the UK selling everything from lingerie to accessories, perfume and cosmetics, but like a lot of chains, they didn't survive Covid and eventually went into administration three years ago. The Face of Experience range ran for nearly six years and was successful enough, but it was discontinued. The model was someone called . . . hang on whilst I check my notes . . . yeah here it is — Rosalind Courtenay. Now there's a made-up name if ever I heard one!' she snorted. 'But don't worry, I'll get her real name and details in a jiffy. But what's even better, I've found our Mr Morgan Fisher. He was the CEO of Fisher King Advertising. Don't know why they didn't put it the other way round — King Fisher. Makes way more sense, doesn't it? Anyway, *they* also went belly up during the lockdown, and it looks as if Mr Fisher had had enough of the London rat race and moved to — guess where? Oxford!'

she added, before Hillary could grumpily inform her that she was too damned hot and tired for guessing games.

'Please tell me you have an address?'

'Not one, but two, guv,' Claire crowed. 'A work address and a home address. He now runs a much smaller ad agency in Summertown.'

Hillary checked her watch once more. 'We're only about half an hour from Oxford now — he'll still be at work.' She glanced at Gareth as she spoke. 'We probably won't be finished by five, so it'll mean unpaid overtime, but since we're on a roll, we might as well keep on going?' She raised the pitch of her voice at the end, in order to make it a question, and Gareth quickly nodded his agreement without taking his eyes off the road.

Hillary made a note of the address in her notebook as Claire recited it and hung up. 'We were due some luck,' she observed drily. 'He might have quit the rat race altogether and retired to the Outer Hebrides.'

Mind you, she thought, with a wistful sigh, it must be cooler up there.

* * *

The Park Dean Advertising agency comprised one half of a converted Victorian villa in Park Town, near the Oxford suburb of Summertown.

The young receptionist seated behind a desk in what had once been a lofty entrance hall eyed their ID badges with widening blue eyes, and forgoing the intercom on her desk, left to deliver their request for an appointment with Morgan Fisher in person. She returned a short while later, still looking wide-eyed and curious, and escorted them to the back of the building, where the largest room (once a salon?) had a view of a rather overgrown rear garden.

The man who rose from behind his desk to greet them was in his early fifties, Hillary gauged, of slim build, with receding mousy brown hair and a pair of very white, soft-looking, well-kept hands.

'Good afternoon.' He gave them a wide friendly smile that Hillary trusted about as much as a dog that was wagging his tail but growling low in its throat. 'Police, is it?'

Hillary produced her ID once more and explained the remit of the CRT. 'We were hoping you could help us with inquiries into the Imelda Phelps case, sir,' she finished, eyeing the chairs in front of his desk in an obvious fashion.

At the silent rebuke, Morgan Fisher flushed a little and hastily offered them a seat. He cast a quick nod at the receptionist, who somewhat reluctantly left, and Hillary wondered if she would have enough gumption to put her ear to the door and listen or would return meekly to the hall.

'Imelda Phelps?' Morgan parroted, trying to look vague, but a shrewd light behind his pale brown eyes ruined it for him.

'One of the models shortlisted for The Face of Experience campaign that you ran for Dundas, Mr Fisher,' she responded crisply. 'She was murdered in June of 2010. I'm sure something like that would stick in your mind.' She was careful to make it a statement, not a question.

She was feeling hot, irritable, and it was nearing the end of a long day, so she was in no mood to play silly buggers with the likes of this advertising executive.

Getting the message loud and clear, he quickly shed his vague puzzlement for one of sudden enlightenment. 'Oh yes, of course. Now I know who you're talking about. Such a tragedy — she was a beautiful woman.'

'We'd like to know as much about the campaign as we can. *For some reason,*' she stressed pointedly, 'nobody came forward at the time to mention it, and the original investigators were unaware of its existence. We were hoping you might now be able to help us remedy that.'

If Morgan had been wearing a tie, he might well have reached up to loosen it at that point in the classic sign of a man who was feeling the pressure. Since he was wearing only a white shirt, with the top two buttons undone, he merely went pale and began to perspire.

'I don't know what use I can be, I'm afraid. The advertising company I was working for then is no longer in existence, you see. And of course, I wasn't permitted to keep any of its paperwork.'

Hillary allowed a small, disbelieving smile to form on her lips. 'I would imagine though, knowing as you did that you were probably going to have to set up another firm of your own, a list of former clients and various other contacts would have been very useful?'

Morgan spread his hands wide in a gesture of appeal. 'Oh, that would have been very unethical. And I can assure you, all of us who were left high and dry when the agency folded were very carefully scrutinised to be sure that nothing untoward went on.'

Hillary could have pointed out that he wasn't a mere junior cog in the executive wheel but actually one of the partners, and as such would have had plenty of time to squirrel away any assets he wanted, but she wasn't interested in his past naughty dealings. Well, not the financial ones, anyway. She was only putting the wind up him so that he would start to see things her way about opening up about Imelda Phelps.

'If you say so, sir,' she said sceptically. 'We'll just have to rely on your memory then, won't we? Now, what can you tell me about Imelda?'

Morgan, looking relieved at the change in direction of the questioning, tried to look helpful and honest. Hillary wished he wouldn't — he was beginning to give her a headache.

'Oh, Imelda, yes, a lovely woman. She was one of three, I seem to remember, to be in line for the top spot. Dundas commissioned us to take some photos and mock up some possible lines for the campaign with all three to see which they liked best.'

'Had it got to the point where they'd made their choice?'

'I don't think so. Although, just between us, I got the feeling that they were leaning more in Imelda's favour.'

And if that were the case, Hillary mused silently, it was a fair bet that everyone and their granny could read the writing on the wall — including the other two models.

'After she died, they gave the spot to another model,' Hillary pressed on. 'Rosalind Courtenay, I think it was? Any idea what her real name is by any chance?'

He opened his mouth to say something, caught her glare, and changed his mind. 'I have a feeling it was Rosemary Cox. And the other woman in the running was Autumn Rawlings — and her last name really was Rawlings, but I think she was christened Felicity.'

'Amazing how the memories can come flooding back, sir, isn't it?' Hillary said mildly. 'If you can remember where these women lived that would be very helpful too.'

But here Morgan seemed genuinely not to know, and Hillary didn't push it, since either Claire or Gareth would be able to find out eventually, now that they had some real names to work with.

'I take it you got to know all three women fairly well?' she tried next.

'Well, not really,' Morgan instantly denied. 'I didn't really do the hands-on stuff, you understand, I was more involved in the tactical aspects of it. You know, planning, that sort of thing.'

'Ah, I see,' Hillary said. 'I suppose it was the photographers who had most interaction with the models then?' She didn't miss the little start of dismay he gave when she mentioned the word 'photographers' and made a show of taking out her notebook and pen (even though she knew Gareth would be making full notes) and glanced up at the now openly sweating advertising man with a raised eyebrow.

'And who did these preliminary shots for Dundas, Mr Fisher?'

'You know, I'm not sure.'

'But they would have been employed by your agency, yes?'

'Oh yes, but we had several that we used.'

'But The Face of Experience campaign must have been a huge client for you. You'd have used only your best people on it. I'm sure if you think back, you can bring a name to mind,' she said. And gently tapped the tip of her pen against her notebook.

Morgan swallowed hard, then shrugged and said casually, 'In that case, it would probably have been Mick Trent.'

Hillary nodded and wrote it down, wondering why Fisher was looking a little green around the gills now. 'Mr Trent still in the business, is he?'

'I'm not sure,' Morgan said. 'He was a bit of a booze hound. He might have gone to the dogs.' He gave a little laugh.

'He sounds most unreliable. I'm surprised he was trusted with such a client. But never mind, we'll soon track him down. One thing I know about professionals is that they always keep backups and copies of their work.'

A smug little smile tugged at the corners of Fisher's lips at that and then, when he saw her noticing it, it disappeared at once. But the fact that something was pleasing him irked her far more than it should have done, and she had to take a moment to keep her temper in check.

This heatwave really was beginning to get to her!

She wouldn't have been human if she didn't want to make sure that smirk never returned to his face however, so she began to line up the big guns.

'Can you please explain, sir, why, when you heard of Imelda's murder and the subsequent police statement asking for anyone with information about Imelda to come forward, you and Dundas Limited remained remarkably mute?'

Morgan sat up a little straighter in his chair. 'Well, I imagine Dundas weren't too keen to be put in the spotlight; I'm sure you can understand that, er, Inspector, er . . .'

'Greene,' Hillary supplied flatly, making no attempt to explain that the 'Inspector' part was now redundant.

'Greene, yes. Er, well, you see, no company likes to be seen in such a negative light as a murder investigation, especially when they're about to launch a major campaign. They'd have invested a huge sum of money already and would be expecting to make millions on the new range. If the press had got a hold of the connection . . . Well, you can imagine.' He gave a little shudder. 'And the nude . . .'

He bit off the words quickly, but nowhere near quickly enough.

'Nudes? I thought The Face of Experience was a campaign for cosmetics and fashion?" Hillary said sharply.

'And so it was, oh yes, please don't get me wrong. When I said nudes, I don't want you thinking along the lines of, well, er, pornography or anything distasteful like that.' He rubbed his soft white hands together nervously. 'It was all very tastefully done — it would have to be,' Morgan was talking so fast now he was almost falling over his words. 'Dundas wouldn't have stood for anything else! This was all going to go out on television and before any watershed. When I say nudes, I meant, really, "implied" nudes.'

Hillary sighed heavily. 'Perhaps you can explain that term, sir? Exactly what kind of photographs are we talking about here?'

'As I recall, for Imelda, it was the fur coat experiment. Implied nudes mean exactly what it sounds like — you can look at a photograph and know that the model isn't wearing any clothes, but you never see anything salacious. In Imelda's case, she was naked under a faux-fur coat. Sitting on a fake-fur rug, that sort of thing. She was dripping in diamonds (fakes, obviously, not the real thing) and looking over her shoulder at you. Her shoulder was bare, obviously, as were her legs and arms and . . . well, you just *knew* she was nude, and yet she was still covered. All very tasteful, like I said. There were other models around at the time of the shoot, it was all very professional. She wasn't alone or pressured or anything like that. The image the photographer was after was meant to portray a confident free-spirited woman awaiting her lover, secure in her body image and of course, she was wearing full make-up by the Dundas line.'

It sounded old hat to Hillary but she was hardly an expert.

Morgan was too busy rushing on with the self-justifications to notice her scepticism, however. 'But you can imagine what would have happened if the press had got a hold of those kind of images when she was found dead! Besides, it would have been horrible for her family too, in the circumstances,' he added, in a rather pathetic attempt at showing some sympathy.

'So, you all just conveniently forgot that they'd been considering her to head their campaign, and everyone concerned was ordered to keep quiet about it.' Hillary nodded. 'Including you.'

Morgan flushed, for the first time showing a little anger of his own. 'You can hardly blame us for that surely? The bad publicity would have ruined everything for everyone concerned. Oh, you can look as disapproving as you like, but what good would it have done anyway? Coming forward wouldn't have helped, since the poor woman's death obviously had nothing to do with us! The husband probably did it, didn't he? They usually do, don't they?' he added hotly.

'Why are you so sure that her murder had nothing to do with you, sir?' Hillary shot back sharply. 'By your own admission, the murder victim was about to become very famous and probably very wealthy. And in doing so, denied two other women the same chance. Where fame and fortune is at stake, murder has been known to follow.'

She saw the colour fade from his face as her words sank in. 'But . . . but that's not . . . none of us could have been involved . . . we sell things for a living, we're not homicidal maniacs!' he protested.

Hillary suddenly felt immensely weary and leaned back in her chair. 'We're the police, sir, we're not just going to take your word for that,' she said sardonically. 'Now, I suggest you focus your mind, and gather together all of the facts and figures that you can track down concerning Imelda's involvement in the campaign. Then start making notes of anything you can remember about that time — starting with personnel. Who would have had direct contact with her, that sort of thing. And then email it to this address.' She handed over one of her cards. 'And, Mr Fisher,' she said, as she began to rise from her chair, 'don't take too long about it. Yes?'

'Of course,' he said hastily, but quickly put her card down as if it was red-hot.

* * *

Hillary's bad temper wasn't helped any when they got stuck in the city's notorious rush hour that encompassed the Woodstock and Banbury roads and their roundabouts, and were forced to sit in the sweltering heat in the resultant traffic jams for nearly an hour.

Gareth, wisely, remained mostly silent.

Trying to distract herself from being baked alive, Hillary got out her phone and texted a full report to Rollo Sale on their new lead. It would mean Gareth and Claire would both be busy tracking down all they could about the new players. And she wanted to find the photographer who'd taken their publicity shots. There was something there that had made Morgan Fisher particularly antsy.

Had the photographer been a problem of some sort? Was it possible that he had become obsessed with Imelda? It had been known to happen before. Conversely, had he fallen for one of the other two? Perhaps Rosalind Courtenay or Autumn Rawlings had seduced him in the belief that he could help her secure the contract. And if so, it wasn't beyond the realms of possibility that he might have taken their strongest rival out of the running. What had Fisher said — he was a bit of a booze hound. Perhaps he was a highly strung type and might simply have snapped.

What else did she need to consider? She had the nagging feeling at the back of her mind that she'd meant to do something — tick some box or other — and had forgotten what it was.

Hillary sighed as the car crept forward another inch and stopped. It was no good — she was just too damned hot and tired to think properly. And according to the weather forecast, tonight's temperatures were hardly going to drop at all. Thirty degrees at night — what the hell was all that about? No pun intended.

She was sorely tempted, once Gareth had dropped her off back at Thrupp, to just pick up Puff and see if she couldn't check into a local B&B somewhere for a while. At least a house made of bricks and mortar couldn't become such a sauna as the *Mollern* was fast becoming. Narrowboats, whilst they could still be cosy enough in winter, provided little protection in a prolonged heatwave.

Hang the expense — she just couldn't function properly without at least one night's decent sleep. It was hard enough conducting a murder investigation when your brain was working at normal capacity, let alone when it felt as if it was being broiled!

CHAPTER NINE

Forty minutes later, she was walking along the towpath towards her narrowboat, dreaming of icebergs and chilly north winds. The owners of the *Ramblin' Rosie*, a boat that had moored up just behind hers last week, had set up a barbecue and deck chairs on the towpath, and greeted her cheerfully with a raised glass of white wine.

Both in their seventies, they were a spritely pair, sun-tanned and lean. 'Hello there, neighbour, you look frazzled,' the man said. 'Want a glass? Supermarket plonk, but it's been in the fridge.' He gave it a little waggle.

'Don't tempt me,' Hillary said with a smile. 'I've just finished work and now all I want to do is collapse in my chair and zonk out.'

'You look like you could do with a holiday, luv,' the old lady said, eyeing her up and down. 'You should take a break. It's the perfect weather for it.'

Hillary smiled and wondered what their reaction would be if she told them that the last time she'd been daft enough to take a holiday she'd had one of her teeth knocked out and had nearly been forcibly chucked off a cliff.

'I'll think about it,' she lied, and with a smile, trudged on to her boat. Too tired to search for local B&Bs, she contented herself with a lukewarm shower, and did, indeed, zonk out, only to wake a couple of hours later, hot and cross, but at least remembering what it was that she'd meant to do and had forgotten. Hooray for the good ol' subconscious!

* * *

The next morning, Gavin Otterley was up with the lark (well, the more reasonable city pigeons anyway) and headed out intent on an ambush. It was Friday, so he was looking forward to having the weekend off — but if he got on to something good today, he'd maybe have to work through some part of it.

Now he'd got the name of the CRT consultant who was heading up the murdered model case, he was feeling pleased with himself at having tracked down her address, and intrigued to discover that she lived on a narrowboat. Could he use that as a bit of local colour? He'd certainly take a snapshot of the boat and canal in any case. Readers liked a pretty picture.

As he parked just outside the Boat pub at Thrupp, he duly set about snapping some pictures before setting off first one way down the towpath and then, not finding any moored boat called the *Mollern*, retracing his steps and trying the other direction. He spotted the boat a few minutes later. Unlike most of the other, more colourful boats, it was painted predominantly in grey, with black, white and gold accent colours. A painting of a heron on one of the panels made him think the name had something to do with the waterbird. He wasn't an investigative reporter for nothing!

He hung around until just gone half past eight and was finally rewarded when the back metal doors opened and a woman appeared. She was dressed nearly all in white, with a just-touching-the-shoulder bob of dark auburn hair that was starting to turn grey. She locked the doors behind her and stepped off onto the towpath.

'Ms Greene?'

Hillary turned to see a slight, fairly short young man walking towards her. He had fair hair and pale eyes and a charming smile. Instantly she was on her guard.

'And you are?' she said sharply.

'Gavin Otterley. Hello, I work for the—'

'Yes, I know your newspaper,' Hillary cut in. She had made a point to memorise the name of the reporter who'd put the news of her latest investigation online. 'I have no comment.'

She turned and began to walk briskly towards the pub, but wasn't at all surprised to find him jogging persistently alongside her.

'Can you tell me if you've uncovered any new leads in the Imelda Phelps case, Ms Greene?'

'No comment.'

'Oh, come on! It's not as if I'm asking questions about a dodgy politician — you're hardly risking your career giving me a quote. It's not even as if it's a current case,' he wheedled.

'No comment.'

Hillary found it odd — but strangely satisfying — to repeat the mantra she'd so often heard from suspects across an interview-room table. Although she'd been trained never to react to this phrase, it had always annoyed her, and she was rather amused to see that it was having the same effect now on her unwanted companion.

'Look, I could do you some good you know,' Gavin changed tack. 'I can put out appeals for new information in my next article. You scratch my back and all that.'

'Speak to the PR liaison officer at Thames Valley,' Hillary said.

Gavin ignored the advice with an inner snort. He didn't want the usual standard handout the PR officer would fob him off with, which would no doubt be guaranteed to have any reader snoring over their cornflakes; no, he wanted a nice juicy quote that would make them sit up and take notice. The follow-up article he was currently writing badly needed a hook, and he thought he might just have the perfect needle to get under Hillary Greene's skin and obtain it.

'I'm due to see a major witness in the original case this afternoon,' he dangled the bait casually. 'She contacted me and said she might have something rather juicy for me. Care to comment on that?'

Hillary didn't, but that didn't mean that her mind wasn't now working furiously. Either he was bluffing, or he wasn't. Assuming he wasn't, who could he be talking about? She doubted he could have got onto The Face of Experience thing, since everyone seemed to have gone out of their way to keep quiet about that. So, who were the other women in the case? There was Jessie, but she couldn't see the vet consenting to talk to a reporter. Rejuvenating her mother's ghost would be the last thing she'd want. And Imelda's mother certainly wouldn't have anything to do with the press! It would be fathoms beneath her. So who did that leave?

Connie Brightman. Hillary could see quite a few advantages to Connie in talking to a journalist. Perhaps she was hoping for a big payout? If so, Hillary thought she'd be in for a big disappointment instead. Local newspapers hardly had huge coffers. More likely she wanted to see her name in print and at the same time take the opportunity to badmouth Imelda. She was still bitter enough to take satisfaction from that all right.

Gavin, on getting not even a 'no comment' for his pains, bit back a sigh. 'Come on, Ms Greene, the public wants to know how come the police never closed the case all those years ago. Are you hiding something? Imelda Phelps was known to be having an affair at the time of her murder — perhaps she was seeing more than one man? Was she having an affair with some VIP? Is that why you're keeping a lid on it? Some minor aristocrat or self-made billionaire putting on the pressure to keep it all hushed up and . . .'

Hillary had to endure more of the same far-fetched waffle all the way to her car. Once inside Puff, she was finally able to shut out the worst of his tiresome voice. She turned the ignition key, mentally threatening to heap all kinds of retribution upon her Volkswagen's head if he didn't start, but the silvery grey-green car was on his best behaviour and started first time. So at least her mechanic's bill had been worth it.

She pulled out of her parking spot, watching in amusement as the small fair-haired man leapt back to prevent his toes being squished, and with a small sigh, set off towards work.

Gavin Otterley swore at the departing car, then shrugged philosophically. After doing his homework on the former DI he wasn't all that surprised to find she wouldn't play ball.

Luckily for him, he had more irons in the fire than the uncooperative former copper.

* * *

At HQ, Hillary trooped to her office, checked her emails, then sat, just thinking and making a mental 'to do' list of her own for the day.

She needed to contact the family members again and get to the bottom of The Face of Experience thing. It was easy to understand why Dundas and Morgan Fisher hadn't volunteered any information about it to DI Clovis, but why Imelda's family had also kept silent about it was yet to be established. And she thought the best one to start with was Thomas. She found it almost impossible to believe the dead woman's husband couldn't have known about his wife's grand opportunity. No matter how much Dundas might have warned her not to mention the campaign to anyone, she couldn't see Imelda being able to keep it from her nearest and dearest. She would have been too excited, wouldn't she?

On the other hand, she was pretty sure that Imelda *would* have gone out of her way to make sure that her mother was kept in the dark about it. Hillary just couldn't see that very fine and upright lady in Cheltenham being pleased to hear that her only child might be about to hit the spotlight again as a woman of experience, dressed only in a fur coat and sparklers!

But she mustn't let herself become one-track-minded, she warned herself sternly. It was so easy to fall into the trap of becoming invested in just one line of investigation to the detriment of keeping an open mind about all the others. Just because they'd unearthed a hot new lead that the original team hadn't, didn't mean they were about to crack the case. For all she knew, the modelling contract the dead woman had been on the verge of winning might have nothing to do with her death.

Yes, they had to track down the major players and interview them in case they could find a connection, but it was possible that, even if DI Clovis had been aware of them at the time, she might not have found any evidence linking them to the murder.

And this still, to Hillary anyway, had the feeling of a more *personal* crime, as opposed to one of opportunity or for financial gain.

But only a fool wouldn't pursue all options, so it made sense to get Claire and Gareth cracking on following up The Face of Experience side, whilst she kept her focus on the family and the lover. And, of course, Connie Brightman. She'd have to be sure and pay her another visit today, just in case she had more to tell Gavin Otterley than mere vicious gossip. And if it turned out she'd been deliberately withholding evidence . . .

The decision made, she went to the communal office and broke the good news to her team. Today, the hottest day so far of the heatwave, they got to spend in the relative coolness of the basement, hitting the computers in comfort, whilst she did all the running around in the thirty-plus degree heat.

Lovely.

* * *

Before heading out into the bright and baking world, however, Hillary returned to her office in the hopes of at least saving herself the trek back into Cheltenham. Although she was confident that Catherine Burton would know nothing of her daughter's near brush with modelling fame and fortune, she still had to make sure.

And she was hoping that Catherine — or at least, the housekeeper — was savvy enough with modern technology that she could make a Zoom call, rather than have to drive all the way to the spa city for an interview in person.

And she was in luck. Within five minutes, she was looking at Catherine Burton's impeccably made-up face on her computer screen. Behind her, the large sash windows that she remembered from her first visit were this time open to the light, giving her a clear image of the older woman.

'Mrs Greene,' Catherine said, no welcome in her voice whatsoever. 'I understand you needed a few more words with me?'

'I do — and thank you for your time. I'll be brief. I was wondering if you knew anything about a modelling contract your daughter had high hopes for, in the weeks preceding her death?'

'We never talked about her so-called work, Mrs Greene, I thought I made that clear the last time we met? Imelda knew I didn't approve of it.'

'I understand that. But the contract I'm talking about would have made her very well known and would have been the highlight of her career. It was to be the face of a new range of cosmetics, accessories and fashion. I believe she'd already done a photo shoot for the advertising agency they were using. Some of them being rather, er, slightly risqué photographs.'

Even over the digital airwaves, Hillary could sense the old lady's spine stiffen. 'I can assure you, you must be mistaken,' Catherine Burton said frigidly. 'My daughter would never consent to anything that demeaning.'

Hillary nodded, knowing it was pointless to argue with her. 'Does the name Morgan Fisher mean anything to you?'

'It does not.'

'Do you recall any photographer calling on your daughter during one of your visits to her?'

'Definitely not.'

'What about a male caller that she seemed embarrassed about? Someone she might have gone to the door to talk to, but didn't let into the house?'

'Nothing like that, I assure you.'

Hillary nodded. Just as she'd thought. Imelda would have been careful to keep her big break a secret from her disapproving mother. 'Well, thank you, Mrs Burton. I'm sorry to have taken up your time.'

'Indeed,' the lady said. 'And I feel it only fair to warn you, Ms Greene, that I've had a conversation with your MP. He knew my husband, and I've made it quite clear to him that I will be very displeased if your activities bring my daughter's name into disrepute yet again. I expect you'll be receiving a warning from your superiors very shortly.'

'I'm sure I will, Mrs Burton,' Hillary lied, bidding her a pleasant 'good day' and terminating the connection. Any complaint about her would have gone straight from the MP to the Chief Constable, who would then quickly have shunted it over to Commander Marcus Donleavy, who'd have probably smiled his shark-like smile at the memo before tossing it into the wastepaper bin.

* * *

The new housing estate in Bicester — which was fast encroaching on the village of Chesterton — looked exactly the same as when Hillary had last visited it, except, perhaps, the recently laid lawns were now more straw-coloured than ever, and everything was wearing that slightly dusty, desiccated look that came with a prolonged heatwave.

Thomas Phelps opened the door to her ring and then immediately stood aside for her to enter. As before, he'd made no demur when she'd called to ask if he'd be available for a second interview. This time, however, he escorted her through the house and out into the back garden, to where a shaded patio had been fitted out with the ubiquitous white plastic garden chairs and a table with an umbrella in the middle.

Hillary accepted a glass of iced water gratefully, and took a sip. If he was surprised to see her alone this time, he made no comment.

'My wife is out, but should be back soon,' he informed her as they settled themselves down. She wasn't sure whether he meant the statement to be a warning or a reassurance.

'I see,' Hillary said, since those two rather meaningless words could usually be relied upon to cover a multitude of scenarios. 'As I said the last time we talked, I would probably have to see you again as and when new information came to light — and it has.'

She saw him brace his shoulders a little, and his mouth firmed into a thinner line. 'Do you have a suspect at last?'

'It's still too early for that, sir. But we have been making progress. Just yesterday we discovered a line of inquiry that was withheld from the original senior investigating officer.'

She watched him carefully and thought she saw a slight darkening of his expression. 'Oh?'

'It had to do with your wife's professional life.'

And this time she had no doubt that she saw a flicker of relief pass across his eyes. It went so much against what she had expected to see that, just for a moment, she was disconcerted, and made a rapid mental note to give that some serious consideration later, when she had more time to donate to it.

'Oh?' he asked, reaching out casually and taking a sip of his cold drink. His eyes scanned around the back garden — a rather plain square of grass, bordered by wooden fencing, with the occasional non-native ornamental shrub dotted around the borders for a bird to sit in and wonder where it might actually find something to eat.

'Yes. We understand that at the time of her death, your wife was competing to win a very lucrative and prestigious modelling contract for a company called Dundas. They were about to launch a new advertising campaign, and your wife was on the shortlist to be their "Face of Experience". Why did you not mention this to DI Clovis, Mr Phelps?'

She deliberately did not ask him if he knew about it, since she didn't want to give him the simple expedient of denying it. Now she watched him closely, and saw his eyes widen a little. Although he was sitting down, and nothing about him moved, she got the distinct impression that he was mentally dithering. Indeed, she felt as if she could almost hear the cogs in his brain turning.

'I seem to remember something about that, yes,' he finally admitted.

'Mr Phelps, that contract, if she'd won it, would have been the highlight of her career. She'd already had interviews, been shortlisted, and had photographs taken for a potential ad-campaign mock-up. She must have been extremely excited and nervous about it. Are you seriously expecting me to believe it barely registered on your radar?' she allowed the incredulity to ring clearly in her tone.

He looked at her briefly, then away again. Finally, he shrugged. 'I suppose it went out of my mind, that's all. My wife had been murdered, you have to remember. It was a totally mind-numbing bolt from the blue and it knocked me sideways. My children were in shock. I was in shock. I suppose it just didn't strike me as being important.'

Hillary deliberately let the silence stretch, and then took a long, slow breath. As she'd hoped, he was now tensed, waiting for whatever was coming next.

'I've recently spoken with the man who had been given the commission to organise the advertising campaign — a Mr Morgan Fisher.' She saw that this piece of information in no way surprised him, and it instantly aroused her suspicion.

Just what the hell was going on here?

'Do you recognise the name, sir?' she prompted sharply.

Once again, she got the feeling that he was mentally dithering, and instinct told her that now was a good time to say nothing at all. When you had a witness on the horns of a dilemma, hard-earned experience had taught her that it was good practice to let *him* decide which way to jump, rather than giving him a push, and risk finding out later that it might well have been in the wrong direction.

After a couple of tense, silent seconds, she saw his shoulders slump a little, indicating that he'd come to some sort of decision, and she felt her heart rate rise in expectation. And, indeed, his next words were music to her ears.

'I'm going to be very honest with you, er, Mrs Greene. Mr Fisher called me right after you left his office.'

Hillary hoped her deadpan expression hadn't slipped. 'Oh?'

Thomas Phelps looked at her uncertainly, then rubbed a hand across his forehead and sighed. 'You're quite right, of course — I knew all about Imelda's big hopes of a final "hoorah" for her career. And I was happy for her. Genuinely, I was — I knew how much she'd always wanted it, and how very much it meant to her. It wasn't until after she died that I began to realise that that sort of opportunity came with a price. A price my wife had been quite happy to pay, it seems.'

Hillary thought that she was beginning to see where this was all going, but she needed to proceed cautiously. 'Oh, yes?'

'At the time, the first day or so after Imelda died, I really didn't know what I was doing — that was true enough. I just couldn't seem to make myself think straight. Oh, I know I answered all the questions that DI Clovis asked me as honestly and truthfully as I could, but I wasn't capable of *volunteering* anything. I was so damned disorientated. So, it wasn't as if I *intended* to keep anything back, I swear. But then a few days later, the phone rang, and it was him. Morgan Fisher. He said he needed to see me. He told me who he was, and I said anything about Imelda's work didn't matter now. But he was persistent.'

Yes, Hillary thought grimly. She just bet he was.

'In the end, more to get rid of him than anything, I agreed to him coming over to the house. I have to say, I detested the man on sight.'

Hillary bit back the urge to say that he wasn't the only one.

'Anyway, he had come, or so I thought at first, on behalf of these Dundas people. When he began to hint at what he wanted, which was of course that I didn't mention the name of Dundas or his own wretched company to the press or even the police, I was sorely tempted to pick him up by the scruff of his scrawny little neck and chuck him out the front door.'

Now *that* Hillary would have paid a reasonable amount of money to watch.

'But as it turned out, there was worse to come,' Thomas went on, looking momentarily so bleak that Hillary felt compelled to help him out.

'Are we talking about certain photographs, sir?' she asked quietly.

He shot her a grateful look and nodded. 'Yes. He told me Imelda had done a nude session the last time she'd been called in. I can tell you, I was surprised. Really surprised. From what Imelda had said, she'd be modelling face creams and make-up, clothes, handbags, that sort of thing. I wondered, for a minute, if she'd been lying to me all along, but then Fisher showed me the photographs, and I realised that they were, by and large, innocuous. Have you seen them? Oh no, sorry, you wouldn't have, would you?'

Hillary, who'd been opening her mouth to tell him that they had only been described to her, changed the direction of her words before they could leave her mouth, and said instead, 'Why are you so sure of that, sir?'

Thomas gave a small, rather sad smile. 'Why do you think? I paid the bastard to delete the files, and promise me they weren't backed up anywhere.'

At this, Hillary leaned back in her chair a little and regarded him thoughtfully. She needed just a moment to take stock. There was a lot to take on board here, and she didn't want to ruin her chances of learning everything there was to know by going too fast and missing things.

'Are you saying that Mr Morgan blackmailed you, sir?' she asked cautiously.

Thomas gave a small grunt that was almost a laugh. 'Did he, I wonder? You know, looking back, I'm not sure that you can say he did. Somehow, we just got to talking about how inconvenient the whole thing was for himself and Dundas, and for myself and my family. And that led to an agreement that it would be pretty catastrophic for all concerned if the photos leaked to the press and that they'd be better off destroyed. But he had, naturally, incurred expenses in having the photographs taken, and naturally, he would need to recoup his losses.' He spread his hands in a 'you-know-how-it-is' gesture.

'Naturally,' Hillary repeated dryly.

'In the end, we mutually decided that I would pay him a set sum of money and he would hand over all files to me and neither of us would say anything to the police about the campaign. And before you start to berate me, Mrs Greene,' he added hastily, seeing her annoyed reaction to that last statement, 'can I just say three things in my defence?'

Hillary spread her hands in a 'go-ahead' gesture.

'Firstly, if I'd thought for one moment that Imelda's murder could have had anything to do with that bloody modelling contract, I'd have spoken up about it without a second thought. Secondly, I knew Imelda would have hated it if the press had got a hold of those photographs and used them to smear her name and drag her reputation through even more mud. Having them shown as part of an advertising campaign on a public billboard, as an example of a beautiful and glamorous woman living the good life, was one thing. Having them appear on the front page of a scandal rag as proof that a murder victim had somehow "had it coming to her" was another thing altogether. She'd have rather died . . .' he suddenly stopped as he realised what he'd just said, and for an appalled moment, he lost the power of speech.

Hillary waited to let him recover and said gently, 'And the third thing?'

Thomas looked down at his hands, then back up at her. 'Thirdly, I had to do what was best for my family — my children. And, of course, Imelda's mother,' he added, as something of an afterthought. 'It might literally have killed Catherine if she'd had to endure salacious photos of her daughter in the papers and the snide innuendos of her so-called friends on top of everything else that was already going on. The media attention was bad enough as it was, but can you imagine . . .' He shook his head. 'Jonas was at university and his life would have been made hell. Can you imagine the headlines? "*Murdered mother's nude pics shock*!" And probably far worse. What lad of twenty could be expected to handle that? And as for Jessie . . . she was even younger. No, I just couldn't have it.'

'So you paid him off?'

'Yes.' Again, he gave a snort that was almost a laugh. 'Do you know, when he rang me up yesterday, after telling me who he was and explaining that you'd just been there questioning him and putting the wind up him good and proper, the first thing he asked me was if I'd left a paper trail that could be connected back to him? The little creep even warned me to check any old bank statements I might have and destroy any record that might exist of the payment. He was in a right state, threatening me that he would sue me for slander and all sorts if I mentioned him to you.'

'I'm not surprised, sir. Mr Fisher struck me as the kind of man who is inordinately fond of his own skin.'

At this, Thomas openly laughed, and then reached again for his glass. He didn't, though, take a drink from it, but merely nursed it in his hands.

Hillary watched him carefully. She understood why he'd acted the way he had, of course. And could even sympathize. But that didn't mean that she was happy about it. She briefly contemplated asking him how he could possibly know that his wife's career could have had nothing to do with her death, but she didn't want to alert him to just how revealing that statement of his had been.

Because if he was so sure that the whole 'Face of Experience' thing was irrelevant, that could only mean one thing: that he had no doubts at all that his wife had been killed by someone close to her. And from DI Clovis's notes, she knew that this man hadn't gone out of his way to point the finger with any great vehemence at either Dermott Franklyn or Connie Brightman. And he'd freely admitted he wasn't at all close to his mother-in-law, so if he had any reason at all to suspect her, why not just say so?

So who did that leave?

As Hillary thanked him for his time and left, her mind was churning. Did he suspect his son — or his daughter — of murdering their own mother?

Or was it because *he* was the one who had killed his wife?

CHAPTER TEN

The journey from Bicester to Chipping Norton passed pleasantly enough, mostly because with literally all the windows rolled down, Hillary was able to luxuriate in a nearly cool breeze. The weather for the upcoming weekend was set to be as hot as ever, with the promised break in the heatwave now looking a little less certain. Whilst some parts of the south would catch the edge of a weather front bringing some rain, the forecasters were now hedging their bets on just how far north the rain might come. With Oxfordshire being the very furthest north that might just be lucky.

Somehow, Hillary Greene wasn't feeling particularly lucky.

She might be being unduly pessimistic, but the more dead ends they hit, the more nervous she was becoming that this case would remain open indefinitely.

As she finally pulled up in front of Connie Brightman's small ground-floor flat, she glanced around. The heat was brutal, and literally nothing was stirring. Not even a cat — and their propensity for seeking out sunlight to doze in was legendary.

She walked up the broken-concrete path which reflected the heat back up at her, turning the thin soles of her sandals uncomfortably warm, and pressed the bell for Connie's flat. There was no porch to provide shelter from the heat, and she could feel the sun's rays trying to burn a hole in the middle of her back.

Nothing stirred inside the hallway. She rang again and waited, uncomfortably aware that a trickle of sweat was forming on her forehead and beginning to itch.

Still there was no answer. Then she realised that she'd forgotten to ring ahead to make sure that Imelda's former business partner would be available for another interview. Cursing herself and the succession of near-sleepless nights for making her feel so groggy, she grabbed her phone from her handbag and called Claire.

'Hey, Claire, it's me. Can you check the files and tell me where Connie Brightman works?'

As she was waiting for the answer, the door suddenly opened in front of her and Hillary looked up hopefully. But the woman who stopped abruptly in the entranceway, clearly surprised to find someone standing right on her doorstep, wasn't Connie, but a young Asian woman with a child in a stroller.

'Oh, sorry,' Hillary said, sidestepping to let her pass. 'You wouldn't happen to know if the woman in the bottom flat is out, would you?' she asked casually.

'Connie? No, sorry, I don't know. But now that I think about it, I don't think I've seen her since yesterday, which is odd, because I usually *do* run into her. We're both in and out all day you see.' The young woman glanced down as her toddler threw a toy out of the stroller onto the concrete path, and bent down patiently to retrieve it. 'And for once, she wasn't playing her music into the early hours of the morning either,' she added as she waggled the stuffed bear in front of her infant. Then she gave Hillary a grimacing laugh. 'I wouldn't mind but it's that ghastly heavy metal stuff. Not my thing, and it keeps the little one awake.'

Hillary, seeing the door to the house starting to close, instinctively put out a hand to stop it, and as the young mother nodded goodbye and set off on her errand, Hillary slipped into the hall and listened to the sound of silence.

Realising she still had Claire hanging on the phone, she put her mobile back to her ear. 'Sorry about that — I was talking to the neighbour. You have her work phone number?'

'Yes, guv, but it won't do you any good. I've looked at her work schedule and she's not due in until tomorrow. She works shifts at a custard factory in Banbury.'

Hillary frowned. 'All right, Claire, thanks.'

She snapped the phone off and tapped loudly on the door to Connie's flat.

Nothing moved, which didn't surprise her. By now, Hillary had that feeling you get when you know you're all alone in a building. Perhaps Connie was out doing the shopping, or had taken herself to the nearest pub for a drink. One thing was for sure — if she'd been sleeping off a nightshift, Hillary's knocking would have roused her by now. Every copper who'd ever walked a beat knew how to knock on the door loud enough to make their presence known.

So why did she feel uneasy?

Hillary wished there was a letterbox she could raise and peer through, but the mail for the two flats went into the wire box affixed to the main door. And there was no old-fashioned keyhole she could look through either; nowadays, it was mainly Yale locks.

There was nothing else for it, but to be patient and wait it out. Not that she was about to go back out into the oven that was the world outside, so she made herself more or less comfortable by sitting down on the fourth wooden stair to wait, and hope that, wherever she was, Connie would be back sooner rather than later.

At least it wasn't as hot in here, although the air felt stale.

And there was definitely some kind of odour.

The presence of a smell had been tickling away at the back of her brain ever since she'd first walked in, but she was feeling so sluggish that it had taken some moments for her to register its significance. Now that it had, she took a long, slow breath in through her nose and then almost levitated off the stair, she shot up so quickly.

Her heart started hammering away in her chest.

She recognised that smell.

It was a smell that some police officers were fortunate enough never to encounter in the whole of their careers, but she wasn't one of them. Instantly, her mind went back through the years to when she'd been twenty-two years old and accompanying an older sergeant on a search through some derelict buildings. They'd been searching for an old man who'd managed to wander off from a nearby old people's home and had been missing for days.

She walked to Connie's door and held the handle down and pushed. As she feared, it was locked. She went down first on her knees, then lay full-out on the dirty linoleum hall floor and pressed her nose as close as she could get it to the gap at the bottom of the door.

She recoiled instantly, got back unhappily to her feet and reached for her phone.

But she didn't call HQ. Instead, she called 999.

To the woman who calmly answered her call, Hillary cited her name, Connie's address, and briefly explained her business at the residence. She concluded by asking that a police unit and an ambulance be dispatched at once, and requested the first responders came equipped to gain entrance to a locked domicile.

She then went back to the stairs and sat back down. Her knees were feeling a little weak and again she cursed her lack of sleep. Or was she just feeling her age?

No doubt if she were in a television programme, she'd have a burly and handsome male officer with her, whom she'd order to break down the door and she'd take responsibility for any consequences. Or else she'd be a twenty-something, svelte and impossibly lovely judo expert who could bust the door open with one high-flying kick, leaving her handsome sidekick looking at her in admiration or irritation (depending on whether there was a love-interest between them or the handsome sidekick was having macho issues.)

But she wasn't a character in a television programme, and she didn't have her lockpicks with her, and she wasn't a serving police officer either, come to that. She had no more right to break and enter someone's home than anyone else.

So she sat and waited, and felt just a little sick.

She might be wrong about what was going on behind that locked door — but she couldn't make herself believe that she was.

* * *

It was something like four minutes before Hillary heard the first siren. She got up and opened the outside door, getting out her ID in readiness. A quick glance told her that it was the Jam Sandwich that had arrived first, and as she watched, two constables in uniform got out of the car, glanced around, and then spotted her waving them over.

As they approached, she saw one was a tall thin woman, possibly in her mid-twenties, who strode like someone who liked walking, whilst her companion was shorter, heftier, and wore glasses with a black frame.

'Mrs Greene?' the woman police officer spoke. 'You called in a possible medical emergency?'

Hillary nodded, and showed her ID. The male of the pair actually took it from her, studied it, and then passed it on to his colleague. 'Civilian consultant?' he said.

'Yes. I'm here to interview a witness in a cold case the CRT are currently reviewing. A murder case. I spoke to the resident, a Miss Connie Brightman, a few days ago and this is a follow-up. Her neighbour upstairs told me she hadn't seen Miss Brightman for more than twenty-four hours, which she stated was unusual. Also, Miss Brightman hadn't played her music last night — also unusual. And there is a definite odour coming from Miss Brightman's flat.' She went on to give them a detailed physical description of Connie.

They listened with classic cop blank faces, nodded, and then moved past her. Hillary watched them, wanting to follow them into the flat once they'd gained entrance and see for herself what there was to be seen.

But she knew she couldn't. She'd only contaminate the scene.

So she stayed where she was, leaning tiredly against the doorframe. She heard the murmuring of voices inside, then a few minutes later, the male officer stepped outside the flat. He regarded her thoughtfully. 'Mrs Greene, we'd like you to remain on the premises please. We have requested a more senior officer attend immediately, and he or she will want to speak to you.'

Hillary nodded, then indicated the stairs. 'I was waiting here — sitting on the fourth stair up, so I might as well carry on . . . ?' He hesitated for a moment, unsure of the protocol, then shrugged.

'That's fine.'

Hillary resumed her makeshift seat.

He waited, dividing his attention between watching her and looking inside the flat to see what his colleague was doing. Hillary could have reassured him that it was too damned hot for her to do a runner, but she didn't think, somehow, he would take that very well.

From their behaviour, it was clear they'd found something suspicious inside. And Hillary had a fair idea that that something suspicious was a dead body. And odds on, it was Connie Brightman's dead body.

She sighed, reached into her bag and withdrew her phone. This attracted the constable's immediate attention, but before he could object, she said flatly, 'I need to call HQ in Kidlington and inform my boss, Chief Superintendent Roland Sale, of the situation.'

The constable, perhaps not surprisingly, had little to say to that.

Hillary made the call, gave Rollo the basics, and listened as he told her to stay at the scene, cooperate fully and give a statement. 'Yes, sir,' she said, and hung up.

She noticed that he hadn't said she couldn't use her eyes and ears and anything else she could think of to try and find out all she could about what was going on though.

* * *

And in this endeavour, Hillary soon had a massive stroke of good luck. And she felt as if she was due one! After ten minutes or so, the sergeant who walked through the door took one look at her and grinned widely. He was in his early fifties, skinny as a whippet and looked a little like one too, being sharp-faced, and with a thin pointed nose, grey hair and a close-cropped goatee beard.

'DI Hillary Greene, as I live and breathe! I thought you'd been put out to pasture years ago?'

'Cheeky sod,' Hillary shot back, then rose and held out her hand, which he shook heartily. 'I was just thinking the same thing about you!'

The two young constables watched this by-play avidly.

'How are you doing, Bill?' Hillary asked Sergeant Bill Rumbold with a grin. They'd worked some cases back in the day, but she hadn't seen him about for some years, and now realised that he must have transferred to this region a while ago.

'All the better for seeing you. So, what brings you to my patch?'

Hillary quickly filled him in on her retirement as an active DI and her coming back to work for the CRT, and specifically about the cold case she was currently working. When she'd finished, he slowly shook his head. 'Sounds as if your cold case has just got hot again. Sorry, but you know I can't let you inside,' he nodded to the open door to Connie's flat.

And gave her a slow wink.

Hillary nodded solemnly, aware of the watching eyes. No, he couldn't let her in, but that didn't mean that he couldn't *fill* her in. Casually, she said, 'It's as hot as blazes out there, Bill. I was just dreaming about heading to a cold pub for an even colder beer. Any chance I could give my statement to you there?'

'Don't see why not,' he agreed amiably. 'There's a place called the Jugged Hare, about half a mile or so away. See you there in an hour or so?'

* * *

It was closer to two hours before Bill showed up, but Hillary wasn't complaining. The pub turned out to be a former coaching inn at least two centuries old or more, with thick walls and uneven original flagstone floors, and thus was blessedly cool inside. What's more, she'd found herself a nice spot in a dark corner with a comfortably padded bench seat that suited her just fine.

Better still, at this time of day, the place was almost deserted. She hadn't ordered beer, since she was driving, but she kept the ice-filled lemon-and-lime soft drinks coming and had made herself so comfortable she was in danger of nodding off. She was just yawning mightily when her old crony appeared at the bar and ordered a half-shandy before joining her at the table.

'Bad?' she asked quietly, noting the pallor beneath his tan, and the tense, tight look around his eyes.

'Bad enough. And this bloody heat doesn't help matters any.'

Hillary thought about that for a scant second or two. So, the death must have occurred at least twenty-four hours ago or more, otherwise, even with the heat, the condition of the body wouldn't be bad enough to make a seasoned copper like Bill go pale around the gills. Unless, of course, the body had been in bad shape due to other factors — a beating, for instance.

'Was it the homeowner, Connie Brightman?' she asked.

He nodded. 'Far as we can tell. We'll need formal ID, of course, but from your description of her, it seems highly likely. If we can't find a nearest and dearest, we might ask you to come in to confirm her identity.'

'Sure — let me know. So, are we talking about natural causes?'

Her friend snorted. 'Not on your nelly.'

Hillary sighed. No, she'd thought not. 'What can you tell me about the crime scene?'

Bill took a long drink of his shandy, giving him time to arrange his thoughts. 'Well, there was nothing out of place at first glance — certainly no signs of a struggle or a burglary. She was lying on her left side on the living-room floor, between the biggest pieces of furniture. The medical technician thinks she was hit over the head with our old friend, the blunt instrument.'

He paused and looked at her, and she met his eyes. She suspected that they were both thinking the same thing, but Hillary obliged him by saying it out loud.

'Just like my cold case victim then?'

Bill nodded. 'Did the medical report on your victim indicate that any other external force had been used?'

At this, Hillary's brain began to pick up a gear — which was about bloody time, she told it. The fact that Bill was asking meant that Connie Brightman hadn't just been coshed, but something else had been in play. Which meant — what? Defensive wounds on her arms? Most victims who could see an attack of any kind coming tried to shield themselves as a matter of reflex, if nothing else. Putting up your hand to try and shield your face from a bullet made not the slightest difference (unless the calibre of the gun concerned was really small) but people did it automatically anyway.

'In Imelda Phelps's case she had no defensive wounds at all,' Hillary said slowly.

'No, neither did Connie Brightman,' Bill said carefully.

Although they knew that Bill should not be discussing anything with Hillary at all without official sanction, and certainly not in depth, they were both wily enough to know there were ways around that. And whilst he couldn't *tell*, she could certainly *guess*. And if she happened to do her guessing out loud, Bill could hardly help hearing it, could he?

So, she mused, Connie didn't put up a fight. Yet Bill had asked a question that seemed to indicate something more than a bash on the head had happened to Connie. Which left . . . what?

Her brain, forced to work and fight off its heat-induced torpor, grudgingly obliged with an obvious answer.

'Pepper spray? Or mace?' she hazarded.

Bill said nothing, but smiled and took a sip of his drink, leaving Hillary to search her memory for what she knew of defensive sprays. Both were illegal in the UK of course, falling under the Firearms Act of 1968. Which meant that anyone caught carrying them would be subject to the same laws as if they'd been carrying a gun. It was funny, she mused, what stuck in your memory banks and what your brain discarded. But during her training, she'd had to memorise so many facts that it was hardly surprising that all these years later, they still lurked there, waiting to be called upon. Now, ask her what she'd been doing last week, and she'd really have to struggle to remember!

What else did she know about them? Mace sprays had been invented in the 1960s by Alan Lee Litman, and the original version had phenacyl chloride in it, also known as tear gas. When sprayed in the face it caused serious pain to the eyes, nose, throat and skin.

Pepper spray had much the same effect.

Of course, like most illegal things nowadays, the internet could provide them to anyone who wanted such items without too much effort being involved.

Unless . . .

'Are we talking Farb-Gel here?' she asked. This was a legal alternative, being 100% a defensive spray. It contained no harmful chemicals and could operate up to four metres away. A coloured gel spray, it caused temporary blindness and provided enough of a distraction for a potential rape or mugging victim to get themselves away from a harmful situation.

Bill said nothing.

Hillary sat back in her chair. So, whoever had killed Connie Brightman had somehow obtained either mace or pepper spray.

Now Hillary found that interesting. *Very* interesting. In fact, it gave her certain ideas.

'Ground control to Major Hillary,' Bill said, making her snap her attention back to him. 'Sorry, thought I'd lost you for a minute there. Your eyes went all out of focus and everything.'

Hillary gave him a knowing grin. 'Sorry — might have had a bit of a lightbulb moment there. Or then again,' she grimaced ruefully, 'maybe not. You know how reliable hunches are.' She shook her head, trying to focus on the here and now. 'Any idea who's been assigned SIO?' she wondered aloud. She wasn't risking anything to either of them by asking this, as it fell under the sacrosanct heading of legitimate station gossip, and everyone from the lowliest constable to the chief constable indulged in it to their heart's content.

As a sergeant, she knew it was unlikely that Bill would be given a murder case, which definitely warranted a DI. And the more she knew about who was going to take over Connie's case the better.

Disappointingly though, Bill shook his head and grimaced. 'It won't be one of ours, that's for sure. It'll be one of your lot.'

Meaning someone would be assigned from Kidlington. Hillary didn't blame him for being resentful of this, but at the same time, they both knew how the system worked. 'You'll be called on to provide local intel though,' she pointed out, trying to cheer him up a little.

'Well, whoop-de-doo,' Bill drawled.

Hillary smiled grimly at him. 'You think you've got beef? I won't even be able to get a look in. As a civilian consultant to the CRT I'm not even *in* the pecking order anymore, let alone at the bottom of it.'

* * *

After she'd gone with Bill to his office to give and sign a formal statement, she'd bid him good luck with things, and with a vague promise to meet up with him for another pint sometime, she'd headed back to HQ where Rollo Sale confirmed her gloomy prognosis.

It was now late afternoon. Sitting across from her boss's desk, she'd just finished relating a more in-depth account of the situation. She didn't mention having had Bill's help, of course, not wanting to drop him in it, and found it rather soothing to her ego that Rollo took her well-informed report for granted.

But when she'd finished, he did confirm that she was to play no active part in the investigation into Connie Brightman's murder.

'When they've assigned the SIO, I'll ask that we be kept informed, naturally. But depending on what they discover, that might not amount to much, as I'm sure you can appreciate. It's not, on the face of it, particularly likely that their case and ours are linked, is it?'

Hillary looked at him thoughtfully. 'You don't think so? Same MO, Connie was a witness in Imelda's case, and she ends up murdered just when we start asking her questions?'

Rollo nodded. 'Sure, I'm not saying it isn't possible. But until the Brightman team have had a chance to assess the situation, we can't take anything like that for granted. For all we know, it could be a straightforward domestic. They could unearth a disgruntled ex-partner with a penchant for booze and beating up on his women. Or you say she was into designing jewellery? Suppose they find a local addict who thought he might find some gold hidden in her cupboards?'

Hillary knew he had a point. It was probably way too early to go jumping to conclusions. Even so. 'Can you at least make sure the pathologist compares the head wounds in both cases?'

Rollo nodded, but slowly, and then began to frown. 'Do you really think it's likely that the murder weapon will turn out to be the same? I can't see it myself. Just supposing it *is* the same killer, why would they keep the murder weapon for so long? It's hardly credible, is it? As you know, getting rid of a murder weapon is usually a number-one priority for a killer, along with any bloodstained clothing. Unless you think Imelda's killer kept hold of it as a trophy?'

'Or maybe because they knew they might want to use it again?' Hillary said, but her heart wasn't really in it. She knew she was behaving like a dog with a bone that she was reluctant to have taken away from her, but she just couldn't help it.

'If so, they waited a hell of a long time,' Rollo pointed out dryly. 'But yes, I'll put in a request that the head wounds are studied for similarities.' He watched her, and she knew he was thinking exactly the same as she was. 'Like I said, I'll ask that we be kept informed, and it'll certainly be somewhere on the SIO's radar that Connie's death might have links to our own investigation. And for sure, he or she will want to know if you turn up anything else on the Phelps's case that might tie in with their own. But Hillary — I mean it. Don't go poking your nose in where it won't be wanted. After all, if the positions were reversed, and you were the DI with the current case, you wouldn't want a civilian consultant constantly peering over your shoulder, would you?'

Hillary had to admit, he had her there. She would have hated it and wouldn't have tolerated it.

'We're agreed then — you stick to working Imelda's case, yes?' Rollo gave her a level look. He knew her of old, and knew that she could be like a terrier at a rathole when it suited her. 'You've just come up with this new line of inquiry about that modelling contract business, so it's not as if you don't have enough on your plate to be getting on with.'

He reached pointedly for a file on his desk and opened it.

Hillary, accepting the tacit dismissal, murmured, 'Yes, sir,' and rose tiredly.

Rollo watched her leave, a knowing smile on his face. 'Cheer up, Hill, remember it's the weekend,' he called after her. 'And no sneaking back into the office either, or I'll have you thrown out on your ear. There's no such thing as overtime anymore,' he warned her. 'Just take the two days off and revel in the fact that you've got nothing better to do than laze about in the sun.'

At this, Hillary's lips twisted in a near-snarl. 'Well, whoop-de-doo,' she said, echoing Bill Rumbold's earlier response. She might have felt inclined to slam the door after her if only she'd been able to summon up the energy.

CHAPTER ELEVEN

The weekend passed in a mixture of frustrated boredom and sweltering heat, and it wasn't until Hillary finally drove Puff into the HQ car park on Monday morning that she was aware of just how tense she'd been, and the extent of her impatience to get back to work.

All that weekend her mind had been constantly going over possible scenarios about the two cases, and she was anxious to do a bit of brainstorming with her team to try and get her thoughts in some sort of coherent order. So, for once she didn't head straight to her stationery cupboard, but instead opted for the communal office.

She'd only had time on Friday afternoon to give Claire and Gareth the barest of details about discovering Connie's body. She knew her team would now be raring to hear more, and she owed it to them to give them a couple of hours to regroup and become focussed before handing out fresh assignments.

They, like her, had also arrived a little early, and were in the process of settling down as Hillary appeared in the doorway.

'Morning, everyone,' she began, eyeing her favourite spot on the corner of Claire's desk. 'How were your weekends?'

Claire, who'd been about to hang her summer jacket on the back of her chair, hastily withdrew a desk tidy that was in the way and Hillary perched a third of her bottom on the cleared space and let one foot swing idly an inch or so off the ground.

'We had the grandkids so their parents could have a weekend break at some swanky little country house hotel,' Claire said with a smile that looked a little forced to Hillary. 'We love having them, but they sure do wear us out.'

Hillary nodded, but couldn't help but wonder if there was more behind Claire's son and daughter-in-law's trip away than the mere desire to have a romantic weekend without the kids.

Gareth hastily clicked open his laptop as he took his seat. When he saw her glance his way, he gave a brief smile.

'Went swimming mostly,' he said. 'It's good for my muscle tone. Had a takeout Saturday night, watched some football on the telly with my mates. Nothing special.'

Hillary nodded. It all sounded very routine. Perhaps too routine? Then she gave a mental shrug. If he didn't want to share, then she wasn't going to press him.

'Right — Connie Brightman,' Hillary began crisply. 'An SIO will have been assigned to her case by now, and Superintendent Sale will be filling me in on him or her later. The Brightman team's now had two clear days to gather as much intel as possible — and of course, we're not involved in that — but Superintendent Sale has asked us to continue as usual on the Imelda Phelps case, so that's what we'll do. But that doesn't mean we must overlook the latest developments on Connie's murder, as it might well relate to our cold case. So, let's just take a while to give all this some thought.'

She paused and eyed the board, to which either Gareth or Claire had added a large photograph of Connie and a few more of her details.

'When I went to her flat and realised someone was dead inside, my first thought turned to natural causes,' Hillary began to think out loud. 'We'd had some very hot weather, and if you've been listening to the news reports, you'll know it's killed off quite a few people already — mainly the elderly, but also those with certain underlying health conditions. And since I had no idea whether or not Connie Brightman had any medical issues, that had to be the front-runner. I don't need to remind you about the statistics, right? Nearly all bodies discovered unexpectedly turn out to have a natural explanation behind them. Despite what the television and crime books would have you believe.'

She had to pause then, remembering that she'd recently had a crime novel published herself, and winced at the unintended hypocrisy. Then she gave a small shrug. She had other things than self-analysis to worry about right now, and contemplating her navel. Or even her novel.

'I now know,' she carried on quickly, without saying just *how* she knew, 'that Connie was killed by a blow to the head after being sprayed with some sort of chemical substance like mace or pepper spray, to first disable her.'

At this, Claire shifted on her chair. 'A blow to the head, the same as Imelda, then?'

Hillary nodded. 'Yes — I've already asked Rollo to make sure that the pathologist on Connie's case was made aware of the similarity and possible connection to ours, and he assured me that they'd compare the wounds for any factors they may have in common. I think it unlikely, though, that they'll match exactly,' she warned them, seeing that both Claire and Gareth were beginning to look really excited.

'No, I can't see a killer keeping a murder weapon in their possession that long,' Claire reluctantly agreed. 'But you think it's the same perp, guv?' she asked hopefully.

Hillary nodded. 'Personally, yes, I do. But as you know, that's irrelevant. It's facts that will matter, and it'll be up to the new SIO to find them. But for now, I want us to proceed with the working hypothesis that we're dealing with the same killer, of two women, nearly fifteen years apart. So, let's speculate. Why would that be? Gareth?'

She put him on the spot first because, as a former soldier, he still had the habit of never speaking unless spoken to, and she needed to get him engaged quickly.

As she glanced his way, she saw him shift to a more comfortable position on the chair. He didn't rush into speech, but after a moment, began tentatively. 'Well, we'd already done a search for any other cases that matched the Phelps murder MO over the past fifteen years, and we hadn't found any that made us sit up and take special notice. Which means we can rule out the likelihood that we're dealing with a serial killer and that Imelda and Connie were just two in a long line of murders. And I think it's safe to rule out the idea that the two murders are nothing more than just a massive coincidence, right? And that they're not connected in some way?'

Hillary slowly nodded. 'Yes, though always bear in mind, coincidences can and *do* happen, and we need to be aware of that. But yes, let's rule it out for now.'

Gareth nodded. 'Well, given that, it also seems too much of a stretch to think that the murderer killed Imelda for one reason, and then, all these years later, it was just chance or bad luck that he or she had to kill Connie for another reason altogether.'

'Yes — it's likely they would be linked,' Hillary agreed.

'There can only be so many reasons why Miss Brightman had to be killed now,' Gareth continued, feeling his way carefully through the minefield. 'One was to silence her. Either because the killer suspected that she'd known or guessed something all along about Imelda's murder, or maybe she had found out something more recently — perhaps as a result of our reopening the case — and the killer couldn't risk her revealing what it was,' he said. Then frowned. 'But if it's the former, doesn't that beg the question — why wasn't she killed sooner?'

'She might not have been a threat to the killer until now,' Claire helped him out.

Gareth thought about it, and obviously didn't like it. 'Possible, I suppose. Could she have known all along who killed Imelda Phelps and simply never said? We know she really didn't like the woman and held a grudge for her shutting down their jewellery business. She might have felt so spiteful towards Imelda that the idea of her killer never having been indicted and living free gave her a kick. But now that we've started reinvestigating, perhaps she began to get cold feet? Maybe she thought keeping quiet all these years might make her an accessory after the fact and land her in jail? Perhaps she even said something along those lines that tipped off the killer that she was wavering or losing her nerve, and so she had to be dealt with?'

'Or perhaps it was the exact opposite,' Claire tossed into the pot. 'Perhaps she saw the opportunity for a little blackmail? Let's face it, she was living in a tiny flat, working a couple of jobs. The idea of some extra cash must have been pretty tempting.'

Hillary nodded, mulling over the possibilities. 'What else, Gareth?'

The former soldier, who had started to relax against the backrest of his chair, suddenly sat bolt upright, as if he was at attention again. 'Maybe that journalist you told us about had something to do with it,' he put forward cautiously. 'We know that he was intent on bigging up Mrs Phelps's murder, and he told you that Connie had agreed to give him an interview. We don't know what that was all about yet. Perhaps someone knew about this, and didn't like it?'

Hillary made a mental note to interview the journalist. (Now wouldn't that be something for her to look forward to?) He'd turn it into a story for his paper of course, but if he knew what Connie had wanted to talk to him about then . . . Abruptly, she realised that she couldn't do any such thing. As a lead in the current murder investigation of Connie Brightman, she'd have to turn the information over to the new SIO, and one of *his* team would then have to tackle Gavin Otterley. The feeling of being so handicapped in what she could or couldn't do depressed her slightly.

'You could be right, Gareth,' she said, 'but we have to bear in mind that the whole journalist thing could be a distraction. Unless, of course, he makes some wild claim that Connie was going to name Imelda's killer or give him some sort of proof as to the killer's identity — which, frankly, I don't think was ever on the cards. She probably just wanted to string Otterley and his paper along with some human-interest angle or scandalous gossip in the hopes of getting a bit of cash out of them.'

She shook her head, then said, 'What about collaboration?'

For a second Gareth looked puzzled, but Claire was on it like a cat on a mouse. 'You think Connie might have been in cahoots with someone else over the Phelps murder, and now that the heat's been turned back on, the partners in crime had a falling-out? And Bob's your uncle, Connie is now a danger that has to be neutralised?'

'It has been known to happen,' Hillary said dryly. 'The question is, who do we like in the role of collaborator?'

'Well, not the dragon in Cheltenham, that's for sure,' Claire said at once with a wide grin. 'I can't see her ladyship deigning to partner up with the hoi polloi. Unless, of course, that was all an act she put on for us, and if it was, then she could give Dame Judi Dench a run for her money.'

'The husband?' Gareth said. 'For some reason I can't see either Jonas or Jessie Phelps teaming up with Connie to kill their mother.'

'Hmm. Thomas,' Hillary said, turning to look at the board and seeking out Thomas's photo. 'He's probably our best bet, if the collaboration theory is right.'

'But you're not liking it, are you, guv,' Claire said softly.

Hillary sighed. Somehow, she just couldn't see it. 'No matter how it turns out, if Connie's killing *is* proved to be connected to Imelda's, then we're all going to have to come to terms with a very unpalatable fact,' she warned them quietly.

Once again, it was Claire who was on it first, and Hillary saw her colleague's normally cheerful face slowly fall into an expression of gloom. 'Yeah. You're right. We are.'

Gareth looked from one to the other, and then slowly began to nod as he too caught on to the significance of

Hillary's warning. 'You mean, if we hadn't started asking questions about Imelda Phelps, the chances are that Connie Brightman would still be alive today?'

For a moment, all three of them were silent as they digested this. Then Hillary slowly got to her feet and straightened her shoulders. 'Nobody in the job likes to deal with this kind of thing, but it's something we have no choice but to face, if and when it happens. You can try and rationalise it however you like, but it probably won't prevent you from feeling guilty. Just try and always bear in mind that the only person truly responsible for what's happened is the murderer.'

Again there was a contemplative silence for a while, before Claire finally broke it. 'So what are our priorities now, guv?' she asked, as Hillary walked over to the board and scanned it.

'Superintendent Sale wants us to keep on "The Face of Experience" thing. It's new ground and we need to interview all those involved.' But her voice so clearly lacked enthusiasm that Claire sat up a little straighter in her chair and looked at Hillary with speculative eyes.

She'd seen that expression on her boss's face before.

'You have a front-runner, don't you, guv?' she asked quietly.

Gareth blinked and went very still.

Hillary nodded slowly. 'Oh yes,' she admitted. 'I now have a definite front-runner, but I may well be wrong. There is also one loose end that needs to be tied up as well — and it's possible that doing that might just bring up something that turns my thinking on its head. But I don't somehow think it will. And if it turns out that I'm right . . .' She turned from the board and looked across at her team, her face grim, 'We're going to have one hell of a job proving it.'

'Who?' Claire said softly, and Gareth immediately added, 'And why?'

Hillary told them.

* * *

DI Liam Heddon walked across the lobby, looking for the staircase that would take him down into the bowels of the building. He walked fast because he was in a hurry, even though a quick scowl at his watch informed him that he was easily on time to keep the appointment that had been made for him to liaise with Detective Chief Superintendent Roland Sale.

Anyone watching him would have seen a man in his mid-thirties, around five feet eight inches tall, with close-cropped brown hair and bright blue eyes. He had the slim, rangy physique of the truly super-fit, and indeed, the DI had been into martial arts since he was a lad.

They would also have seen a well-dressed man in a light linen suit and matching tie, because Liam Heddon had always been a dapper dresser. As a kid, his older brother used to tease him that he was like a bantam cockerel — all showy feathers and nasty temperament, until Liam's growing judo expertise had put an abrupt and painful stop to it.

He'd transferred to Kidlington from his native Warwick just over a year ago, chasing a promotion which had duly come his way. And there was no doubt that being in the heart of Thames Valley, the biggest police force outside of the Met, suited him, as did being handed lead on a murder case — his fourth so far.

The desk sergeant watched him go by with a knowing eye. Everyone knew Heddon was an up-and-comer and ran a tight ship, which meant, theoretically, that he should get on well with Hillary Greene, who'd always run a tight ship herself; but somehow the desk sergeant didn't think it would pan out that way. There was something about Heddon that seemed to rub most people up the wrong way, making him respected rather than liked. Perhaps it was the air of impatience that wafted from the DI — giving the impression of a man who would rather be somewhere else, doing something else. Perhaps it was the fact that Heddon was still an outsider and hadn't yet learned his proper place in the rank and file's hierarchy.

Whatever it was, it had the desk sergeant lifting the phone and dialling Hillary's number to give her a warning that Heddon was on his way.

As in most things, the desk sergeant already knew that Heddon had been assigned the Brightman case, and that Hillary had found the woman's body. Like a spider in the middle of the web, desk sergeants always knew everything that went on in the nick.

Heddon, oblivious to what desk sergeants did or didn't know, found the stairs and headed down into the gloomy, warm and slightly stale air of the basement, already mentally shaking his head.

He hadn't been at all happy on entering his office this morning to find that his boss had scheduled this meeting; he didn't think it a high priority. Last Friday evening, though he'd listened dutifully as his super informed him of the CRT's ongoing case of the fifteen-year-old murder of a model, and how it might dovetail with his current case, it hadn't particularly impressed him.

It wasn't as if being hit over the head was an uncommon form of attack. And to him, the link between Connie Brightman and Imelda Phelps was tenuous at best, and the possibility of having another team piggybacking onto his own was deeply annoying.

The last thing he needed was some has-been DI sticking her nose into his murder investigation.

And it hadn't sweetened the pill any to keep on hearing Hillary Greene's name being lauded by all and sundry during the last two days either. OK, so he got it — she'd been a good copper and was something of a station legend. Her solve rate had been high. Fine, she was well regarded by both the bosses and the grunts. And yes, it did give him pause when he kept hearing that she and Commander Donleavy seemed to have some sort of weird mutual appreciation society going on between them.

But none of that meant that he was going to cut her any slack. He was SIO on the Brightman case, and she was now just a civilian consultant working on a very cold case — there could be no doubt as to who was in charge here and he wasn't going to tolerate any interference on her part.

Which was something he intended to make very clear to her boss in their imminent meeting.

He paused as he turned left, then right, and then found himself in a long, gloomy corridor that ended who-knew-where, and swore softly to himself. His own office on the third floor was light and spacious and open-plan — down here, he felt like a rat in a maze.

He followed the sound of computers beeping and the susurration that came from human conversation at a distance and eventually found a large room of IT experts, who helpfully directed him to Roland Sale's office. Even then, he got lost twice before he found it, which made him a minute late, which in turn made him feel wrong-footed. Which was something he'd always hated.

Swearing under his breath, he tapped on the door and was bidden to enter. As he stepped into a surprisingly large and well-lit office, he was annoyed to find it occupied not only by a heavy-set grey-haired man in his early sixties who must be the superintendent, but also a woman in her mid-fifties, whom he strongly suspected was the former DI Hillary Greene herself. An inch or so taller than himself, she was wearing a cream linen trouser suit, teamed with a mint-green t-shirt that suited her colouring perfectly.

'Ah, DI Heddon,' Superintendent Sale said, rising from behind his desk. 'Please meet Hillary Greene.'

'DI Heddon,' she nodded at him and shook his hand, her sherry-coloured eyes raking over him briefly.

'Please, sit down,' the superintendent offered, pointing to the other chair in front of his desk.

Heddon, mentally cursing his luck, sat down. He'd been hoping to meet the head of CRT in private and make it plain that he wanted them to stick to their case whilst he stuck to his, and thus have as little to do with the civilian consultants as possible.

Now he would have to be more tactful, and he didn't like wasting his energy on extraneous stuff like that.

'Sir,' Heddon said crisply.

Hillary sat down silently, and Heddon followed suit. Then they both looked at Rollo, who found himself clearing his throat.

* * *

'So what's he like?' Claire asked a quarter of an hour later, as Hillary returned to the communal office. She'd already heard from one of the tech people down the corridor that the Brightman SIO had come calling, and she knew that the superintendent would have wasted no time bringing about a meeting between them.

Hillary neatly sidestepped the question by merely giving them his name, then immediately changed the subject to issue them their orders for the day. 'I'm going to arrange a Zoom meeting with Jonas. I have a few follow-up questions for him, then I want to tackle Thomas again. After that, Jessie. Who wants to stay here and work the computers on The Face of Experience end, and who wants to come out and about with me?'

Claire glanced at the small electric fan on her desk and sighed. Gareth, noticing, took pity on her and came to the rescue.

'I wouldn't mind getting out of the office, ma'am. And I've heard so much about this big rabbit of Jessie's that I'd quite like to see it for myself.'

Claire shot him a grateful look, as Hillary nodded and headed to the door.

'All right. As soon as I've spoken to Jonas, I'll come and pick you up.'

As Claire watched her leave, she slowly leaned back in her chair, twiddling a biro pen in her hand. 'I think we're going to have problems with DI Heddon,' she said thoughtfully.

Gareth looked at her curiously. 'Why do you say that? She barely said a word about him.'

'Exactly.'

* * *

Back in her office, Hillary phoned Jonas Phelps's home telephone number, but his wife informed her that he wasn't working from home that day and had gone into his London office. She quickly gave Hillary his direct line at work however, promising that he'd pick it up at once.

Sure enough, Jonas Phelps answered the line directly. If he was put out by Hillary's request for a Zoom meeting, she couldn't tell it by his voice (which was one of the reasons she wanted to see his face as they talked) and within a short time, they were looking at each other on the screen of their respective devices.

In the background behind him, Hillary could make out some posters on the walls showing some ultra-modern desirable residences which, presumably, their firm had been instrumental in designing, and to the right of the screen, she could just make out a few leaves and the colourful petals of some kind of pot plant. An African violet maybe? She wondered how many modern executives still indulged in office greenery and suspected that it had been a gift from his plant-loving sister.

'Thank you for this, Mr Phelps, I'll try not to take up too much of your time,' Hillary began.

'That's fine,' he said, his hazel eyes holding hers steadily. 'How's the investigation going?'

'It's developing, Mr Phelps, and we've had several new leads to follow up,' she responded positively. 'Were you aware that at the time of your mother's death she was in the running to win a very significant modelling contract?'

'No, I had no idea,' he said at once, showing neither surprise nor much interest. Again, if she'd hoped to catch him out trying to toe the family line, she was disappointed, but that was hardly surprising. If he genuinely hadn't known about his mother's possible career boost, his response now was the obvious one; and if he *had* known about it at the time and had been purposely asked to keep quiet about it, his father would have had plenty of time to catch up with him over the weekend and warn him that the police were now aware of The Face of Experience and that Jonas should play dumb all over again.

'I see. You will have heard that your mother's one-time business partner, Connie Brightman, was found dead in her flat last Friday.' She made it a statement, not a question. For although DI Heddon had been very unforthcoming about what had been happening in the Brightman inquiry so far, she was sure that someone on his team would have spoken to the Phelps family, if only as a matter of routine and to ascertain their whereabouts at the time Connie was being killed.

And even if that wasn't the case, the murder of the local woman had made the Oxford papers and must surely have come to their attention. The significance of the death of someone once connected to their murdered mother and wife couldn't have escaped the notice of the Phelps family, and if they hadn't already discussed it amongst themselves then they must all have almost superhuman powers of self-control.

'Yes, I was contacted by someone from the police yesterday evening. And for the record, I was working from home both Thursday and Friday of last week, as my wife can confirm. And no, I didn't take the car out on either of those evenings and I was certainly nowhere in Oxfordshire during the times they asked me about.'

Hillary nodded. So, his alibi was only backed up by his wife then. As alibis came, it was about average. It was reasonable, but hardly airtight. It was no great shocker that wives had been known to lie for their husbands before.

'Thank you, sir, but the reason I specifically wanted to talk to you concerns your mother's death. We've been informed that for a period of, say, around a week to ten days in the months shortly before her murder, your mother, who was normally very social, wasn't seen out and about at all. She didn't attend any gatherings, nor did she follow her normal routine but remained in the house. Do you recall that?'

As she saw his eyes flicker and his mouth tighten, Hillary was glad that she'd insisted on a Zoom call. Not wanting to give him the opportunity to lie to her face, she added quickly, 'Ah, I can see by your face that you *do* recall the episode I'm talking about. Can you tell me about it please?'

But he was not going to be railroaded. 'I'm afraid you're mistaken, Mrs Greene. As you know, I was away at university at the time, and wasn't at home all that often. Which means that I wasn't there to take note of her comings and goings. But it does sound very unlike my mother to remain closeted in the house, so personally, I think you've probably been misinformed.'

Hillary nodded and said blandly, 'I see. Well, thank you for your time, sir.'

'That's it?' He sounded surprised, and she strongly suspected that it was the first spontaneous thing he'd said to her.

'Yes, sir. For now,' she added with a brief smile. 'I hope you're not suffering too much with the heat down there in London. I hear the temperature's always a good couple of degrees higher in a major city than it is anywhere else.'

'We have air conditioning here in the office building I'm glad to say,' he said, and after the usual awkward murmurings that come with ending an electronic conversation, they terminated the link.

Hillary sat back in her chair, which was pressed so close to the wall behind her that it creaked loudly in protest, and slowly nodded to herself. Yes. Things were progressing pretty much as she'd expected.

CHAPTER TWELVE

As they drove into Bicester, the road seemed to shimmer and undulate ahead of them due to the effects of heat haze, and Hillary tried to persuade herself that she was getting used to baking alive. She only hoped the tarmac didn't melt altogether and finally drag Gareth's car to a halt, like an animal trapped in quicksand.

Thomas Phelps answered the door with a resigned look of patience on his face. Once again, he'd agreed to stay in to be interviewed, and she wondered if he was having flashbacks to the original investigation, during which he must have become accustomed to the disruptions and obligations that having a murdered wife had thrust upon him.

'Thank you for seeing us again so soon, sir,' she began politely, once they were seated in the lounge. She could hear noises emanating from the kitchen, and presumed it was his wife making the noise, although it might just as easily have been someone that he employed to help out with the housekeeping.

'That's all right, I want to be kept informed about what's going on, as you can imagine. By the way, there's some journalist called Otterley who's been making a bit of a nuisance of himself, trying to get one of the children or myself to give him a comment. Is there something you can do about him?'

'Yes, we're aware of him,' Hillary said tonelessly. 'If you want to make a complaint, I can put you in touch with the people you need to speak to.'

But at this, Thomas merely grimaced wryly and sighed. 'There's no point, really, is there? He'll only scream something about the rights of the free press. It's just that after our chat about Morgan Fisher, I keep checking the papers for some so-called "exclusive" scoop about the whole Face of Experience connection, but so far there's been nothing printed about Imelda's photographs. Which is a massive relief! I take it he can't have ferreted out anything about that, at least?'

'*We* certainly haven't made that information public, sir, and have no intentions of doing so,' she said crisply, and saw him flush.

'No, of course not. I'm sorry, I didn't mean to imply . . . It's just that I remember from the first time being ambushed and harassed by reporters every time I stepped outside my front door . . .' He trailed off and shrugged helplessly. 'So, what can I do for you this time, Mrs Greene?'

'You're aware that Connie Brightman was found dead in suspicious circumstances in her flat last week?'

'Yes, I was. But, forgive me, I was told that you weren't investigating that,' he said, rather too pointedly for her liking. Were Heddon and his team actively going around warning her witnesses not to talk to her about Connie Brightman?

'No, sir, I'm a civilian consultant now, as I told you,' Hillary said, keeping her tone light and unconcerned, 'so that investigation is being conducted by DI Heddon.' Beside her, Gareth had been taking notes quietly, but something in her voice must have caught his ear, because he paused to cast her a quick look before dipping his head again.

'I'm only here to talk to you about Miss Brightman as she relates to the murder of your wife,' Hillary swept on, not quite truthfully. 'Tell me, had Connie contacted you at all recently?'

'No.'

'Did she make any contact with you at the time of the original investigation?'

'No. By then she'd already made her feelings about Imelda and the shutdown of their jewellery business very clear, and I suppose she must have felt that it would be hypocritical of her to suddenly offer her condolences after some of the things she'd said.'

'Yes, I see. Especially since she herself was a "person of interest" at the time.'

Thomas winced slightly at this. No doubt as a man with his own share of intelligence, he must have been aware that he, too, was on the same list.

'As you say,' he agreed dryly.

'Has anybody contacted you recently about Imelda? I mean friends that you might have lost contact with, suddenly getting in touch again. Things like that?'

'No.'

As he spoke, the door opened, and his wife walked in. Today she was dressed in a brightly coloured floral-patterned trouser suit and had a matching wide headband holding back her long, pale hair. She smiled as she set a tray of cold drinks on the table, then took a seat next to her husband on the sofa.

'Hello, please help yourself to some orange juice. It's ice-cold.'

Hillary didn't need asking twice, but Gareth shook his head that he was fine.

'I'm sure you've already been asked and answered this question, but where were you during the period that Connie Brightman was attacked?' she asked as casually as she could. She knew she had no business asking it, and no doubt Liam Heddon wouldn't like to hear the direction of her questions if he were to find out about them, so she kept her mental fingers crossed that word didn't get back to him.

From the slightly amused expression that suddenly flickered across Thomas Phelps's face, she strongly suspected that he might be something of a mind-reader; nevertheless, he answered her readily enough.

'I was at home all Thursday, luckily. Phil was with me,' he turned to his wife, who nodded vigorously.

'Thank you, sir. We have to ask routine questions sometimes and they can be a bit of a chore, going over things twice,' she cast the couple a vague smile, and saw that at some point, Thomas's second wife had slipped her hand into his. And she wondered — was she offering support and comfort, or seeking it?

As if sensing her interest, Philippa suddenly crossed one long leg over the other and tried a little too hard to look casual.

Hillary could tell the other woman wasn't comfortable about this latest upset in their life, but she was inclined to put that down to the general wariness and unease that most people felt when violence impinged on their normal, everyday lives. Indeed, if this pair *had* seemed genuinely nonchalant about her questions, her radar would have pinged loudly and clearly with suspicion.

'There is one more thing I need to ask you about Imelda. It concerns a certain time period during the few months leading up to her death.'

Thomas looked at her without much expression, other than a mildly quizzical readiness. 'Yes?'

'We understand that, sometime within her last few months, Imelda stayed at home for a long period of time — say about ten days or so.'

She saw him go slightly pale. Then he said, 'Sorry? What?'

'What I mean is, your wife was a very social person, often out and about, attending parties, meeting up with friends, lunching out, enjoying herself outside the home. But for some reason, she was totally absent from her usual social scene during this ten-day period, and never left the house. Can you confirm that, sir?'

Thomas's tongue flicked out quickly and wet his lips, before he began to speak. 'I'm sorry, I can't say that it rings a bell.'

'Surely you'd have noticed if your wife suddenly became more or less housebound though?' she pressed.

He shrugged. 'I was at the office every day — sometimes on a Saturday, so . . .' Again, he shrugged.

Hillary saw Philippa cast him a slightly puzzled look. Like Hillary, she was picking up on something odd in his manner.

'But you were home in the evenings, yes? Didn't you used to go out regularly in the evenings, sir? To the theatre, dinner, visiting friends, things like that?'

'This was fifteen years ago that we're talking about,' Thomas said, clearly rather more shortly than he'd meant to, for he suddenly smiled, and moderated his tone. 'I remember the big things, obviously — birthdays, special occasions, but I don't remember just casual things like that.'

Hillary nodded. 'I see. Well, thank you for your time, sir,' she said, finishing off the cold fruit juice and rising slowly to her feet.

Thomas got up quickly and showed them with barely restrained eagerness to the door. He thanked them politely on the doorstep then hesitated for a moment, as if unsure whether to watch them leave. Finally, and somewhat diffidently, he closed the door on them when they were halfway down the drive.

Gareth, limping silently alongside her, said nothing until they were in the car. Then he turned on the engine, and as the air conditioning mercifully began to blow cool air on their faces, laps and feet, said quietly, 'He's normally a very self-controlled customer, but he was badly rattled by that last question you asked him, wasn't he?'

Hillary nodded. 'Yes. I rather think he was. And you'd expect it to be the murder of a woman that he'd once known that would cause the said rattling wouldn't you, instead of the fact that his wife stayed home for a couple of weeks one time, fifteen years ago?'

'Yes, ma'am, you would.' He looked out of the windscreen at the deserted modern estate, and then looked at her. 'Do you have any idea what that's all about, ma'am?' It was a rhetorical question on his part though, for, by now, the former soldier had worked under Hillary Greene's command long enough to know the answer already.

Hillary slowly nodded. 'As a matter of fact, I think I do. And it's about time to find out if I'm on the right track.' She put on her seatbelt and lowered the flap down over the windscreen to shield her eyes from the bright glare. 'All right, time for you to meet the biggest rabbit you've ever seen in your life.'

* * *

Jessie glanced at her watch as she let them into her house. 'I'm sorry, but I don't usually take a lunch break,' she began nervously. 'But when you phoned me at work this morning, we'd just had a cancellation at noon, so I was able to get some time away. But I must be back soon — I have a tom cat that needs castrating.'

At this Gareth swallowed hard, and Hillary was hard put to keep a straight face.

She showed them into the same room as before, when Claire had been with her, and sure enough, stretched out in a patch of sunlight coming through the window, was Jester. Laying out fully, he seemed to take up almost half the length of the short back wall.

'That,' Gareth said, deadpan, 'is one big rabbit.'

'Isn't he lovely?' Jessie said, pride in her pet warring with her obvious nervousness. She bent down as she passed the animal and gave him a gentle stroke behind his ears. Then she indicated the seats and sat down abruptly, as if the strength had suddenly left her legs.

She gazed at them with a curious look of hopelessness in her eyes that made Hillary feel tense. She never liked it when the job made her feel like a bully.

'I imagine your father rang you the moment we left his place?' Hillary began quietly.

Jessie made a quick, nervous start on her chair, opened her mouth to automatically deny it, then thought better of it and nodded. 'Yes. He said you'd just been around to his place.'

'Did he tell you what we discussed?'

'About Connie? Yes, wasn't that awful? Do you think what happened to her had anything to do with what happened to Mum?'

Hillary looked at her thoughtfully. 'Do you?'

Jessie hesitated for a moment, then spread her hands in a helpless gesture. 'I can't really see how. I mean, after all this time. Unless, I mean, you think Connie might have known something about Mum and kept quiet about it. And . . .' she went a little pale and swallowed hard. 'Well, you know . . . someone panicked and thought she might be about to tell the police, and . . .' her voice trailed off, as if she was failing to convince even herself of this theory.

'*Did* Miss Brightman contact you any time after your mother's murder? Either back then, or more recently?' Hillary inquired.

'Oh no. I would have told you if she had.'

And Hillary rather believed her — on that point at least. But she hadn't come to talk about Connie — and she knew that Jessie Phelps was only too aware of that fact. It was time to get down to the real business of the day.

'In the months before your mother's death, there was a period of time when she didn't go out of the house. Two weeks or so. Do you remember that?'

At this, Jessie's eyes grew a little wider and began to sparkle ominously. Tears, Hillary could see, were not far away.

'No, I can't say as I do,' she mumbled miserably.

Hillary nodded but let her eyes deliberately drift over to look at the rabbit, basking in the sunlight on the carpet. 'When I first heard about your mother's odd behaviour, I was immediately struck by it,' she said, keeping her voice totally level and neutral, much as she imagined hypnotists did when they were testing a subject for susceptibility. 'Because you see, by now I'm beginning to get a much fuller picture of your mother, and that picture is of a mature, confident woman, who always enjoyed the benefits of what mother nature gave her. A woman who liked life and enjoying the things that life offered her. A social woman, who liked people and being in a crowd of people and being admired by people.' She continued to watch the rabbit, which had now closed his eyes and appeared to be sleeping.

'And I had to ask myself — why would a woman like that suddenly shut herself up in the house and not go out? My first, obvious thought, was that she had probably been ill — a bout of flu, perhaps. But Dermott Franklyn didn't think that was the case, and when I asked your father just now, he didn't seem to recall that she'd been ill either. Or if he did, he didn't mention it.'

She turned her gaze back to Imelda's daughter and saw that the threatened tears had now begun to fall. Gently, she returned to contemplating the enormous rabbit. 'So that meant I had to think again. Why would a woman like your mother shut herself away if she wasn't ill? Did she have some sort of mental breakdown? But that didn't fit either, because after a couple of weeks she went back to her usual routine and active social life and seemed much the same as ever. And you don't throw off a fit of depression or something even more serious just like that. So, what could have happened? It had me stumped for a while, but then I stopped looking at it from *my* perspective and began looking at it from hers. I said to myself, "I'm a very beautiful woman, on the verge of winning a very large modelling contract. What matters the most to me in this moment?" And when I did that, the answer was obvious, wasn't it, Jessie?'

In her seat, the young vet began to nod. But she still didn't trust herself to speak. Hillary didn't mind — she could do the speaking for her, for now.

'Her looks,' Hillary answered her own question.

'It was always her l-looks,' Jessie finally quavered bitterly. 'It was never anything el-else as far as she was concerned. She was so vain — I know she didn't really *mean* it . . . not like you or I would mean it, if *we* did something wrong. It was just, like . . . it was like she never really *understood* that she *was* being so self-obsessed all the time. To her, it was just . . . normal. Just how it *was*. Like a kid, doing something wrong but not knowing she was doing anything wrong, which made her sort of innocent. But at the same time — you just wanted to rant at her to stop it. Oh, it's no use. I can't explain it, exactly.' She sniffled and reached towards the box of tissues residing on the table. Once she'd helped herself to a handful she wiped them around her face.

'I understand — her self-image was everything to her. So, if something were to happen to her lovely face,' Hillary carried on, focussing now on Jester's twitching nose, the only part of him that seemed to be moving, 'she would be sure to hide away, wouldn't she, where no one could see her? It would be like her worst nightmare come true. But what, I asked myself, could possibly have happened to her looks? If she'd had an accident and bruised her face up, why all the secrecy? And it wasn't as if she wasn't used to looking after herself and her appearance. She didn't stint on having the best make-up, the best clothes, *the best skin creams* . . .'

Hillary emphasized the last four words meaningfully, and Jessie gave a muffled sob.

'Yes. Skin cream. That's where I found myself concentrating my thinking. What if she'd had an allergic reaction to something?' Hillary mused out loud, still addressing the oblivious giant rabbit. 'If she broke out in an unsightly rash, it would send her into a tailspin of panic, wouldn't it? It would be the ultimate disaster for her — especially then, when she was so close to getting that wonderful Face of Experience modelling job.'

Hillary nodded, but then changed it to a slight shake of her head. 'But then, I began to wonder even more. Did that make sense? Why would she suddenly become allergic to the products she was using? She was a professional model — she'd probably had her favourite creams and moisturisers for years. Why would they do her any harm now?'

'Perhaps those people you were talking about — the people with the modelling contract, perhaps they gave her some samples of their stuff, and one of them didn't agree with her? Don't they do that, those people? Give out samples for people to try?' Jessie said.

Hillary pretended to give that some thought, cocking her head a little to one side. 'Yes, that's possible.' Then she frowned. 'But your mother was a professional — she wouldn't just slather stuff all over her face without doing a patch test first, would she? Probably on the back of her hand or the sensitive skin on her underarm perhaps?'

In her peripheral vision, she saw the younger woman slump down a little in her chair. And the sniffles came back.

'No. I don't think that's what happened at all, Jessie. I think what happened is that someone deliberately doctored her usual cream. And then, of course, I had to wonder who would want to do something like that. And then I wondered who would *know* how to do something like that. And that's when I thought of *you*, Jessie — with your love of botany and all that marvellous knowledge you have of poisonous plants. I imagine you knew your stuff, even back then. Weren't you studying botany at school, as well as zoology?'

Hillary finally turned her gaze from the giant rabbit to the young vet, who now had tears openly running down her face. 'There you were, just seventeen, and full of the usual angst and worries that all teenagers are prone to. How angry and alone you must have felt, with your beautiful mother, who everybody already fawned over, now set to become a really famous model. And if that had happened, she would probably have had even less time for you than before. Am I right?'

Jess nodded sadly and gave her face another wipe with the already sodden tissues. 'It was always all about her,' she said, gulping a little, as the sobs wracked her again. 'But this was even more manic than usual. All she could think about was becoming famous at last. People recognising her in the streets. The money she'd earn — serious money, the sort of money that could send you to Monte Carlo for a couple of weeks, or where the hell ever.' She suddenly became angry.

'It began to make me really sick. All this "we could move to Mayfair" rubbish. I just wanted to . . .' And then, as quickly as the anger came, it seemed to leach out of her. 'I just wanted her to shut up about it for once. To see that there was more to life than being Queen Bee! That *we* needed her. Jonas pretended he didn't, but he did. And Dad . . . Poor Dad. I wonder if she ever loved Dad at all. Or me. Or Jonas. Or did she only love herself?' Her voice had now petered out to a defeated near whisper.

She frowned down at the tissue in her hand and began to restlessly pull it apart.

'So you decided to teach her a lesson?' Hillary prompted her.

In his seat, a fascinated Gareth Proctor took notes, careful not to make the slightest sound.

Jessie nodded. 'Yes. I did. I admit it,' she said, finally showing some spirit and raising her chin defiantly. 'I used some giant hogweed I found near the river. *Heracleum mantegazzianum*, if you want to get technical. It's nasty stuff — but I was careful. I made sure it wouldn't cause any lasting damage. Just enough to give her a real fright.'

Suddenly Jessie gave a short bark of laughter, and then looked surprised, as if the sound had come from somewhere else. She put a hand quickly to her mouth, as if afraid that once she'd started to laugh she would never be able to stop, but after giving Hillary a slightly panicked look, she slowly lowered her hand again, and then stared down into her lap. Then she heaved a massive sigh.

'Are you going to arrest me? Will I lose my job?' she asked in a small voice.

'I don't have the power to arrest you, Jessie. And I really can't imagine that anyone would be interested in prosecuting you now. So — did it make you feel better? Seeing your mother so upset?' she asked, genuinely curious to know the answer.

Jessie Phelps raised her head to look at Hillary, and slowly smiled. 'You know, it did! She was always so in control, so superior, so confident in her looks and her place in the world, to see her unsure and worried for a change — and in a downright panic, and looking *not beautiful* for once in her damned life . . . Yes. It made me feel better. *Now you know how I feel for once,* I thought. *How do you like it? Welcome to the real world, and the real human race.* For a few days, I went around the house, outwardly sympathising with her and supporting her, and telling her everything would turn out fine, but underneath, I was mentally clapping my hands with glee. I suppose that horrifies you?' she asked, half-defiant and half-appalled, shooting Hillary a quick look.

'I don't horrify easily.'

Jessie's eyes flickered and she looked away, shook her head, and then sighed. Slowly her shoulders slumped again. 'But it didn't last,' she said miserably. 'And, funnily enough, as the rash began to fade, and Mum began to feel better and get back to her old self, I began to feel worse and worse about what I'd done. Instant karma, right?' She again gave a snort of laughter, but a half-hearted one this time.

Hillary shrugged. 'I didn't come here to make you feel bad, Jessie. Only to gain evidence and facts. All I want to know is — is that *all* you did to your mother?'

Jessie looked up at her, puzzled. 'What do you mean? Isn't that enough?'

'Jessie, is that the only way in which you hurt your mother?' Hillary repeated patiently, and watched as the colour faded abruptly from the tearful woman's face as Jessie finally understood what it was that she was being asked.

'Oh hell yes!' Jessie yelped. 'I didn't *kill* her! I swear. I wouldn't. I couldn't. I didn't. I . . . I . . .'

And she began to weep bitterly.

Hillary watched her, feeling about two inches tall, then reached out and put her hand over hers, feeling the sodden tissue squishing between Jessie's fingers under her own. 'All right, Jessie. All right. Why don't you go and cuddle Jester, hmm? He looks like he could do with a hug.'

* * *

When they left the house ten minutes later, Jessie was much calmer and a lot happier, as if finally confessing to what she'd done as a teenager had lifted a massive weight off her shoulders. They left her sitting on the carpet next to her pet, gently stroking the huge, elongated ears, taking deep, calming breaths, and about to ring the surgery to tell them she would be in time to make her next appointment.

'She was getting really shaky for a while back there. Do you think she'll be all right now?' Gareth asked with genuine concern as they made their way back to his car under a sun that — now at its zenith — had all the charm of a blow torch.

'I hope so. For the tom cat's sake,' Hillary said, deadpan.

* * *

Back at HQ Hillary typed up the notes on the Jessie Phelps interview for the Murder Book herself. She could have delegated Gareth to do it, but it was now well into the mid-afternoon, and there was no way she was going back outside again until it was time to drag her sorry, wilting body back to the *Mollern*, where she could melt into a puddle on her single bed in decent solitude.

Notes typed up, she took them through into the interview room and then, with a dragging sense of reluctance headed upstairs and into her old stomping grounds. As she opened the door and walked in, she deliberately kept her eyes averted from the area of the large open-plan office where she'd used to have her desk, but she could sense the room perk up at her appearance.

Those who knew her from the olden days smiled at her, and those that didn't looked at her with a mixture of speculation and interest. She gave a general nod and smile, all the time making her way to DI Heddon's hang-out.

Since she'd last been a DI here, the interior had changed a little, some areas having been cordoned off for the 'higher-ups' with that sort of semi-glazed cubicle configuration that neither afforded the inhabitant any privacy, whilst at the same time, managing to block them off just enough to leave them the last to know anything about what was going on. Hillary didn't know which genius had come up with this, but she was heartily relieved that whoever it was had at least had the decency to wait until she'd retired before inflicting it on her old workmates.

Of course, Heddon saw her coming before she was halfway there, and already had his scowl in place when she gave a gentle tap on the glass panel of the door (careful not to tap too hard, in case the whole thing fell to pieces, like a house made of cards), and opened it before waiting for a direct summons.

Inside were two men, both younger than Heddon, who turned to look at Hillary as she leaned her head and shoulders inside. One was sitting in the room's only other chair beside the DI's, whilst the other leaned gingerly against a wall. They'd been discussing something but had broken off their conversation the moment the door opened.

'Can I have a quick word, DI Heddon?' she asked pleasantly.

'Is it important?'

Hillary was so sorely tempted to snap back that she would hardly be here if it wasn't, that she literally had to clamp her lips firmly together, giving her a vital second to control what eventually came out of her mouth.

'Potentially, yes. I was wondering if you had any updates about anyone seen visiting Connie Bri—' She broke off in surprise as Heddon almost threw himself back in the chair and began to cut across her.

'I thought my boss and your boss made it quite clear that the Brightman case is *our* investigation,' he said, indicating his two companions with a flick of his fingers. One of the men looked delighted at being included, and gave Hillary what almost amounted to a smirk, whilst the other looked a little discomfited and refused to meet Hillary's eyes.

'They did,' she began tightly, 'and I have no intention of interfering . . .'

'That's nice to know. So why are you here asking me about it?'

'I have a prime suspect in the cold case, and I was just wondering if you had any information linking—'

'So far as I'm aware, none of the lot you're interested in has appeared in our data. Jordan, that's right, isn't it? You've read the file Superintendent Sale sent us on the Phelps case?'

The one with the smirk nodded. 'Yes, guv. So far, none of the Phelps family, or any relevant witness from fifteen years ago, have made contact with our murder victim.'

'There you have it. I'll be sure to let you know if that changes, Mrs Greene,' Heddon added pleasantly.

Hillary nodded, said a curt 'thank you' and ducked back out, shutting the door silently and carefully behind her. The people at the desks nearest Heddon's office had gone quiet, and she felt a bit like that stranger in a Western who had just wandered into a saloon and now all the locals were watching every move she made.

She sighed, shook her head a little, and walked to the door.

Well, so much for inter-departmental cooperation then.

She went back down the stairs, knowing that before she left for the day, the news would already be circulating around the building. Hillary had gone upstairs and been kicked out again almost immediately. She could imagine the gleeful desk sergeants already taking bets from Traffic, PCs and chief supers alike about how long it would take before she got her revenge.

But as she made her way back down into the basement, she wasn't contemplating retribution (well, not much) so much as fighting off a sense of growing frustration. She was simply too uncomfortably hot and way too tired from spending so many nights unable to sleep properly, to be able to work up any enthusiasm for a bout of one-upmanship with Heddon.

She was also becoming too concerned about her case to want to spend any excess energy on distractions.

As she slunk into her stationery cupboard and poured herself into her chair, she reminded herself that there was no shame in being unable to close a fifteen-year-old murder investigation when even the original team had been unable to do so.

What's more, for some time now, she'd been aware of a growing conviction that this might just turn out to be one of *those* cases. Every copper, unless they were extraordinarily lucky, ran into them from time to time. The case that just won't come right, no matter what. The case where you were *almost* certain you knew who did it, but just couldn't prove it. The case whose solution kept coming almost within your grasp, only to slither out of reach time and time again, until it made you want to spit.

The temptation to sit and wallow in misery was almost overwhelming, but she was beginning to feel too angry to enjoy it. If only the bloody weather would break it would be something! She got up, went to the ladies, and had a makeshift wash at the sink, keeping one eye on the door in case anyone came in. She then brushed her sweat-dampened hair off her forehead and regarded herself in the mirror.

Deciding that she was as presentable as she was ever going to get, she smiled grimly at her reflection. 'Time to spread the misery around then,' she told it, and with that left the loos, marched down the corridor, turned a few doglegs and then tapped briskly on Rollo Sale's office door.

'Come in.'

Hillary did.

Rollo took one look at her face, sighed wearily, and indicated the chair in front of his desk. 'How much of a stiff drink do I need?'

Hillary grinned. 'Not in this heat, sir,' she warned him. 'A belt of straight whisky would probably send your inner temperature into meltdown.'

'Bad as that?' he asked, not without sympathy. 'I take it the case has hit the buffers? Are the new leads not panning out? You know, even you can't get blood out of a stone, Hillary. If you want to call it a day . . . ?'

'It's not that, sir,' she said. 'I'm more than two-thirds sure that I know who killed Imelda Phelps and why. Not quite so sure why they also killed Connie Brightman — although I could take a damned good guess — but with DI Heddon not wanting to play nicely, I might not have the opportunity of finding that out either. But you can't have everything, can you?'

Rollo, who'd been idly eyeing the electric clock on the wall, counting down the minutes until he could reasonably pack up and get off to his home and then his allotment shed, abruptly transferred all his attention to the woman in front of him.

'You have a prime suspect? Then what's the problem?' he demanded.

Hillary's lips twitched. 'What isn't? Too much time having passed, no forensics worth a damn, a very odd motive that is going to take some swallowing, it's too bloody hot for me to think in a straight line anymore, and if all that isn't enough, a DI who's too concerned with guarding his patch to realise we'll probably need each other if we're going to have any hope of even getting within a cat's whisker of closing either of our cases . . .'

She ran out of puff, shrugged and spread her hands. 'Take your pick.'

Rollo slowly sank back in his chair and regarded her warily. It was not like Hillary Greene to look and sound so defeated. And he didn't like it. He didn't like it at all.

He also wanted to demand answers then and there but was rapidly having second thoughts. Perhaps the end of an exhausting day was not the most auspicious time to hold a council of war.

'You look totally done in,' he told her brusquely instead. 'It's this bloody heat, I know, we're all feeling it. Look, go home, try and get cool, try and get some sleep. Then first thing in the morning, come back to me with your head in the right place, and lay it all out for me, and we'll go through it together and see what's to be done. Then we'll come up with a plan of action. Understood?'

Hillary nodded. 'Yes, sir,' she said. Then, after he'd nodded a dismissal and she was halfway to his door, she said dryly over her shoulder, 'and thanks for the boot up the backside, sir. I needed it.'

Rollo watched her go, a small smile pulling at his lips. 'You're welcome.'

Now that was more like it!

CHAPTER THIRTEEN

The thundery weather that had been promised for some days began to make itself felt during the latter part of the night, but frustratingly, not a drop of rain had yet fallen from the sky when Hillary drove into work the next morning.

The radio assured her that various parts of the south coast were now nearly awash with water, along with the cooling-off period that rain inevitably brought with it, but right here, in the middle of the country, they just had the muggy, soggy, repressive humidity of an approaching storm, with no guarantee that they'd get the pay-off at the end. The weather front might — or might not — reach Oxfordshire by mid-afternoon.

Sheer exhaustion had meant that she'd had nearly five hours' sleep, but when she pushed into Rollo's office, ready to do battle, she could feel a dull headache beginning to settle into the back of her head, and she felt as if some unseen weight was trying to push her downwards — both probably the result of the low-pressure weather system overhead. Or maybe, given her growing anxiety over how her case was going, it was something more psychological in nature? Either way, she could have done without it right now.

It didn't take her long to tell her boss the way her mind was working, and it took him even less time to agree with her that, though her thinking might well be sound, it wasn't very much to go on in terms of providing either proof or bringing them any closer to getting something together that could be taken to the prosecution service.

'So, what do you think we should do next?' Rollo asked, his fingers idly fiddling with a ballpoint pen. 'Personally, I don't think there's much to be gained by waiting and hoping something useful falls into our laps. It's been fifteen years, and the chances of you finding anything tangible now have to be close to zero.'

Hillary nodded. 'I agree. The only way forward is to tackle her again and hope for a confession. And even then, that might not be enough.'

Rollo's eyebrow rose half an inch. 'And what do you think your chances are of that?'

Hillary shook her head. 'Who can really say? On the one hand, she's as tough as old boots — she must be, to do what she did and keep it together all these years. And yet, on the other hand, she's vulnerable. Maybe very vulnerable — at least on certain points. But let's face it, our best chance lies with DI Heddon coming up with something that links her to Connie's murder. We might have to settle for that and let the Imelda Phelps case — technically at least — remain open.'

Neither of them liked this much — Rollo because it affected his figures and closure rates, and Hillary because she thought that Imelda Phelps and her family deserved more. But sometimes life presented you with unpalatable facts and you just had to deal with it.

'Are you bringing her in here, or tackling her at her residence?' Rollo eventually asked.

Hillary sighed. 'Her residence, I think, initially anyway. I want to test the waters, try and find out just what I'm up against before going down the more formal route. Also, we don't want to risk the appearance of bullying. That could backfire on us pretty quickly.'

'You think softly-softly is going to work though? From the picture you've painted of her, I can't see kid gloves will achieve much,' Rollo said sceptically.

Hillary shrugged. 'It's going to depend on what buttons I can press, and how successfully I can press them. I'm pretty sure she'll want to try and handle things herself at first, but once she senses real danger, she'll soon start yodelling for a solicitor. And it's not as if anyone in this case can't afford the very best legal representation.'

'Once they realise what's happening, do you think the family will close ranks?'

'Only one way to find out, isn't there, sir?' she said, and with that Rollo gave her the go-ahead, and she left his office, if not with a spring in her step, then at least with a determined look on her face.

She tried to keep that look firmly in place as she put her head around the door of the communal office and Gareth and Claire looked back at her expectantly. They knew she'd just been consulting with the super and must have been discussing amongst themselves how she was going to handle things tactically.

'All right — we're going to risk it,' she said bluntly. 'Confront her with it and see how she reacts.' Hillary glanced from Gareth to Claire and back again, thinking hard. Whilst Gareth would undoubtedly gain much from watching the process in action, and of the two of them was definitely the one most in need of the experience, it wasn't that simple. Had their suspect been male, she probably would have taken him without a second thought.

But the potential for disaster was already far too great for her liking, and she felt an officer like Claire — given her years of experience with dysfunctional families and domestic violence — was too valuable an asset to leave behind. Also, it would undoubtedly look better if they kept this an all-female affair.

'Claire,' she said flatly.

Gareth looked disappointed and watched a little enviously as Claire quickly grabbed her bag and followed Hillary out the door.

The drive to Cheltenham was tense, traffic was bad, the weather was even more stifling than ever, and Hillary's nerves were stretched far more than she would have liked. As they approached Catherine Burton's impressive residence, Claire kept glancing at Hillary every chance she got to safely take her eyes off the road.

'Strategy, guv?'

Hillary told her the conclusions she and Rollo had come to, and ended, 'So we play it by ear. And bear in mind the suspect's age. First sign of any distress and we break off and bring in a medical professional.'

But there was an old saying about how man plans and God laughs, because, before Hillary had even had the chance to walk up the front steps of the Georgian townhouse and ring the bell, she was abruptly knocked off her intended course. And all her speculations about how the crucial interview ahead of her might go were destined to disintegrate and scatter after she heard a tentative voice pipe up behind her.

'Excuse me. By any chance, are you from the police?'

Hillary turned to see a white-haired woman dressed in a neat short-sleeved white blouse and a pale primrose-yellow skirt regarding her anxiously. She was dressed in very sensible and comfortable-looking white sandals, and her gaze kept flicking nervously from Hillary's face to the house beyond her. 'I don't think she's in right now, if you're looking for Catherine. I saw her and Nanette going out a little while ago.'

Nanette, Hillary thought, momentarily distracted. The dragon at the gate was called *Nanette*?

'Oh, I see. Thank you, Mrs . . . er . . . ?'

'Featherstone — Eloise Featherstone.'

'I don't suppose you know how long Mrs Burton will be out?'

'Oh, I don't expect she'll be long. This awful weather is so draining, isn't it, so she won't have gone far. I do wish the storms would get here and clear the air, don't you? I live just over there,' she vaguely indicated one of the buildings behind the central garden. 'You're very welcome to come and wait inside. I have some lemonade in the fridge and . . .' She paused and looked around, but nothing was stirring in the small cul-de-sac. The woman's friendly, round face clouded over. 'I actually wanted to have a little talk with you anyway. If you are from the police, that is? You never said . . .' she chided gently.

Hillary hastily produced her credentials and introduced Claire. Eloise peered at them carefully, the cards almost touching her nose, before nodding in satisfaction. 'Oh, and you're from Thames Valley too — that's Oxfordshire isn't it? Oh, I'm so glad. Tell me, are you investigating the murder of that woman in Chipping . . . something-or-other?'

Hillary, who had been weighing up the pros and cons of sitting in an old lady's flat to pass the time away — with cold lemonade on tap — as opposed to waiting in a sweat-producing car, suddenly felt her interest truly sharpen for the first time.

'I know the DI who's heading the investigation, yes,' Hillary said blandly, earning an approving glance from Claire, who could appreciate a truly awe-inspiring act of temporisation when she heard it.

'Oh that's good. Because . . .' The old lady leaned a bit closer to them, once again looking around her nervously. 'I could have sworn I saw that lady here, and it must have been only a few days before she died. At least — from the picture they printed in the newspaper, I'm fairly sure it was her,' she added hastily. 'Sometimes, though, those photographs can be a little blurry, can't they?'

Hillary smiled gently at Mrs Eloise Featherstone. 'They certainly can. And thank you, we'd be very happy to accept a glass of something cold to drink, wouldn't we, Claire?'

'Oh, it would go down a treat,' Claire agreed.

* * *

If the Featherstone residence was very similar in room sizes and layout to that of the Burton residence, it was a world away in terms of decoration. Here riotous floral wallpaper climbed every wall, and chintz ruled the furnishings. Whatnots, tallboys, cabinets and occasional tables of every geometric size cluttered an ancient Aubusson carpet, and vases, trinkets, mementoes, souvenirs of past holidays, photographs in real silver frames and China ornaments of dizzying variety lined every surface, making both women very careful about how they moved and what they did with their elbows.

But eventually they were seated in front of a large bay window with a view out over the gardens, and sipping very tart, very cold and very welcome homemade lemonade.

'I was sitting right here, as a matter of fact, when I first saw her,' Eloise was saying, glancing out of the window. 'I often spend my time just watching the world go by nowadays. It gets so lonely here now, since my Clarence died.'

'Your husband?' Hillary asked, glancing at some of the photos, trying to pick out a likely-looking departed spouse.

'My parrot,' Eloise corrected with a woebegone sigh, making Claire nearly choke on her drink.

'He was an African Grey — and I'd had him so many years. They live a really long time, you know, parrots. He was so cheerful and so funny. I'm afraid he picked up a little bit of bad language though, somewhere along the way. I really can't think how. But I do have one nephew with such an odd sense of humour . . .'

Claire began to cough helplessly.

'And what time was this, Mrs Featherstone,' Hillary said, careful to keep her eyes from meeting those of her colleague. 'When you thought you saw the woman from the papers?'

'Oh, the afternoon — early.'

'And you're sure of the day you saw her?'

'I think so,' Eloise said, but a small frown tugged at her brows. 'Let me think now — it was Saturday the story came out in the papers, wasn't it?'

'I believe so yes,' Hillary agreed.

'So it must have been . . . not the day right before, or the day before that, but the day before that.'

Hillary, despite her growing headache, managed to sort out the mathematics of this somewhat garbled statement. 'Wednesday?'

'Yes. Must have been. Or perhaps Tuesday? Anyway, she came through the entrance way,' she gave a vague nod towards the narrow lane that led into the square, 'and looked around, as if checking door numbers, you know. Then she walked up Catherine's steps and was let in by Nanette.'

'And you saw her plainly?' Hillary asked, just a shade sceptically, as she glanced out of the window. There were some trees between this house and that of Catherine Burton. They didn't block all the view, but even so . . .

'Oh yes. I'm long-sighted you see. I've always been that way. Or is it short-sighted?' Eloise immediately contradicted herself. 'I can never remember which is which. Well, whichever it is, it's the one where you can see very well far away, but not quite so good close to.'

Which is why she had to peer at our IDs, Hillary thought. Slowly, she brought out her phone and scrolled through her picture gallery until she came up with the best photograph she had of Connie. It was one from Imelda's case, so it was fifteen years old, but she didn't think Connie had changed too much.

'Is this her?' she asked, handing it over to Eloise, who predictably had to hold it up close to her nose and squint at it.

Hillary was so prepared for her somewhat erratic witness to regretfully admit that it wasn't her after all, that when Eloise beamed and nodded her head emphatically, she felt momentarily disconcerted.

'Yes, that's the woman. She was dressed in one of those horrible tracksuits that everyone seems to wear nowadays, but that's her all right.'

Hillary took her phone back and stared thoughtfully down at the picture.

'Do you think it's important?' the old lady chirruped on. 'I mean, that she came *here*? The papers said she was killed in her own home, so I wasn't sure . . . I was thinking about phoning the police yesterday, but didn't want to be a nuisance. It's so hard to know what to do for the best, isn't it? So when I saw you again today . . . I saw you when you first came, you know. And of course, I know all about poor Catherine's daughter, and that her murder has been under investigation again. And, well, if you don't mind me saying so, Mrs Greene, you do so have the air of a police officer about you somehow. So competent and, well, upright and so on, that when I saw your car arrive again . . . Oh, that reminds me. I meant to say — I don't think *she*,' Eloise nodded at Connie's image still on Hillary's phone, 'came by car. She didn't park it here if she did, and she walked through from the main street outside.'

'No, she didn't own a car,' Hillary agreed vaguely, her mind already racing ahead. And coming up with some rather unpalatable facts.

Because this, of course, changed everything.

It would have been one thing for her to interview Catherine Burton as a suspect in the murder of her daughter, since that case was hers. It was something else entirely to interview a suspect in an ongoing murder — and the fact that Connie Brightman had, apparently, visited Catherine sometime shortly before her death was definitely something DI Heddon and his team needed to check out.

Whether she liked it or not (and she didn't, she *really* didn't), she was going to have to take a step back and put her own agenda on hold. She sighed gently and gave Eloise Featherstone an encouraging smile.

'I was wondering, Mrs Featherstone, if you would mind helping us out a little?'

Eloise looked in equal measure both delighted and dismayed. 'Me? Help the police? Oh dear, I don't know,' she quavered. Then said eagerly, 'What would I have to do?'

'Would you mind if we drove you back to Oxford with us — don't worry, we'll bring you back home again afterwards. But I think it best if you had a talk with a nice man called Detective Inspector Heddon. I think he's going to be very interested in what you have to say.'

* * *

When they arrived back at Kidlington an hour and twenty minutes later, however, Hillary did not steer the excited but nervous old lady up to Heddon's lofty office, but instead steered her down the steps towards Rollo's.

Her eyes widened slightly as they descended, and Hillary could imagine the poor old dear wondering nervously if she was about to be thrown into some dungeon and given the third degree. She wasn't surprised when Eloise almost wilted with relief as she was shown into Superintendent Sale's office. Although it had only a slit of a window, and that was high up where the wall met the ceiling (which was actually ground level), it was well lit, reasonably cool, and most of all, had the reassuring presence of a gentleman in it.

Rollo Sale, already warned by Claire of the latest developments, rose to the occasion at once, walking around his desk to shake Eloise's hand and thank her fulsomely for her civic-mindedness. He even went so far as to look straight at Claire and demand tea for everyone, and Claire, biting back a grin, and the desire to curtsy at him, left to see what she could rustle up.

Hillary gently led the old lady through her testimony again, and Rollo agreed that her story was so important that it warranted immediate action. This so thrilled Eloise Featherstone that she almost couldn't sit still long enough to drink the tea that Claire had just provided.

When the last cup was drained however, and Hillary and her witness rose from their chairs, Rollo couldn't help but give Hillary a crocodile smile and indulge in a little stirring. 'I think, Hillary, Mrs Featherstone would prefer it if you were to take her to DI Heddon in person? Rather than ask him to step down here? And perhaps Mrs Featherstone would prefer it if you stayed with her for the interview?' he asked, eyes glinting and lips twitching.

Hillary gave him a knowing look. 'Thank you, sir. I think that might be for the best,' she agreed mildly.

* * *

As before, the moment Hillary pushed open the door to her old stomping grounds everyone looked up again, but this time their eyes quickly went to the old lady beside her. Eloise, for her part, glanced around agog at what she fondly assumed was the sordid side of life in a police station.

Hillary headed straight for Heddon's cubicle, knocked on it briefly, and ushered their witness inside. And if she deliberately let the door remain open, so that everyone could hear her opening words, well, that was just very forgetful of her. Wasn't it?

'Ah, DI Heddon. I have a witness for you. This is a neighbour of Catherine Burton, the mother of Imelda Phelps, my cold case victim. She saw Connie Brightman visit Mrs Burton in the days before her death . . .'

At this, Heddon's bright blue eyes sharpened on the old lady and his face tightened ominously. At the same time, the skin around the back of his neck visibly reddened. Beside her, Hillary could almost feel Eloise begin to shrink into herself with fright as she suddenly sensed the prevailing atmosphere, and Hillary turned to her at once with a gentle smile, and set out a chair for her to sit on, facing Heddon's desk.

'Don't be alarmed, Mrs Featherstone, there's nothing to it. Just tell DI Heddon what you've been telling me,' she said, and over the top of the old lady's head, shot Liam Heddon a warning glance. And, to his credit, he immediately took the hint.

His face softened and he even managed a smile. Of sorts. 'Yes, just take your time. Do you mind if I record this?' he added, reaching for his phone.

'Oh no. Isn't modern technology wonderful? My nephew can do all sorts of things on a telephone . . .' the old lady said, rallying a little.

Hillary smiled, belatedly shut the door, then drew up a chair and sat firmly beside her witness. Outside, she saw DI Sam Waterstone, a long-standing friend, reach out and tap someone on their shoulder and wiggle his fingers. And what looked suspiciously like a twenty-pound note exchanged hands.

Hillary conscientiously pretended not to notice. But whoever had bet that it would take her less than a day to regain the upper hand, apparently were due for a bonanza.

* * *

It took some time for Eloise's rather rambling statement to be taken, but on certain points she was reassuringly positive. On being shown a more up-to-date photograph of Connie Brightman, the old lady was more certain than ever that she was the same woman who had called on Catherine Burton just days before her death had been reported in the newspapers.

It was further established that, until then, Eloise had not seen the woman in Cheltenham before.

And something new — something she'd failed to tell Hillary. Namely, that on the day of Connie's death, Catherine Burton had left her flat in a large, swanky car that had all the appearance of an upmarket chauffeured car service and had been gone for several hours.

When Hillary finally escorted a rather triumphant Eloise from the office in the company of a junior officer who would type up a statement for her to sign, everyone in the outer office kept their heads down and assiduously avoided both Hillary's and Liam Heddon's eye.

When Hillary stepped back into the cubicle, Heddon was already on the phone to his super. She had to admit to being impressed by the way he relayed the latest developments without even the hint of a gnashing of teeth, and after a few terse 'yes, sirs' and 'no, sirs' and 'I agree, sirs' he hung up and slowly let his gaze return to her.

'We're bringing this Burton woman in,' he said flatly.

Hillary had expected as much, but that didn't mean she felt particularly happy about it. Whilst she could see that Catherine needed to be formally interviewed — if only to ask her why she had not come forward with information after the widely reported request from the police that any member of the public with knowledge of the murdered woman should contact them — she still thought a more softly-softly approach would have been preferable.

'Going storming in is just likely to put her back up,' she tried to warn him. 'She's of the old school — stiff back, stiff neck and stiff upper lip. You antagonise her and she'll just freeze you out.'

'We'll see.'

'She's old, rich and still feels entitled. And I'm not at all sure that a few flying mammals haven't made their way into her belfry over the years. Her former husband was an MP, and she probably still fondly believes she can call in reinforcements at the flick of her fingers. You're going to have to tread care—'

'I have no doubt your input is well intentioned, but we'll make our own assessments and take it from here,' Heddon said flatly.

Hillary nodded and without another word, got up and left.

Back downstairs she told her team the news, which was met with concerned scepticism. Claire was the first to break the silence. 'The old bat will run rings around him,' she prophesied glumly.

'DI Heddon is an experienced officer,' Hillary said.

Claire snorted. 'Not with her type he isn't. She's a dying breed. The likes of modern DIs are used to dealing with a different class of scrote altogether. He'll probably assume she'll be a pushover in comparison and go in thinking he can simply scare her into some admission or slip-up, and then build on it. What does the super say about it all?'

Hillary shrugged. 'Rollo won't have any say in the matter. I'm going to go to him now and ask if we can at least listen in on the proceedings from the viewing room. It's possible that Mrs Burton will let something slip about Imelda.'

'Surely everything depends on what she has to say about Connie Brightman's visit to her, ma'am,' Gareth said quietly. 'I mean, if she can come up with a reasonable explanation for that, and account for her whereabouts during the time Connie was murdered, she need not say anything about our case at all.'

Hillary smiled grimly. 'If she can come up with some reason for Connie's visit that *doesn't* relate to Imelda's death in some way, I'd really be interested to hear it. I can't think of a single thing those two women might have had to say to each other about any other topic, can you? Let's just hope Rollo has enough clout with Heddon's own super to at least let us listen in.'

It turned out that Rollo Sale did, for two hours later, when Catherine Burton was ushered into an interview room, all four of them were seated in the viewing room, watching and listening intently.

Hillary watched Heddon first. He looked calm and confident, as did his sergeant, who took the seat beside him. Catherine Burton, dressed in an outfit that had probably cost an eye-watering sum and had come straight from some Paris boutique or other, looked around with distaste, and eyed the chair in front of her without making any attempt to sit.

Heddon looked puzzled for a moment, then he got up, walked around the table and pulled the chair out for her. Catherine gave him the barest of nods and deigned to sit.

Hillary wished that she could shake off the persistent feeling she had that nothing good was going to come of this afternoon's work. She tried to put it down to sheer pessimism, or the heatwave, or her tiredness and growing headache.

But try as she might, she couldn't persuade herself that her instincts were wrong.

CHAPTER FOURTEEN

'I do hope this won't take too long, Inspector Heddon,' were Catherine Burton's first, crisp words, as she put her Gucci handbag on the table in front of her and cast a disparaging look around the small, dingy room. 'I have an appointment this evening with my masseuse.'

Heddon calmly introduced himself and his sergeant for the tape, adding that Mrs Burton had not requested the presence of a solicitor or legal representative, but had been told that she could ask for one at any time.

'We just have a few questions that we believe you can help us with concerning the murder of Constance Brightman,' he began smoothly. 'We understand Miss Brightman visited you last week, a day or two before her death?'

If he'd hoped to knock Catherine Burton's confidence with such a forthright opening statement, however, Hillary could see that he'd clearly failed. Instead, the old lady's impeccably coiffured head merely dipped briefly. 'Yes, that's right,' she agreed, leaving Heddon the one feeling disconcerted.

He hid it well though, and merely made a brief note in the notebook beside him. 'You must have been aware that the police were interested in hearing from anyone who'd had any dealings with Miss Brightman in the days before her death.

So can I ask, why didn't you contact us about this right away, Mrs Burton?'

'Young man, I'm not a teenager,' Catherine drawled, her transatlantic accent thickening somewhat as she feigned amusement. 'I'm not constantly on one of these modern phones or computers or what-have-you. And I rarely watch the news on television — it's so depressing, and I'm sure these television people have their own agendas as to what they tell us. No, I still prefer to get my information the old-fashioned way — from *The Times*. Over breakfast. It's such a fine newspaper, don't you think? And I really don't recall reading anything about Miss Brightman's unfortunate demise.'

Hillary had to smile admiringly at this. No doubt the upmarket newspaper, never known for its sensationalism, hadn't reported on the murder at all.

'Oh, she's good,' Claire whispered, to no one in particular.

'I see,' Heddon said flatly, knowing — but not acknowledging — that he had been outmanoeuvred. 'Perhaps you can tell us now, then, why Connie Brightman called on you? Had you seen her often in the years since your daughter's death?'

'Never. That was the first time I'd laid eyes on the woman in nearly fifteen years. She simply turned up on my doorstep, out of the blue,' Catherine informed him primly.

Beside Heddon, Hillary saw his sergeant — the one with the unfortunate habit of smirking — tense in anticipation. No doubt he was hoping this might be plainer sailing than they'd thought.

Hillary could only admire his optimism.

'So you *were* surprised to see her then?' Heddon said, trying to ramp up the momentum. With some witnesses, it helped to build up the drama of their storytelling, as most people enjoyed being the centre of attention. And people with narcissistic tendencies in particular thrived on telling a good story with themselves as the principal character.

Hillary admired his tactics, but was worried that the old lady, self-absorbed though she undoubtedly was, was too canny to let herself be led by the nose in this way.

'I was, yes,' Catherine admitted tersely.

'And what was it that she wanted?'

'Money, of course,' Catherine said with a sniff and an elegant shrug of one shoulder. 'What else do women like her want?'

This time Heddon looked visibly surprised. He hadn't expected such a straightforward and blunt answer, and for a fraction of a second, he struggled to assimilate it and find the right path forward. In the end, he decided to go straight for the jugular. 'She tried to blackmail you? How — and with what? Did she have information about your daughter's case? Something that cast you in a bad light perhaps?'

'Of course she didn't,' Catherine said shortly, giving Heddon a look full of censure. 'I doubt that woman knew anything more about what happened to my poor daughter than the man in the moon.'

Heddon shifted slightly in his chair. 'Then what was the purpose behind her visit?' he asked shortly. Hillary could see that he was beginning to lose his patience, and she was pretty sure that the American woman could see it too. And was feeling gratified by it.

'It was all to do with that awful young man, Otter or some such silly name,' she responded, absently twisting a large emerald and diamond ring into a more comfortable position on the index finger of her right hand.

Heddon looked at her blankly.

'He's a nasty little reporter who's been sneaking around, trying to dig up dirt for his second-rate newspaper,' Catherine obliged. 'Really, DI Heddon, I'm surprised you don't know what these guttersnipes are getting up to, right under your nose.'

Hillary wondered if Heddon had ever come across the word 'guttersnipe' before and doubted it. She was pretty sure Catherine herself had only used it in order to further underline the difference in their age and social status.

'You're talking about Gavin Otterley, I take it? The journalist for a local Oxford newspaper who first reported on the fact that Thames Valley are taking a second, in-depth look into your daughter's case?' he said smoothly, letting her know that he was, in fact, well acquainted with what was going on under his nose.

'I expect so,' Catherine said dismissively, waving a hand vaguely in the air. 'I only know he'd been snooping around my residence, talking to my nosy neighbours and had the gall to ask me for a quote. My housekeeper sent him packing, naturally.'

'Naturally,' Heddon repeated dryly. 'We know that he'd also approached Connie Brightman for a quote as well,' he added, proving that he really had been reading Hillary's reports. 'According to our information, Miss Brightman had promised him something of a scoop.'

Catherine's lips immediately twisted into a sneer. 'No doubt she had. Personally, I'm inclined to believe that she was merely leading him on in the hopes of a payday. He struck me as the overly ambitious sort, young and arrogant, and just the type to fall for a con woman. It's the ones who think they know everything and see themselves as big bad wolves who are the easiest to fool, don't you agree, Sergeant?' she added, deliberately demoting him to a lesser rank.

And it worked, for Liam Heddon flushed slightly in anger.

Now who was being led by the nose, Hillary thought uneasily. She hoped Heddon got back control of the narrative — and quickly.

'Let's get back to Connie's visit, Mrs Burton,' Heddon said, and in the viewing room, everyone let out a sigh of relief. 'You said she wanted money *from you*. So what, exactly, was she selling?'

Catherine shrugged one shoulder elegantly. 'Her silence. What else?'

'About what?'

'About whatever it was that she was going to tell this Otterley individual, obviously.'

In the interview room, Heddon's sergeant cast a quick, slightly puzzled look at his guvnor, who was staring fixedly at the woman seated across the table.

'And what was she going to tell him, Mrs Burton?'

'I have no idea.'

Rollo Sale swore softly and muttered something under his breath about the woman playing them for idiots, whilst Hillary began to pace up and down.

Heddon leaned slightly forward across the interview table. 'But she must have told you, Mrs Burton. Why else would she travel all the way to Cheltenham to see you?'

'Because she wanted money, I've already told you that. Really, Inspector, you must pay attention.'

'Don't lose it,' Claire warned under her breath.

'How much money did she want?' Heddon asked.

'Ten thousand pounds,' Catherine said, leaning back in her chair a little, and letting a small, amused smile cross her lips. 'She had the audacity to say that she thought that was a reasonable sum for me to pay to avoid any more unpleasantness. Though she used more colourful language than that, of course.'

'And did you agree to pay her?'

Catherine snorted. 'Certainly not.'

Hillary put her hands on her waist and continued to pace. She didn't like where this was going — not one bit. And, as if in agreement, the headache in the back of her head throbbed in sympathy.

'Perhaps we should get down to specifics, Mrs Burton,' Heddon tried a change of tactics. 'What exactly happened when Miss Brightman called on you? Talk me through it. She arrived at your house, your housekeeper showed her in. You recognised her. I take it you dismissed your housekeeper?'

'Naturally. I don't like to discuss private matters in front of the staff.'

'Right,' Claire muttered. 'She wouldn't want the domestic help hearing the skeletons in the family cupboard rattling away.'

'What exactly did she say?' Heddon persisted.

Catherine allowed herself a weary sigh. 'She asked if I was aware that the police were reinvestigating my daughter's murder. I told her that I was and had already been interviewed by a Mrs Greene. She then asked me if I was aware that the case was being "bigged up" I believe is how she phrased it, by a local journalist. I told her that an individual had called, asking for a comment, and that I'd sent him away unseen.'

She broke off to pour herself a glass of water from the jug provided and took a slow sip.

'She then told me that this journalist had telephoned her, asking for a quote. She said she was considering giving him a full interview, and that she could tell him a thing or two about my daughter that hadn't come out at the time of her murder that would, and I quote, "make him wet himself" if she were to reveal them. She then went into a whole song-and-dance routine about how she really didn't want to do it, and that it wasn't nice to speak ill of the dead, but then whined on about how badly Imelda had treated her over shutting down their little jewellery business, and how times had been hard, and how she could do with some cash, et cetera, et cetera.'

Catherine gave a small, grim smile. 'She then said that she would far rather keep quiet than tell this repulsive man "Imelda's dirty little secrets" and would do so if I could make it worth her while. That was when she suggested the sum of ten thousand pounds.'

Heddon nodded. 'That sounds very much like a threat to me, Mrs Burton. And an attempt at blackmail. It must have made you angry. Very angry?'

Catherine regarded him with a withering stare. 'My dear man, I can assure you that it did no such thing. I merely told her that she was wasting her time and mine. I told her that the days when tabloids paid out huge sums for muckraking stories were a thing of the past, and even if they weren't, what she had to say could hardly be worth ten thousand pounds! I pointed out that Imelda's death was hardly breaking news, or even of much interest anymore after all these years. I then suggested she leave.'

'And what did she do?'

'She left.'

Heddon slowly tapped his biro on top of his notepad, and took a long, slow, calming breath.

'But that wasn't the end of it, was it, Mrs Burton?' he said softly. 'We know that, on the day she died, you left your residence in a hired car and were gone for some time. Would you care to tell us where you went?'

Hillary abruptly stopped pacing. She shook her head. 'No — that's no good. She's just going to admit to visiting Connie,' she said quietly.

At this, all three of her colleagues looked at her in surprise.

'You think so?' Rollo said.

At the same time, Claire said, 'Do we even have any witnesses putting her in Chippie?'

'She's got no choice *but* to admit it,' Hillary pointed out. 'She can't be sure what forensic evidence we might have found in Connie's flat, and she needs to have a plausible explanation for anything that puts her at the scene.'

In the interview room, Catherine said calmly, 'Certainly, Inspector. I went to Chipping Norton, to talk to Connie.'

Heddon cast a quick look at his sergeant, who was beginning to look happier again.

'So you admit to visiting Miss Brightman hours before she was found dead?' Heddon said, for the tape.

Catherine Burton sighed elaborately. 'Since I have no idea when Miss Brightman was killed, I can't possibly say. I can tell you that I arrived at her flat around early lunchtime. She was not in when I rang the bell, so I waited in the car until she came back about ten minutes after I arrived.'

'She knows we'll track down the car company and the driver she used,' Hillary said, nodding her aching head. 'Which means she gains the moral high ground by admitting to being there rather than giving us the satisfaction of forcing it out of her. Now she's going to simply defy us to prove that she killed Connie, and then stand pat.'

'That's going to take some nerve,' Rollo said. 'She's already admitted Connie had threatened her and was trying to blackmail her. Now she's admitted to being one of the last people to see her before her death. She must know she's on shaky ground. Especially since she has no way of knowing, like you said, what forensic evidence we might have on her. She's not going to be able to keep on denying everything in the face of all that.'

'Just you watch her,' Hillary said grimly.

In the interview room, Heddon shifted slightly on his seat. 'Can you tell us why you visited Miss Brightman if, as you've already said, you had no intention of paying her hush money?'

Catherine sighed. 'Because, Sergeant, in the meantime I'd heard from my son-in-law about certain . . . developments in my daughter's case. Rumours about some photographs, if you must know, that had begun to emerge.'

'These are the photographs taken by a modelling agency, yes? For a contract your daughter had hoped to win?' Heddon said, proving once again that he'd been paying Hillary's reports far more attention than he'd been willing to let on.

'Yes, those,' Catherine said tightly. 'My son-in-law went into enough, er, detail to make me feel concerned. Although he assured me that the photographs had now been destroyed.'

'These were the nude shots of your daughter, Imelda?' Heddon said brutally, trying to ruffle the old lady's feathers.

'Hardly! From what I understand, Imelda was wearing a fur coat.'

'But with nothing on underneath,' Heddon pressed.

'I can't say, never having seen them,' Catherine snapped, then immediately got a firm hold of herself once again. 'But the fact that they had once existed were enough to give me pause for thought. Especially since Miss Brightman had intimated that she had something scandalous to sell to this Otterley man.'

'And you went to confront her?' Heddon said.

'I went to *ask* her if she'd spoken to this journalist yet, and if she had, what she'd told him,' Catherine corrected him icily. 'Really, Sergeant, you must learn to curb your obvious love of melodrama.'

Heddon ignored the barb. 'So, let's go through this second meeting then,' he said mildly. 'You were waiting for Miss Brightman. She came back home. She let you into her flat?'

'Yes.'

'Was she pleased to see you?'

'Yes. Which reassured me. Obviously.'

Heddon blinked, his face tightening.

Hillary, who had resumed pacing around the interview room, suddenly stopped and stiffened. 'And here it comes,' she said morosely.

'Why did that reassure you, Mrs Burton?' Heddon asked.

The old woman sighed heavily. 'Because, Sergeant, it meant that she either hadn't got much joy in prising money from this wretched journalist, or else she hadn't yet spoken to him. Either of which was good news as far as I was concerned.'

'Which was it?'

'As it turned out, the latter,' Catherine said, with a twist of her lips. 'After she invited me in, she offered me a drink, which I refused. The flat didn't look that clean, and I doubted her kitchen would have been any cleaner. She asked what had brought me to her, and I asked her if she'd spoken to the journalist yet. She said she hadn't. I asked her why. She dithered, saying that she was going to talk to him the next day. I asked her what she intended to say. She asked if I'd reconsidered paying for her silence. I told her that depended on what I was paying for.'

Catherine shook her head. 'It was all so silly really. But if she'd said that she knew about the ill-considered photographs Imelda had agreed to have taken of her, I might have offered her something to keep that quiet. Not ten thousand pounds, of course, but *something*. A few hundred. But it quickly became clear to me, from her manner, that she knew nothing about the photographs whatsoever. Eventually I got it out of her that she was going to give this Otterley man the names of some men she said my daughter had been . . . intimate with — and that hadn't emerged at the time of the original investigation.'

'Men other than her acknowledged lover, Dermott Franklyn?' Heddon put in smoothly.

Catherine's lips tightened. 'Indeed.'

'That must have made you very angry,' Heddon mused. 'She was threatening to expose your daughter's promiscuity. Drag her name through the mud again. I can understand how upset that would make you. After all, your daughter was dead and unable to defend herself. And here was this woman, this *nobody,* threatening to make her notorious all over again. Did you mean to hit her? I can easily see how you must have fell to arguing, especially since Miss Brightman was known to have an aggressive personality. Or did she perhaps attack you first? I can just see her getting frustrated and resorting to pushing you about or trying to physically bully you. We call that an attempt to obtain money with menaces. Is that what happened, Mrs Burton? Did things just escalate out of control, leaving you no other choice but to act in self-defence perhaps? If that's the case, you can be sure—'

'My dear man,' Catherine's amused voice cut across his words like a whip. 'What an imagination you have! I've warned you about that. I can assure you that none of those scenarios are correct. Once I was sure that Connie Brightman had no idea about the photographs, I told her that she could do her worst as far as I was concerned. I told her that I didn't believe for one second that she had a list of men who would corroborate her story about my daughter's private life. If so, she'd have blackmailed them, not me!'

She gave a brief, unamused bark of laughter. 'I suppose it was just possible that she might have persuaded some man to give a kiss-and-tell piece for money, whereby they'd split the proceeds afterwards. But even if she had, I told her, even second-rate journalists had enough sense to corroborate such stories and would soon smell a rat if that was their game.'

She paused, took another sip of water, and then gave a Cheshire-cat smile. 'And if that wasn't enough, I then informed Miss Brightman that if she *did* go ahead and make up some scandalous story, that I would sue her in the civilian courts. I told her in no uncertain terms that I would hire the best lawyers, forcing her to pay for her own legal team to defend her, and that any money she may have received would very quickly be gobbled up in legal fees. Believe me, she saw sense pretty fast after that. When I left her flat, she was fuming and, quite frankly, hurling foul language and abuse at me like a fishwife, but she was very much alive and well.'

And with that, Catherine Burton leaned back in her chair, raised a silver eyebrow and said, 'Is there anything else I can help you with?'

In the viewing room, Hillary stopped in her tracks. 'And there it is,' she said wearily.

Of course, Heddon wasn't about to let it go at that, and took her over it all again, prodding for loopholes and weaknesses, hinting about bloodstains and fingerprints and DNA. But Imelda's mother merely sat and let it all wash over her, maintaining throughout it all an irritatingly superior smile.

In the viewing room, Hillary talked quietly to Rollo. 'Do they have any forensics on her, do you know?'

Rollo shook his head. 'Not that I'm aware of. And if they had, I think DI Heddon would have felt secure enough to make an actual arrest.'

Hillary nodded in agreement. 'Yes. I was afraid of that.' She then walked to the glass and watched Heddon and Catherine play cat and mouse with neither giving an inch. They'd been at it for over an hour, and if the old lady was growing fatigued, she was giving no sign of it. In fact, Hillary thought that she was almost enjoying herself.

And why not? With every minute that passed without her being formally charged, Catherine was becoming more and more convinced that there could be no real evidence against her, and so her confidence continued to grow.

And that needed to stop.

Hillary turned to Rollo. 'Sir, do you think you can get us in there?'

'Us?'

'Yes, sir. You and me. Can you sell it to DI Heddon's boss?'

'I don't know. It's very irregular,' he said, looking unsure.

'But you can make the case that Heddon could do with a break, can't you? Or that he needs to check up on any new information that might have come in? And in the meantime, you can point out that we do have one or two questions of our own that we'd like to put to this witness about Imelda's murder. After all, it makes sense, seeing as she's right here, right now, for us to talk to her too. And a change of personnel in there, plus a change in emphasis in the questioning, might just lull her into a false sense of security and give Heddon an advantage when he returns for a second bout.'

Rollo frowned. 'I suppose I might be able to swing it. You think you can find a crack in her armour? I know you and Heddon didn't hit it off, but from what I saw, he's doing a decent job in there.'

'Yes, sir, I agree. But I don't think he's pressing the right buttons with her. He hasn't quite got her measure yet — which is no reflection on him. I've interviewed her before, and he hasn't, that's all. I just think we might have a better chance of getting under her skin. And if we can soften her up for him — well, that's a win for both of us. Right?'

'You're not actually thinking that you can get a confession from her though, are you?' Rollo asked doubtfully. 'From what I've seen so far that woman is definitely not for turning.'

Hillary shrugged. 'It all depends, sir.'

'On what?'

'On whether or not Mrs Burton is a hypocrite. And, personally, I don't think that she is.'

CHAPTER FIFTEEN

The superintendent frowned at her. 'No — you've lost me there. You'll have to elaborate on that.'

Hillary glanced through the one-way mirror again, trying to arrange her thoughts into a coherent explanation. If only her damned oppressive headache would just let up!

'I think Catherine truly *believes* that she murdered her daughter for a good cause, to save the family from scandal — as outlandish as it might sound. In fact, I'm pretty sure that she really killed her because she didn't want Imelda ruining her *own* social status and standing. She was due to collect some silly award and couldn't bear the thought of being made a laughing stock by her only child. Naturally, she can't consciously admit that to herself, any more than she can face the fact that she's always resented her own daughter so much. The first thing she told us was that she'd nearly died giving birth to her. And every other statement out of her mouth concerns how Imelda was always disappointing her. But if we can put her in the position whereby she believes that she *herself* might be about to bring ruin to the family name . . . I think, psychologically, it might leave her without a leg to stand on, and she might just cave in. *Unless* she's a hypocrite. In which case . . .' Hillary shrugged graphically, 'she simply won't give a damn, or will come up with some internal excuses that let her off the hook. But, somehow, I don't think she *will* put herself first. I just don't think she's been programmed that way by her own parents. What went for Imelda — always be upright and respectable, a lady and a credit to the family name or what-have-you — was drummed into her too. I might be wrong — but there's only one way to find out. And let's face it: at this point, what have we got to lose?'

Rollo looked at her thoughtfully for a long couple of moments, whilst Gareth and Claire watched and waited, hardly daring to breathe.

It wasn't hard for Hillary to guess what her boss was thinking. He'd be sticking his neck out, asking to muscle in on Heddon's turf. And if, at the end of it, they had nothing to show for it, it wouldn't go down well with the top brass — especially if DI Heddon wanted to make an issue out of it. On the other hand, he knew that Hillary's success rate in interviews was very good, and if she could pull a much-needed rabbit out of the hat, the kudos for the CRT team would be correspondingly high.

And a feather in his cap.

'All right. I'll see what I can do,' he said, and left the room.

* * *

There was thunder beginning to rumble away somewhere far in the distance, but still no sign of rain, when Hillary and the superintendent entered the interview room, which had recently been vacated by a disgruntled Heddon and his sergeant. By now the humidity was so high that Hillary felt as if she'd spent the last hour or so in a sauna, and she was aware of how sticky and uncomfortable she felt.

In contrast, the older woman still looked cool and showed no signs of fading. She regarded Hillary with a sharp look however, and her eyes went over Hillary's shoulder, no doubt hoping to see Heddon once more. And Hillary hoped that it was a flicker of disappointment that crossed her face when she realised that he was not present. Which was all to the good. If Catherine Burton was so sure that she had the other man's measure, it could only act to their advantage that they'd changed the players around.

Not that Heddon had been pleased about it, but he'd been overridden by his own superintendent, and now he and his sergeant had joined Claire and Gareth in the viewing room.

Rollo Sale introduced himself for the benefit of both their suspect and the recording device, and Hillary did the same. The superintendent then asked, once again, if Catherine wanted a solicitor present. This time she hesitated briefly, making Hillary's heart thump uncomfortably in her chest, but she finally shook her head.

'No thank you. Not at present. I'm quite happy to give any information to help the police as much as I can. It is, after all, my daughter's murder we're here to discuss now, isn't it?'

Hillary nodded. 'Yes, that's so, Mrs Burton. It's Imelda that I primarily want to discuss with you. When we first met, I got the feeling that your daughter had always been something of a trial to you. Didn't you tell me you almost died giving birth to her?'

Catherine stiffened. 'Yes, that's true.'

'And I can't imagine that you got much gratitude from your daughter for the fact?'

Catherine flushed slightly. 'I didn't discuss it much with her. One doesn't like to traumatise a child, Mrs Greene,' she said reprovingly.

But Hillary Greene was no Liam Heddon, and far from looking chastened or embarrassed, she merely cocked her head to one side and regarded Catherine thoughtfully. 'You told us that you never approved of your daughter's choice of modelling career, and all this latest upset over risqué photographs has only underlined how right you were to be concerned. Don't you agree?'

'If she'd told me what she had been thinking of doing, I'd have put a stop to it, naturally,' Catherine admitted. 'I'm only glad her poor father isn't still alive to know about all this latest business. It would have made him shrivel up and die at the thought of his daughter being seen like that by all and sundry.'

'It wasn't only your husband who was likely to suffer though, was it, Mrs Burton?' Hillary said smoothly. 'When I visited you at your home, I couldn't help but notice a photograph of you receiving a Woman of the Year award. And that you were accepting it the year *after* your daughter's death?'

Catherine frowned elaborately. 'Was I? I can't recall.'

'I happened to notice the date,' Hillary informed her smoothly. 'I take it that you must have known for quite some time that you were in the running for it, yes? I've known several people who've won various awards, and it's all but inevitable that the shortlist of candidates gets out. And usually someone tips the winner a wink, isn't that so?'

Catherine merely sniffed, as if finding the question in bad taste.

'You must have been very flattered by it all,' Hillary continued equitably.

Catherine shrugged. 'One does like to feel one's earned the respect of one's peers, naturally.'

'So, when Imelda informed you that she had strong hopes of being given a very prominent modelling contract soon, it might not have been the best timing? I mean, she must have known how conservative you are in your views and that you were hardly likely to take such news with unbridled joy.'

Catherine gave an elaborate sigh. 'I was used to my daughter disappointing me, Mrs Greene. It was all par for the course I'm afraid.'

'But this time it was different, wasn't it?' Hillary persisted. 'This was not the usual scenario of her appearing in a fashion catalogue, or a women's home-and-garden magazine holding up a bottle of the latest perfume and looking demure in some Laura Ashley outfit. This was full-on glamour — television commercials, billboards in London, your daughter's face fifty feet high on motorways. Your daughter, dressed in nothing but a fur coat and some vulgar diamonds. It must have made you shudder.'

'I knew nothing about those photographs,' Catherine all but hissed, sitting up straight in the chair and giving Hillary the evil eye.

'Oh? Mrs Burton, do you seriously expect me to believe that you were fooled? Imelda never could outfox you, could she?' Hillary chided. 'With all the trouble she caused you, you must have kept an eagle eye on her, almost as a matter of course. She might have been able to keep it from you at first, but not for long. You had her measure, didn't you? The daughter who left home the moment she could, the daughter who was never even grateful that you'd almost died giving her life? The daughter who delighted in disobeying all your rules, who took lovers galore without a single thought to the scandal she was bringing to her family, and made an exhibition of herself whenever she could? Please! In the end, did she delight in flinging it in your face? All her dreams were coming true at last, weren't they? She was finally about to hit the big time, proving once and for all that she'd been right all along, and that your old-fashioned principles of right and wrong were so outdated as to be ludicrous.'

Catherine had gone pale now, and her breathing was shallow, but she still had herself firmly under control. 'Like I said, Mrs Greene, I was used to Imelda's outlandish behaviour by then. I expected nothing less of the girl.'

'I don't think that's true, Mrs Burton,' Hillary said flatly. 'I think you'd finally had enough. All your life you'd been forced to put up with it, but this — this Face of Experience fiasco, was just too much, wasn't it? And to make matters more difficult, your husband was now dead, and he'd always been the chief mediator between you, hadn't he? Wasn't he the one who kept her from the worst of her excesses? Didn't she listen to him, whereas she'd never listen to you?'

'Oh, she was certainly Daddy's little girl when it suited her,' Catherine agreed spitefully. 'And he never could see her for what she really was.'

'But you knew better?'

'Of course I did!' Catherine snapped. 'A mother always knows when she's given birth to a bad seed.'

'Is that what you said to her? When you went to see her that day. The day she died?'

Catherine opened her mouth then abruptly shut it again. 'You're as bad as Inspector Heddon, Mrs Greene,' she said, too rattled now to remember to give Liam Heddon a lesser title. 'You both have far too active an imagination. I didn't visit my daughter on the day she died, and I'm pretty sure that that incompetent woman who investigated Imelda's murder originally never found any proof that I did either, otherwise I'm sure she'd have mentioned it,' she concluded triumphantly.

'Oh no, you were very lucky, I admit,' Hillary said, almost approvingly, and nodded her head. 'But then, if you went to your daughter's house intending to kill her, I'm sure that a woman of your intelligence took all due precautions. I imagine that you parked your car — you were still driving then, weren't you? — in some back street somewhere well out of the way. And chose just the right time of day for the visit, when you knew it would be quietest out in the street. After all, your daughter had been living there for many years, and you would have had plenty of time to get the lie of the land.'

'You're being ridiculous,' Catherine said, sounding disgusted.

'No murder weapon was found at the scene, so you must have brought it with you and taken it away again,' Hillary continued, as if the other woman hadn't spoken. 'I must admit, I've been wondering what it might have been. One of your husband's walking sticks, perhaps?'

It was a random guess, but from the swift, surprised look that Catherine gave her, Hillary felt a jolt of adrenaline shoot through her as she realised it had been an incredibly *lucky* guess. 'I'm sure, if we put our minds to it, we could find some family photographs of your husband carrying such a thing. A man as dapper as he was, was bound to have had something distinctively eye-catching. Something with a shaped head perhaps? A brass knob or something similar?'

Catherine pulled herself together quickly. 'He may have done — but I gave most of his things to a charity shop that I support. They're always happy to receive such items.'

Hillary nodded. 'Yes — very wise, Mrs Burton. But I'm afraid you can't expect to go on being so lucky,' she admonished. 'Take Connie Brightman's murder, for example. How long do you think it will take DI Heddon and his team to start bringing together a case against you? He's even now got people tracking down such things as the spray used on Connie to incapacitate her. Oh yes, didn't you know we were aware of that?' Hillary said quickly, as if Catherine had been about to interrupt her. 'Nowadays very clever officers with all sorts of scientific specialities can learn vast amounts of things with just the tiniest scrap of trace evidence. Mind you, as soon as I heard that Connie had been sprayed with something before her death, it only took plain common sense to understand its significance. And why it pointed straight at you as her killer.'

Catherine laughed; not convincingly, but managing to convey her contempt nonetheless. 'I'm sorry? I'm afraid I must be rather dim, but I'm not following you at all.'

'I can see that, Mrs Burton,' Hillary said kindly, making the older woman flush with resentment, 'but it's really rather simple. The first thing I asked myself, when I learned that Connie had been sprayed with some sort of pepper spray, was why? And the answer to that was obvious. It was necessary to help incapacitate her. And why did the killer need to incapacitate her? Because the killer couldn't be sure that he or she was physically capable of overpowering their victim without chemical assistance. Which meant someone either much older or less strong than Connie. Or both. Someone like you, in fact.'

'That's just an assumption,' Catherine dismissed scornfully.

'Yes — but when DI Heddon traces the purchase of the spray used back to you, Mrs Burton, that won't be an assumption, will it? And no matter how clever you think you've been, I can assure you, you won't have been clever enough. If you got someone to get it for you, back in the States, say, we'll find out who it was. And believe me, friendship won't count for much if it comes down to facing an accessory-after-the-fact charge, or an aiding-someone-to-commit-a-felony charge. And if you bought it yourself or paid somcone to get it for you on the internet, we'll find that out too. You see, that's where someone like you is at such a disadvantage, Mrs Burton. All your life you've lived a decent, civilized, law-abiding existence. You don't know the right people to contact about things like this. And nowadays, with all these modern technologies available to us . . . We have experts here in the CRT unit who do nothing all day long but use the latest scientific methods to track down criminal activity.'

Catherine gave a slight toss of her head. 'Now you're becoming insulting, Mrs Greene. I had nothing to do with my daughter's death, and I'm outraged that you should even suggest I did. And as for Connie Brightman — I wouldn't sully my hands on her.'

'But you had no choice, did you, but to do just that? What did she really have on you, Catherine? Did she see you near your daughter's house the day Imelda died, is that it?'

'Now you're just clutching at straws,' Catherine said contemptuously.

Hillary shrugged, looking unconcerned. 'In the end, we'll find out. We always do. As we will with this latest killing. Perhaps in the end your patience with Connie Brightman ran out, or you just lost your temper. Is that it? Did she get under your skin, mocking you and threatening to milk you dry? I can certainly see how that could make you lose control — she did have a rather annoying way about her, didn't she? Maybe you just lashed out with something to hand? Or did you perhaps save one of your husband's walking sticks after all, and took that along with you? That makes more sense; you already knew how to kill with it, and besides, an old lady with a cane — it wouldn't have looked at all suspicious, would it? You could have left her house, using the murder weapon in plain sight and no one would think anything of it.'

Catherine flushed, beginning to look just a little desperate now. 'I did no such thing,' she spat, 'and I defy you to prove that I did,' she added, falling back with some relief on the method that had proved so effective against her other interviewer.

But Hillary wasn't having it, and deftly turned Catherine's words against her. She shook her head sorrowfully. 'I'm afraid that is *just* what is going to happen, Mrs Burton,' she said quietly, and leaned forward a little on the table. 'That's what I'm trying to make you understand. *It's all going to come out.* Bit by bit, DI Heddon and myself will piece together everything, until we have the full picture. Your daughter's lovers will be found and forced to testify in open court as to her true nature. The photographs that your son-in-law fondly believes to have been destroyed will turn up somewhere, probably in the original photographer's archive, and will be shown to the members of the jury. And if you think the newspaper coverage at the time was intrusive, then this time . . .'

Hillary shook her head. 'I'm afraid it will be far, far worse. You will be filmed arriving at court, and it will be aired on the television news that night. Your testimony will be reported on and quoted *ad nauseum* in the press. Images of your daughter will trend on social media, along with all the vicious comments that inevitably follow. I'm afraid your name, and that of your daughter, will become a byword for murder and sordid scandal. And I know that can't be what you had in mind. After all, you did what you did to avoid all that. Didn't you? Believe me, the cruel irony of it isn't lost on me.'

Catherine swallowed hard, and Hillary could see that she was finally getting through to her. At last, the old lady was beginning to see the potential nightmare and ordeal that lay ahead of her. Now all she had to do was offer her the way out. A clean confession, a deal between her lawyers and the court, a quiet sentencing, almost rubber stamped and going practically unnoticed by the press, and everything would be so much more civilized . . .

It was then that Catherine Burton's eyes went dark, as if a shadow had fallen across them, and she became unnaturally calm. Preternaturally calm.

And Hillary knew that disaster was staring her in the face.

'I think I'll have a solicitor now,' Catherine Burton said quietly. 'I'll phone him at once if you don't mind. And after that, I shall need to use the ladies powder room.'

Beside her, she felt Rollo Sale deflate. He too knew they'd *almost* crossed the finishing line.

Hillary stiff-backed in her chair, swallowed hard and merely nodded. 'Of course. I won't be a moment whilst I arrange that.'

She got up and walked to the door as Rollo stated for the tape that she was leaving the room.

But the moment Hillary closed the door behind her, she shot down the corridor and ran into the viewing room.

'Well that's just great, isn't it?' Heddon snarled at her immediately, but Hillary barely heard him.

'Claire — quick. Go and grab a WPC and get her installed in one of the cubicles in the nearest loo. Tell her to keep quiet and keep her wits about her. Unless I miss my guess, Catherine Burton is going to try and take her own life. *And we've got to stop her.*'

Liam Heddon and his superintendent exchanged quick, anxious glances. Heddon shrugged his shoulders as if trying to wash his hands of the whole affair.

Claire left at a dead run.

Back in the interview room, Rollo Sale listened glumly as Catherine Burton used her mobile to call what was, no doubt, a very high-priced and respectable firm of solicitors who'd probably been overseeing the Burtons' legal needs since Henry VIII was in short trousers.

After a few minutes of tense silence, Hillary returned. 'If you'd like to come this way, Mrs Burton?'

She walked the silent and now pale old lady to the nearest toilet block and opened the door for her. 'I'll wait outside for you,' she offered politely.

The old lady nodded, as gracious as ever, but was unable to totally hide her relief. She stepped into the room where there were six cubicles, all with the doors standing open — one of them only partially so.

She checked the outer door was closed properly, walked to the sink and opened her handbag, searching through it quickly. A moment later, she brought out a small brown plastic bottle of pills.

For a moment she regarded the bottle grimly.

Then her lips thinned, and she unscrewed the cap and tipped the small digitalis pills into her hand. She was just raising them to her lips when a cool hand slipped with vice-like strength around her wrist, and she gave a little gasp of surprise. A young woman in police unform was regarding her steadily.

'I don't think that's a good idea, Mrs Burton,' the young woman said gently. And then called out, 'Mrs Greene?'

Hillary pushed through the door and took in the scene. So, she'd been right. Catherine Burton was no hypocrite — and to prevent scandal, had been as willing to die as to kill. But it gave her no satisfaction at all.

Catherine Burton stared daggers at her. And then began to slide down into a heap on the floor. Hillary stepped back outside, where DI Heddon was watching and waiting. 'Get the police surgeon. Quick.'

* * *

They held a council of war a little while later.

After the police surgeon had concluded that she'd merely fainted, he had called in a mental health expert, which meant that, until a full assessment of Catherine Burton's mental condition could be carried out, none of them could proceed any further as far as questioning her again was concerned.

Heddon was anxious to get started on the laborious task of making a case for two counts of murder against her, so he and his sergeant quickly excused themselves to get on with organising that, whilst the two superintendents got their heads together to work out how best to proceed.

Hillary had a fair idea of how that was likely to go.

'They'll sacrifice Imelda's case if the CPS tell them that's the best way to go,' she warned her two colleagues as they made their way back down to the communal office in the basement.

'And unless we catch the break of all breaks, that's just what they *will* recommend,' Claire agreed glumly as they settled down in their usual places. She caught Gareth's puzzled eye, and elaborated. 'They won't want to muddy the waters with an iffy fifteen-year-old cold case when they've got the chance of bringing home the Brightman murder to her,' Claire explained. 'With lawyers, it's all about the win.'

'That will hold even more true if Catherine's fancy solicitor cuts her some kind of deal,' Hillary added. 'Which, given the circumstances, he'd be an idiot not to.'

Claire, slumped into her chair, yawned widely. 'You think he'll go for diminished responsibility then?'

Hillary nodded. 'His client just attempted suicide. She's old — a case could even be made for dementia.'

'Surely not, ma'am,' Gareth felt compelled to object. 'The old lady was as sharp as a tack — you'd only have to listen to the interview tapes to know that.'

Hillary, perched on the end of Claire's desk, shrugged. 'Maybe so. But everyone will take the quick and easy option if they can get it — Heddon, the prosecutors, the top brass. And let's face it — realistically, there's very little chance that we can *prove* that Catherine killed her daughter. Even given the suicide attempt, which might be taken as a tacit admission of guilt, the case against her for Connie's murder will be far stronger. And it's not as if she isn't going to die in jail anyway,' she pointed out grimly, 'whether she's convicted of one murder or two.'

'Which is justice of a sort, I suppose,' Claire said, not sounding particularly convinced.

Hillary felt a bead of sweat begin to prickle down her back. The air was now so heavy with humidity it was almost like trying to breathe under water. And having her stress levels somewhere up in the stratosphere didn't help. 'At least Imelda's family will finally be able to get some respite from it all,' she mumbled. 'I've always had the impression that Thomas Phelps has been living with the worry that his daughter might have been responsible for Imelda's killing. My guess is that there was always something a little fragile about Jess that made him wonder about her.'

'Yeah, there is that,' Claire said, sounding more cheerful. 'At least now they'll all *know*. And I don't think any of them will mind too much that it turned out to be Granny, do you? What a piece of work she was.'

Hillary grunted. 'At least we stopped her from committing suicide whilst in custody. That would have been a total nightmare.'

'Yeah — there's bound to be some brownie points coming our way for that at least, surely?' Claire mused.

At this, Hillary gave a rather jaded laugh. 'I wouldn't hold your breath.'

* * *

When Hillary emerged into the car park an hour later, more than ready to head for home, she groaned at the sight of the slender, fair-haired reporter running towards her.

'Mrs Greene! Is it true you've made an arrest?' Gavin Otterley panted, shoving his recording mobile under her nose.

'No comment.'

'*Oh, come on!*'

'Go and talk to the media officer,' Hillary snarled at him.

Giving her a dirty look, he turned and ran off towards the station entrance.

Wearily, she made her way to Puff, then leaned heavily against the driver's door as she searched in her bag for her keys.

What a day.

What a case!

Nobody had exactly covered themselves in glory today — not Heddon, not herself, and certainly not Catherine Burton.

Sometimes it just worked out that way, she supposed.

Finally finding her keys, she lifted them out of her bag, and as she did so felt something soft and wet hit the back of her hand.

Then again.

She looked up at the grey swirling sky above her, and a wave of thunder rumbled noisily overhead. And finally, it began to rain in earnest. Big, fat, soft, wonderful rain.

Cooling rain.

Hillary lifted her face up to it and sighed. At last!

THE END

THE JOFFE BOOKS STORY

We began in 2014 when Jasper agreed to publish his mum's much-rejected romance novel and it became a bestseller.

Since then we've grown into the largest independent publisher in the UK. We're extremely proud to publish some of the very best writers in the world, including Joy Ellis, Faith Martin, Caro Ramsay, Helen Forrester, Simon Brett and Robert Goddard. Everyone at Joffe Books loves reading and we never forget that it all begins with the magic of an author telling a story.

We are proud to publish talented first-time authors, as well as established writers whose books we love introducing to a new generation of readers.

We won Trade Publisher of the Year at the Independent Publishing Awards in 2023 and Best Publisher Award in 2024 at the People's Book Prize. We have been shortlisted for Independent Publisher of the Year at the British Book Awards for the last five years, and were shortlisted for the Diversity and Inclusivity Award at the 2022 Independent Publishing Awards. In 2023 we were shortlisted for Publisher of the Year at the RNA Industry Awards, and in 2024 we were shortlisted at the CWA Daggers for the Best Crime and Mystery Publisher.

We built this company with your help, and we love to hear from you, so please email us about absolutely anything bookish at feedback@joffebooks.com.

If you want to receive free books every Friday and hear about all our new releases, join our mailing list here: www.joffebooks.com/freebooks.

And when you tell your friends about us, just remember: it's pronounced Joffe as in coffee or toffee!

Made in United States
Orlando, FL
29 January 2026

77528150R00134